DAUGHTERS OF PARTITION

BY

FOZIA RAJA

ISBN: 978-1-9163384-0-1 (Paperback)
ISBN: 978-1-9163384-1-8 (Kindle)

This is a work of fiction based on the personal accounts of Rasheed Begum and Parwez Raja. Every reasonable attempt has been made to verify the facts against available resources. All names other than Rasheed, Asaff and Parwez are fictional, as are many of the place names.

First Published by Creative Ethnics Publishing: February 2020

www.foziaraja.com

For our angel in heaven,
Sami Jehan Quyoum

AUTHOR'S NOTE

Daughters of Partition is a work of fiction based on the first-hand account of my grandmother, a survivor of the partition of India; and my father Parwez Raja, who both feature as main characters in this novel. What you read is not an authoritative record of the terrible events that took place in 1947. There are many resources that document what occurred in much more detail than can be found here. The sole purpose of this novel is to share the experiences of one woman; although her story will be reflective of many more just like her.

Table of Contents

PART I

Chapter 1

October 1978, London, UK

With his fingers interlocked and knuckles turning white, he sat precariously on the edge of the black plastic chair, rocking back and forth. His eyes fixed on the wooden oak flooring beneath his feet in this small-town community hall. It may have shone once but was now deeply stained from spillages and cigarette burns; and scratched from reckless furniture dragging. The smell of the cigarettes was still alive, leaving a musky odour, mixed with stale beer. Looking out of the narrow rectangular windows, Parwez noticed the sun that was attempting to break through during his coach journey to London had disappeared, and the sky, now ominously dark, promised rain. The orange streetlights began flickering, marking the beginning of the evening. Having been one of the first to arrive, and securing a good view close to the front, he could now hear a hall full of chattering, laughter, drinks orders being placed, and stewards asking guests to take their seats ready for the evening performance to begin.

As the stage lighting dimmed, the tabla player beat faster and faster to a crescendo before reaching a calmer, rhythmic beat. A voice emerged from the darkness,

'Please welcome on stage, our guest for tonight who has travelled all the way from India, Balminder Singh.'

'Thank you. Thank you all,' he began. A spotlight followed him to the foot of the stage, where he stopped, took a gentle bow and graciously touched his heart with his right hand.

A warm welcome was extended which relaxed Balminder. He prepared himself by sitting cross-legged on the large hand-woven rug covering the raised platform; and took a few moments to familiarise himself with his surroundings. The three hundred or so chairs were almost all taken by people with a range of ages, both men and women. Once comfortable, he gently nodded to the sitar and tabla players and they in return acknowledged the signal by allowing their fingers to beat louder notes. Balminder began humming to his first song, Balle Ni Punjab Diye, tuning his vocal cords, and the crowd applauded in recognition. When they quietened, the only sound was that of Balminder's soulful voice and sweet lyrics. Many of his admirers were mesmerised and swayed their heads from side to side, while others had their eyes closed, listening to the tranquil melodious tunes rippling through the atmosphere. Parwez felt every heartbeat pulse through his body. He locked his gaze onto Balminder's eyes and willed him to recognise and understand why he was there. Among the many Indians he felt isolated where, ironically, he should have felt most at home. On completing the first two songs, Balminder stopped to take requests.

'Are you all enjoying yourselves?' he questioned, engaging with his audience, creating a warm, relaxed environment. There was an instantaneous nodding among the crowd, who were in awe of his flawless and highly emotive voice. 'Tell me, what would you like to hear next?'

Many requests came at once, making it difficult for him to understand. Parwez stood, quietly watching. Their features were so alike, he thought; that nose definitely gives it away: straight and slim, widening at the nostrils. They were even similar in height, no more than five feet and a few inches. Balminder was a traditional looking man, with his blue turban, matching kurta and trousers. If he was in a crowd, Parwez would never have guessed, but now that he knew, now that he had found out, the resemblance was evident. How had he missed this? In all the pictures he had seen of Balminder, on posters, in newspapers, never had he thought that this could be the man to provide the answers. When Parwez snapped out of his stream of thought, he noticed that the first requested song had almost been completed. He shuffled through the pockets of his khaki trousers and found a scrap of paper.

'Excuse me, do you have a pen?' he asked his neighbour.

'No,' she replied sternly, unimpressed at being disturbed.

He tapped the elbow of an elderly man sitting to his left.

'Do you have a pen?'

He nodded and took out a ballpoint pen from his inside coat pocket. Resting the paper on his knee, Parwez scribbled on it, folded it up and then passed the pen back.

'Any more requests?' Balminder questioned, after the applause came to a close. He sat with poise: upright, an air of radiance surrounded him, alluring his audience, as he transported many of them back to their homeland with his traditional singing. Parwez waved the paper, trying to get his attention.

'We have another, over there, three rows back. Continue sending them forward.'

Parwez nervously passed the note to the woman in front and she passed it forward. It reached the hands of the steward standing at the foot of the stage, who then gave it to the tabla player sitting on a mat beside the sitarist. Parwez watched the note, not daring to blink or breathe until it reached the hands of the intended recipient. It may only be a simple note, but it had the power to change so much: the consequence so unknown, it could all turn out well, but also potentially not. At the age of twenty-seven, he had defied the advice of the elders he respected, he demonstrated absolute courage and conviction in standing by his decision. Within him he was aware he'd be responsible for any fallout; a burden he didn't carry lightly.

'I'm here for you and honoured to be in London again. I'll be performing your favourite hits,' Balminder said, filling the silence as he unfolded the small square paper. Looking down he saw that it was not a request, but a note, scrawled desperately in block capitals. "I am Taji

Kaur's son. I would like to meet you." Balminder stared at the name. He re-read it, again and again, his hands trembled, his heart beating fast. It couldn't be his Taji, there was just no way. He didn't want to look up, but he must. He slowly raised his head, his eyes searched for the man who was waving the note; but couldn't remember the face. Where was he sitting? Three rows away, he recalled. He scrutinised the third row, right to left. Parwez watched him but remained still until they made eye contact. The audience sat silently, wondering why their performer looked so disturbed.

'What did you write?' the old man to the left of Parwez asked, but he didn't receive an answer.

Balminder looked directly at him, their eyes met. Parwez nodded and gave an apprehensive smile in acknowledgment. Yes, he was the writer of the note.

The host appeared onstage to find out what was happening. Balminder slowly walked towards him, faltering, holding the note securely with both hands. He tried to whisper but struggled to get his words out. He tried again, stammering.

'I, I need to, to take a break, I can't continue with the show.'

'Why? What's happened? Are you unwell?'

'No, no. I'm fine, I need to meet somebody. It's important.'

The audience lost patience and the atmosphere became tense.

'What's going on here?' one man towards the front shouted.

'Balminder, the audience is waiting for you, come on.' The host tried to pull him back.

'Give me some time, please!' Balminder demanded and disappeared behind the curtains.

Parwez jostled through the crowds and walked to the side stage door where two security guards stood. His mouth was dry, as he held his breath and wondered if he'd made a mistake by coming to the concert.

'Sorry, no entrance without a VIP card,' one of the security guards said.
'I don't have one. I'm here to see Balminder.' He tried to push past them, but they restrained him by blocking his path.

The backstage door opened and Balminder appeared between the guards. He looked at Parwez stunned, not uttering a word. Parwez held out his hand, Balminder eventually took it and then embraced him with loose arms, leaving a small gap between their bodies.

'Let him through, he's family.'

'Well, you know who I am, how else do I introduce myself?' Balminder stated, feeling disorientated; his gaze focussed on the wall in front of him, arms folded, refusing to look at Parwez. 'You're Taji's son?' Parwez was unsure if this was a question or statement; a lump formed in his throat, all he could do was nod in response. But Balminder showed no acknowledgement of it.

Taking a seat on the dusty settee behind him, Balminder's head slowly swayed from side to side, the internal dialogue evident on his distressed face. Parwez scanned the rather narrow, dark backstage room for some water, but only saw bulky instrument boxes. He also took a seat, each man on opposite ends of the settee, looking away from one another.

'Where is she?' Balminder queried, finally breaking the silence and turning in Parwez's direction. 'Is she alive?'

Parwez hesitated, not knowing what reaction he would get from Balminder. 'Yes,' he confirmed, quietly. He swallowed, noticing the blood drain from Balminder's face and his body became motionless until it looked as rigid as a statue.

'It's so hard to believe, after all this time...' He recollected memories, the times he played with her, spent summers with her, teased and fought with her, right up until she was married. 'You know we mourned her death?' Parwez listened. 'I was there, the whole family gathered and paid their respects. And now, to be told that for all this time...' His speech faltered, as he replayed watching Taji's parents struggling in a sea of agony and grief; totally broken, having said goodbye to their child. His voice trembled and he shook his head in disbelief.

'Are her parents healthy and well?' Parwez asked.

'Yes.' Balminder confirmed.

'I know this is difficult, it is for us too. Ammi has lived without knowing the whereabouts of her family for over thirty years; and now that we have made this connection, she's completely overwhelmed, with conflicting emotions. When she's excited, she puts pen to paper, recording all that happened in that time, so she's ready with her stories; and then there are times when she loses hope and tears those notes to tiny pieces, yelling at me, telling me I'm doing the wrong thing by getting in touch with you. I know she is longing to see her parents and siblings, but she equally dreads their reaction. The only way you are going to come to terms with this is if you meet her.'

After contemplating the idea he managed to bring himself to say, 'Meet Taji?'

'Yes, meet… Taji.' Parwez knew this was not the time to tell Balminder that Taji was no longer her name. 'We live two hours away from here, in Leicester,' Parwez explained. 'Maybe you could spend the night with us? If you'd like to of course. We wouldn't want to make you feel uncomfortable. But it is getting very late now.'

'Oh, well, the thing is, I fly back to Delhi tomorrow, I don't think I'll be able to visit this time.'

'What time is your flight?'

'Evening.'

'Don't worry, I'll make sure you're back in London on time. Come on, please, I know Ammi will still be awake, waiting to see you.'

'My manager has plans for tonight. We don't have much time left in London. I'll be back in England soon, I promise to come directly to Leicester on that trip and even stay with you.'

Parwez's heart sank. He felt the thudding in his chest; not only pain, but anger raged inside him. He turned away, closed his eyes and tried to calm himself. The awkward silence between them was broken when the door burst open.

'Balminder, are you coming back on stage or what?' There was no response. 'Is everything OK here?' the manager asked, waiting to be acknowledged.

'I will not be coming back on stage… I've had some news.' In his mind, Balminder tried to construct a manner in which to tell his manager what was happening. 'This is my cousin's son.'

The thudding in his chest eased and Parwez turned around to face Balminder.

'Parwez, this is my manager, Jeevan.' They both leaned forward and greeted each other. Jeevan was confused as to how they were related given the obvious religious differences, but he didn't dwell on it.

'I didn't know you had family in England, Balminder?'

'Neither did I,' he replied with his lips breaking into a smile, as did Parwez's. 'I'll be accompanying Parwez back to Leicester tonight, but I will be back tomorrow for the flight.'

Parwez sighed in relief. 'You're coming back to Leicester?'

Balminder nodded, despite still feeling anxious. Jeevan seemed puzzled, annoyed even, but understood enough to know that there was no point in negotiating a return to the stage.

'We'll see you at the airport then?' Jeevan asked.

'Yes. And I'm sorry about tonight. I'll explain.'

'OK. Be at the airport no later than six.' The door closed, leaving Balminder and Parwez alone.

'Come on, what are we waiting for? Do you know how long it's been since I've seen Taji?'

Parwez noticed the smile on Balminder's face was much more relaxed; there was even a tiny spring in his step as he leaned forward to grab his coat.

*

Balminder and Parwez walked along East Park Road, having alighted from the long journey. Despite the heavy rain pouring from the thunderous clouds, the evening could not have ended any better. The church clock struck midnight, streetlamps were shining on the deserted road, no car in sight. As they approached the corner of Cork Street, Parwez told shivering Balminder that they had reached their destination. Suddenly Balminder asked himself if he had done the right thing, maybe the visit was too soon. Parwez walked ahead as Balminder's pace slowed, he looked up to the sky as if seeking some guidance. His throat felt dry, he struggled to swallow, there was an ache in his stomach. He wanted to turn back whilst Parwez wasn't looking, and then the sound of the house keys startled him and brought him back to his senses. Balminder looked at the wooden door, with a rusting letter box and saw the numbers '84' painted in white. He observed the two-up, two-down redbrick terrace houses, standing so desolate and insignificant in this soulless street; no lights burning, or people moving, complete desertion. A world so far removed from her youth, the grand white marble home, which stood tall on the hills overlooking the city, surrounded by lush green gardens and delicate pink and white blossoms, where the two cousins would seek shade and play. From the street paving Balminder and Parwez stepped straight into a dark room, Parwez closed and then bolted the door.

'Parwez, you're back?' A quivering, high-pitched female voice asked from the backroom. It's Taji, Balminder almost shrieked. He sensed the anticipation, the dread, in his cousin's voice. He took a deep breath to calm the hammering in his chest and wiped the water from his eyes.

Parwez opened the creaking door separating the two rooms and there stood a slim woman, in dark green shalwar kameez, a thin dubatta covering her head. A tall, handsome man towered over her, a gentle face, bright hazel eyes with flecks of green looked straight at Balminder. Balminder remained in the doorway, grasping the handle, digesting the scene before him; was it really her? The matured features of his favourite cousin. Rasheed examined Balminder, no longer the young man she knew him as. He had a neatly kept beard, just like his own father and her father had. He even tied his turban as they did. One thing which had not changed was his height: although he was never very short, compared to the rest of the six feet plus relatives, he always felt out of place. However, Balminder had a great gift which nobody else in the family had: a passion for music and a divine voice which no other singer could ever match.

'Taji?' he asked. A smile spread across Rasheed's face, her eyes welled up and blurred her vision. Her childhood name stunned her and the tears streamed down her cheeks, like a waterfall in full flow.

'It's Rasheed now, not Taji,' Parwez interrupted. Balminder didn't respond, but acknowledged the man standing beside her.

'This is my father, Asaff,' Parwez said.

They awkwardly shook hands, but Asaff did not let go when Balminder loosened his grip, instead he pulled him forward and hugged him, with a firm grip; his strong arms and army physique still remained even ten years after retiring from army life. This was the first time Asaff had met any of his wife's family. Rasheed used the end of her scarf to dry her eyes. Balminder stood in front of her, lifted her chin which had fallen so low and looked her in the eye. 'You've found us,' he said, embracing and holding his sweet cousin, as she relaxed into the warmth of his arms.

'Come, take a seat,' Parwez instructed his guest, pulling a chair towards the open lit fire, where the black coal burned.

Asaff sat on the red settee opposite, which was partly covered in blue chintz. The hard concrete floor was concealed by plastic vinyl. The cold draught came through even with shoes on. Balminder stretched his legs, so his feet could rest on the rug covering the middle of the room.

'You must be hungry. I'll get something to eat.' Rasheed said.

'Don't go to any effort.' Balminder pleaded.

Rasheed left the room allowing her husband and son to finally get to know a member of her family. Balminder continued looking around, astounded at what he saw. A makeshift shelf sat on top of the fireplace, which had been drilled into the wall after many failed attempts. He studied the black and white photo on one side of the shelf, but had difficulty making out what it was. He reached out for it, a beautiful photograph of a nervous-looking young bride and confident groom, on their wedding day.

'Me and my wife,' Parwez confirmed.

'You're married?'

'Yes,' he laughed, 'it's been five years.'

'Where is your wife?'

'She's with my two girls visiting her family in Manchester.'

Rasheed returned with some plates on a tray and placed it on the plastic table in front of Asaff.

'Rasheed, you're a grandmother!' Balminder smiled.

'Yes, I'm getting old, nearly fifty now. I'm not the young girl you knew.'

'Take a seat here, Balminder,' Asaff offered, vacating his seat.

On the table there was a small bowl of yellow lentils, some vegetables which could barely be identified, and what appeared to be the remains of a chicken curry. Balminder was touched by the humble nature of the food and the manner in which it was served. This was the Taji whose parents had an enormous dining room which was large enough to seat at least twenty people. Every meal in that house was like a banquet; the chefs prepared something for everybody, favourite dishes in abundance so nobody had an excuse to miss a meal. The aroma would hit upon walking into the dining room, enough to whet one's appetite even if a five-course meal had been eaten earlier. Here in England, the so-called land of opportunity, where people were wealthier, Taji lived in a tiny mid-terrace and wore simple cotton clothes. The daal looked a few days old, almost a stale colour, where the solid lentils had separated from the liquid in an unappetising way. Balminder took a perfectly round roti, freshly made by Taji's hands, the girl who would say: "I'll never make roti, my hands ache when I roll out the chapatis." He helped himself to half a spoon of daal.

'Take the chicken, Balminder,' Rasheed insisted, feeling embarrassed that she was unable to provide a generous meal. 'I was not expecting you; I was certain Parwez would not be able to convince you to visit, so I didn't cook anything special.'

Balminder, out of pity, took the chicken and placed it in his metal bowl. It looked more black than golden and lacked the depth of flavours and fragrance of a well-cooked Indian dish.

Balminder contemplated how he would inform his cousin, Taji's Abba, that she was alive, but living in this manner. And that she was no longer Taji, but Rasheed. How could he break such news to the family? He took the last piece of roti and cleaned his plate with it.

'You've eaten very little, have some more,' Parwez encouraged, but Rasheed remained quiet, aware of how basic the food must appear.

'No, really, you cannot imagine how special this meal has been.'

Rasheed lowered her head, uncomfortable that Balminder had found her living in such conditions.

Asaff appreciated his wife must have so many questions for her cousin, and although he too was eager to learn more about his new family, he wanted Rasheed to spend this precious time with Balminder. He excused himself and retired for the night, under the guise of needing to be up early for work the next morning.

'I'll come home during my lunch break and take you to the coach station,' Parwez offered, after picking up on his father's silent signal to leave them alone. 'There's a coach at two thirty.'

'Parwez,' Balminder said, pulling him in closer and resting his hand on his arm. 'I know how tough this must have been for you. You're a brave man. Thank you for bringing me here.'

'I'm just glad that Ammi has finally found her family.'

Once alone, Rasheed and Balminder examined each other for a few moments and then Balminder broke the silence, not able to comprehend the altered name.

'Taji, why Rasheed? I don't understand.'

'You don't understand?' Rasheed tittered. 'It was either Rasheed, or I died as Taji.' Balminder wasn't going to probe any further. 'Come, let's take these dishes and make you some tea.'

The rain was beating against the kitchen window, the blustery wind bellowing through the cracks in the frame, filling the room with a cold draught and a feeling of dampness. The light flickered, making a distinct buzzing noise the way a mosquito does before an attack; it soon stopped, leaving a florescent yellow glow. A rusting pan sat on the hob; Rasheed filled it with water and ignited the flame with a match, remembering how, when they were young, they'd watch the servants theatrically pour spiced tea from shiny copper pots. She asked Balminder to wait inside, because she didn't want him to catch a chill. Balminder didn't protest, he returned to the living room and huddled up by the fire. Rasheed brought in the tea and joined him.

'You look so different, Taji, sorry, I mean Rasheed,' he said, confused about what to call her.

'I'll always be Taji for my own family. For this family, I'm Rasheed. But what's a name? It doesn't matter if you call me Taji. I've missed it actually: it's been so long since I've been called by my birth name. And what do you mean I look different?' Rasheed laughed, now finally feeling at ease. 'Are you saying I look old? I'm a young grandmother, you know.'

'It's been so long, Taji. We used to play together as children, sneak out of our houses onto the colony drive, and there the guards would catch us, do you remember?'

'Yes, so clearly,' she confirmed.

'Even though your father was actually my first cousin, I always felt we were closer. I guess it was the age difference. He was more like an uncle to me.' Rasheed nodded in agreement. 'Do you remember the last time we met, Taji?' Rasheed thought, scanning her memory as far back as her wedding.

'My wedding. That week of endless parties. Decorating the colony, the floral arrangements, choosing the outfits, the colours, the jewellery, who to invite, the singing, the dancing! It was wonderful.'

'I didn't have the opportunity to tell you then, but you were a vision of beauty on your wedding day, like a flower that had come into full bloom, showing off its deeply coloured, perfectly formed petals.'

'I've never forgotten that day: it was definitely the best day of my life.'

Chapter 2

June 1945, Lahore, India

Taji's Story

'Kishin Colony.' I glanced at the welcome board of my family estate and sighed out loud: the tiresome journey in the heart of summer had come to an end. Although father's car was cooled prior to beginning the drive, the cold vents still absorbed the humid city air. Travelling before midday, when the summer sun reaches its maximum and humidity levels soar, made little difference: the pointer on the manual temperature reader still remained at one hundred and ten degrees. Lahore City came to life at eight o'clock as locals made their way to work. Carriages, rickshaws, cycles, beggars and pedestrians all obstructed our path as we approached the Colony, which meant Lala, Abba's chauffer, sounded his horn repeatedly in an attempt to attract their attention and make them give way. The armed chowkidars began opening the gateway as they saw the car approach and waved at my grandmother and me as we drove through.

'Mubaarak Taji. I hope you are blessed with a very happy married life.' I smiled, acknowledging his blessings.

Ammi had chosen a husband for me while I was staying with Nanni, and we were returning now that the wedding date had been set. We drove through the private estate of twelve grand houses belonging to the paternal side of my family. Great-uncles, uncles, aunts and cousins, all lived in one enclosed neighbourhood. We also shared a small cricket pitch and badminton courts too, where we'd come together for competitive matches. On reaching our house, I noticed the gates were already ajar.

'Wedding preparations have begun,' I shouted to my grandmother, sliding to the edge of the seat. Decorators who were present only a few months earlier, on my sixteenth birthday party, were huddled together on the veranda. Lala drove us to the main entrance and there Nanni and I alighted. Garlands of flowers were hanging from the four large pillars covering the square veranda and the centre light piece was also being embellished. I stopped to watch for a few moments and then walked on, stepping over and avoiding the many tools and decorations on the floor. I struggled to open the heavy doors but managed to squeeze through, relieved to be stepping onto the coolness of the marble flooring.

The house maid had her back to me, on her hands and knees with a polishing cloth.

'Masi, Masi, I'm getting married!' I shouted. She turned around.

'I know, my dear child, you have grown up so quickly.' She looked back towards the door and saw the marks I had left on the polished floor. 'Some things don't change! I've been cleaning up after you since you were five years old, now that you're about to be married, I'm still doing so.'

'You'll miss me when I'm gone,' I said, skipping away in search of Ammi. 'Where are you, Ammi?'

'In here.'

I entered the library and saw her sitting in the furthest corner at her desk. She stood up looking at me proudly; her tall slender figure was dressed in a pale cream sari, her dark black hair all perfectly twisted back.

'Let me see a picture of him,' I pleaded, pulling at her arm as she cupped my face in her soft hands.

'Taji! You know it's bad luck for the bride to see her groom prior to the wedding day. Besides, you only have four days to wait.'

'Four days?' I repeated, shocked at the speed with which everything was happening.

17

'Yes, that's why there is such havoc around the house. Your groom,' she said mockingly, 'has a busy business schedule and a major project to begin and this was the only time mutually convenient for both families.'

'Tell me his name at least.'

'OK, he's called Gurpul Singh, twenty years old and his family lives in Mirpur.'

'How far is Mirpur? And how do you know the family?'

'Your Abba and I have known Gurpul's family since he was a baby; they lived close by, but then moved to Mirpur which is a four hour drive away, when construction and development opportunities became available'. Looking towards the door, Ammi changed the subject quickly.

'Where has your grandmother got to? She needs to look through this guest list. I already have five hundred people, but I want her to check through to ensure I've not missed anyone.'

'She'll be inspecting the house and giving orders.'

'Taji, I need you to look through this schedule and list of functions,' Ammi said passing me a sheet of paper.

My head was spinning with a complicated tangled web of thoughts. Was there enough time to design a perfect wedding outfit? Who would apply my henna? I would need to pack all my belongings as I'd be leaving my parents' home. Would Ammi keep my bedroom as it is? Would it always be my bedroom? But I loved Lahore and couldn't imagine living in another city. What about my siblings and cousins and friends, how often would I see them? I felt dizzy. I kept wondering about my husband to be. I would be spending the rest of my life with him. We would have children together and he would be the most important person in my life. I was both afraid and excited. I could not wait to meet him. He would be perfect for me because Ammi approved of him. Was I pretty enough? I quickly glanced in the mirror and scrutinised the reflection. Good, straight, slim nose, large eyes, long and thick black hair. I wished with all my heart that my complexion had been fairer.

Coming back to my senses I glanced over the sheet Ammi had given me: so many parties just for me. Tomorrow night, Sangeet, an evening where all the local women and girls gathered to sing and set the wedding atmosphere alight. Mehndi night was to follow, the most exciting part of the wedding when the henna is applied, whilst the guests dance away. Lost in these thoughts, I did not even hear Nanni come in with the tailor and her assistants; carrying many bags, fashion books and what looked like samples of different types of material. We all followed Ammi out of the library and into the dressing area, where the tailors frequently came to measure Ammi for her saris and Abba for his kurtas and turbans. It was my favourite room with the most exquisite pieces of furniture and sumptuous fabrics lining the windows. The two wall-length windows and then mirrors across the bricked walls reflected plenty of light. Along one side rested an ornate cabinet; the doors were open and there were lots of boxed gifts piled up to give to the groom's family. Next to it was an imposing dressing table, with a small stool, where Ammi got ready each morning. The furniture in this enormous room was all pink marble, with a soft white rug in the centre covering most of the wooden flooring. To finish it off, the garden staff would ensure there were freshly picked white carnations and pink roses blooming in the window vases; and the smell of jasmine wafted through the rest of house. The Master tailor, Rani, who was always dressed elegantly in the finest attire, spent three hours taking notes and measurements for the different outfits I was to wear at each function. Ammi and I were shown many different styles of sari, the multiple yards of free-flowing sumptuous fabric, to be wrapped around the waist and effortlessly draped over one shoulder, leaving the midriff slightly exposed; shalwar kameez, the more traditional trouser with a long, knee-length shirt; and also my favourite, the lehenga, which was made up of a full ankle-length skirt, with a short blouse. Each of them so incredibly beautiful. It was all too confusing and I became restless and bored, as I had never paid so much attention to materials, styles, fittings, embroidery, thread. I left Ammi to place the final orders for what I was to wear on my wedding day so this would remain a surprise for me.

I walked around the house examining and observing all that was happening: the decorators, the florists, the cleaners, the caterers, were marching about the courtyard and the driveway carrying out their individual tasks. The gardens had been sealed with a green waterproof covering, and it was here the singing would take place. Even on the roof men were at work, placing chairs around the edges of the balcony.

'One hundred and twelve chairs have already been brought up, how many more are down there?' one of the workers complained as he wiped the sweat from his forehead and took long gulps of water, most of which was slipping from between his lips and down his t-shirt.

Further decorations were put up around the balcony. The florists formed a circle, each of them squatting on the floor with large bunches of roses and lilies and jasmines and marigolds; intricately weaving and knotting them into exquisite designs, their fingers moving quickly, eyes wide open, deep in concentration. Ammi only wanted the freshest, brightest and most fragrant flowers available in Lahore to form her arrangements.

I strolled along the balcony and watched the working day in the city come to an end. Lahore was soon to become the city of my past, the city of my childhood. The front gates opened and Abba's red Chevrolet drove in. Abba had finished at the office, picked up my siblings from school and returned home. I ran down the outdoor staircase leading to the side of the house and made my way to the main front doors. Abba gave his keys to Lala so his car could be taken to the rear driveway.

'Taji!' he cheered, picking me up by the waist and swirling me around in the air. 'You've become a stranger: three weeks at your grandmother's!'

'Did you miss me?' I asked as I held him tightly around his neck.

'My favourite girl not at home? What do you think?' he protested, placing me back on the floor and kissing me on my head. 'I don't know how I'll cope without you when you're married.' He looked down at me, as I looked up, and reassuringly squeezed my hand. His loving eyes eventually moved from me to the house. 'The house looks incredible. It stands out all the way from Dhabi bazaar, and all for my Taji.'

While Abba and I were talking, my siblings took the opportunity to slip out to the front of the house and chase each other around the fountain. It had become a novelty to play outside since we were prohibited from doing so in the last few months: Ammi and Abba had become even stricter about our whereabouts. I was not sure why, but Ammi had sat us down one evening and told us to be aware of the people who attended the local mosque just outside the colony. From then onwards Masi was ordered to watch us whenever we were playing outdoors.

'Taji, Paal, Manju, Amardev, Mohan,' Masi shouted from the doors, 'make your way to the dining hall, dinner will be served soon.'

Limping, Amardev eventually made his way back indoors, whilst complaining he wanted to continue playing cricket with the rest of his teenage cousins, despite having fallen and injured his leg. His little helper Mohan struggled behind panting, carrying the cricket bats, ball and gloves. Masi waited until we were all in the house and then bolted the door after us.

Among all the excitement of being back home to prepare for the wedding I had forgotten to eat lunch and was now starving. In the dining hall everybody was already seated. The spicy aroma of the various curries filled the air. There was an entire table of lavish and colourful foods: red chicken tikka, green vegetables, biryani with meat and chickpeas, fresh rotis and naan.

'Yes, all for you, Taji,' Abba said as he saw my eyes widen. 'Your Ammi and I thought we'd have a feast to celebrate. This will probably be the only night before the wedding where we have a family meal: guests will begin arriving tomorrow and the functions begin too.'

I took my usual seat at the table, in between Paal and Manju. Paal remained engrossed in her school science textbook trying to finish her homework; whilst the mischievous eight-year-old baby of the family, Manju, continued to distract her by covering parts of the page with her napkin and pulling on Paal's long plaits. My mouth was watering at the sight of all my favourite food. Hot tandoori chicken, lamb koftas, vegetable samosas and mint chutney were my starters, and for the main course I ate potato stuffed chapattis. I managed to swallow all that down with fresh mango lassi. After dinner we made our way to the drawing room where we spent over two hours talking. Ammi and Abba explained to the children that I was getting married and despite my pleas throughout, I was still not shown a picture of my future husband.

We retired to bed late that evening. On reaching my bedroom I noticed Masi had already been in: she had taken the covers off my bed, turned on the fan to cool my room, and switched the light on outside the window to attract any mosquitoes flying about inside. I lay in bed looking out of the balcony window at the full moon shining at its brightest. The twinkling dancing stars looked magical and drew my gaze up to the heavens, as I heard the silent music playing against the backdrop of a velvety midnight blue sky. The moon and the stars and the heavens were all out to play, celebrating my wedding! The thoughts of the wedding functions beginning the next night stimulated me such that I no longer felt any fatigue. I contemplated sneaking to the library in an attempt to find the photograph: I was anxious to know who he was and what he looked like, but fearing bad luck I decided against it.

Ammi woke us all early the following morning. Paal, Manju, Amardev and Mohan were ready for school and Abba for another day at the office. At seven o'clock we met in the prayer room, where Ammi read Guru

Granth Sahib, the holy book, for a quarter of an hour. She was in her usual place, the slightly raised stool in the centre of the room, with the book placed on the rack in front. I removed my shoes, covered my head and then sat beside Ammi, listening to her reading the morning prayer. The beautiful recitation of these holy words prepared us all for the day. No day at Ammi and Abba's house began without our prayers: they protected us and reminded us to be thankful for all we were blessed with. On completion we collected our shoes and everybody departed.

'The goldsmith will be arriving soon with your wedding gold, Taji, so please stay out of the way and make sure you do not try to take a quick look.'

'Oh, Ammi! Do I have to wait until the wedding day? Just let me have a peep. I can't wait!' Ammi dismissed my pleas and ran through the plans for the day.

'Rani, the designer, will be here in half an hour for a fitting session, so if I'm with the goldsmith, take Nanni with you to the dressing room and try on your outfits to ensure everything fits well. I'm expecting somebody to arrive by lunchtime to finish the flooring in the courtyard. When he leaves we need to advise the decorators so they can complete their tasks, and then we'll be prepared for the Sangeet tonight. I think guests will begin arriving at seven, although I'll have to check what time I had printed on the invitations. As for refreshments, I've informed Masi and she will tell the chef. We'll be serving cold drinks and snacks.'

Ammi left me in the prayer room confused: I had forgotten most of what she told me, although I remembered I was to wait for Rani. She took the goldsmith, who had arrived with a large case, into the backroom and there they viewed everything he had prepared.

'Taji, can I come in?' I heard a voice from behind the door.

'Balminder! What are you doing here?' I leapt on to his back, as I always did, causing him to lose his balance slightly. 'Come, let's go through to

23

the drawing room, unless you've come to say your morning prayers,' I joked.

'I've said mine, I have a lot to ask for.'

'Like what?' I enquired, leading the way.

'My tutor tells me I have a special voice and with a little more practice could become a professional singer.'

'You must invite me to your first live performance,' I insisted, and he nodded before continuing.

'Taji, you'll be so busy once all the functions begin, and then you'll get married and forget me, so I wanted to visit today and give you a small wedding gift.'

'I will not forget you,' I protested.

He passed me a small square box, which I immediately unwrapped to reveal a fine gold bracelet.

'This is perfect! I'll wear this and always think of you and the times we've spent together. I'm going to miss you, Balminder.' His gentle arms embraced me, in that protective manner he displayed.

'You must promise to keep in touch and write with news.' I firmly promised I would.

Balminder left for his singing lesson and I took the bracelet out of its box and tied it around my wrist; it was to remain with me as a memory of my dearest cousin. Although Balminder was actually Abba's cousin and five years older than me we had a greater bond, and I treated him like an elder brother.

As the days passed by they became more and more chaotic. The house, the balcony, the courtyard, the entrance to the colony had all been immaculately decorated with delicate chiffon hangings, twinkling wedding lights and fragrant floral arrangements in full bloom. At sunset the lights were turned on, and the entire colony came to life. The brightly lit wedding house could be seen from a distance, the whole neighbourhood and Lahore City was aware that a wedding was taking place at Kishin Colony. Wedding guests flooded the house each evening, with dancing and singing in the courtyard and on the balcony. When the partying ended at four o'clock in the morning, the guests often found themselves in no fit state to return home, and thus spent the remainder of the night sleeping in a corner, both indoors and out.

Seven hours later, my henna had been applied, it looked perfect; fine, graceful floral patterns on the palms and backs of my hands and arms, and on my feet as well. I was ordered to sit still and not move for the entire day; otherwise it would smudge and be a disappointment for my groom. Ammi fed me and I slept like a scarecrow, careful not to spoil the patterns. The following morning the henna had dried and Masi took me to the bathroom to gently scrape it off using the back of a metal spoon. She then filled the bathtub with warm rose water and I bathed for thirty minutes to then reveal a symmetry of floral petals and scrolling paisley detail on my hands and feet. With it being another night until the wedding, I was told not to wash my hands too often, otherwise the intense brown would fade into an unappealing, dull orange colour.

The morning of the wedding finally arrived. Ammi knocked on my bedroom door and entered at seven o'clock.

'Time to get up, Taji,' she whispered as she kissed my cheek and sat beside me. 'This is going to be one of the most important days of your life. Come on, get up sleepy, take a bath. One of the maids will be up shortly, and Rani will arrive soon to help you with your lehenga.'

I jumped out of bed as soon as I heard Ammi mention my wedding dress. My fingers itched to touch the fabric, to see the embroidery, to feel it against my skin. I could not wait to see what it looked like. After bathing Masi rubbed rosewood all over my body with long sweeping movements, whilst simultaneously removing any knots with her strong hands. Anxious to get to the dressing room, I slipped on a shirt leaving my hair wet. Ammi's maid and Rani were already setting out their accessories on opposite sides of the room. I saw what I presumed was my wedding outfit on three separate hangers with covers over them.

'Ah, Taji you're here, let's get started,' said the maid.

I sat on the dressing table stool where she combed the morning tangles out of my long hair. I was preoccupied with thoughts about meeting my groom and new family at the temple, where the wedding ceremony was to take place.

'Shall we start on the lehenga now?' Rani asked, interrupting my thoughts.

'Yes!' I shouted enthusiastically. The maid stood behind me with a smirk on her face which I saw through the reflection in the mirror.

'I think we should make her wait a little longer,' Rani teased.

'Please don't make me wait.' I was not taken seriously. The maid found a scarf and tied it around my head, covering my eyes. I heard the unzipping of what I believed to be my wedding dress.

'Arms up,' Rani said as she lifted my arms and pulled the blouse over my head and down my chest. She zipped up the back and I felt the blouse fit perfectly around my curves. My fingers examined the texture of the blouse: it was pure silk and not as heavy as I had expected, but delicately soft and light. The blouse fell just below my navel and around the edges there was some embroidery. I knew this was my dream dress.

'Lift,' Rani ordered tapping me on my legs. I placed my left leg into the skirt and then my right, she pulled it up and already I felt the weight of it. She twisted it into position and fastened the hooks. The blouse was pulled over the top of the skirt and they both just met.

'This is so heavy. It must weigh over a hundred kilos,' I exaggerated. 'How am I going to carry this all day?' I asked without giving anyone else the opportunity to speak.

'Oh Taji, you look like a dream. The way the fabric falls to your feet so effortlessly, the blouse accentuates your tiny waist and the neckline shows your bosom perfectly. It looks incredible. It really is beautiful,' Rani commented, and the maid agreed.

'I'm going to pull this thing off now, you've kept me waiting far too long.'

'Not yet!' Rani exclaimed. She guided me a few steps to the right and then she un-knotted the scarf.

I stared into the mirror, not uttering a sound. It was a startling sight, the lehenga tied tightly around my twenty-two-inch waist. There were two layers to it: the maroon full-length underskirt was of lustrous satin fabric with a natural sheen; the gold organza top layer was two inches shorter, revealing a border of heavily embellished silver and gold stones, gems and crystals. The cap sleeves of the golden bodice had detailed handwork all over them and the rest of my bare arms were shimmering from the oil Masi had rubbed onto my skin. The sparkle from the jewels reflected in my eyes. A Mughal maharani is what I felt like in this vintage masterpiece.

'I think she likes it,' I heard the maid whisper to Rani.

I nodded, unable to express how I felt. I savoured the moment.

Ammi's maid took me to the dressing table where she finished towel-drying my hair and then put rollers in it the way all the English ladies asked for in the salons. I loved the way the loose curls in their sun-kissed golden hair fell against their pale skin. I imagined my hair falling in the same way, but it wouldn't have the same effect against my chocolatey colour. I watched in a dream like state, through the mirror which sat on the table, as she took sections at a time and carefully wrapped my thick hair around them. The lotion she used on my face lightened my skin, so I looked almost as fair as Ammi, and the black kohl elongated my dark espresso-coloured eyes. Rouge on my cheeks and lips, finished off what looked like a perfectly symmetrical and sculpted face. I barely recognised myself. Rani came up behind me and carefully placed a heavy casket-style domed silver box on the dressing table. This held my wedding jewels. There were two necklaces: a maroon choker adorned with pear-shaped ruby stones, which Ammi had worn on her wedding. She tied it around my neck and fastened it securely in a bow. The other was pure gold and sat on my bare skin just above the neckline of the blouse. The earrings were bell shaped, featuring the same rubies and fell to the chin line. Six gold bangles encrusted with diamonds on each arm, rode up and down, playfully clattering and clinking like the laughter and dancing of the last few nights. They glistened as the sun's rays hit them, the way my spirit was doing so too. Such pure jewels, rarely seen, but all out in force on this special day

'Just one more finishing touch,' Rani reminded us as she unveiled the matching dubatta.

It was placed over my head and pinned into position. The scarf covered the plain back and was draped behind my shoulders, revealing my small bosom and extravagant jewels. I slid into my plain gold shoes and was ready.

Rani had already sent the messenger to find Ammi, and she entered just as I was getting up from the dressing table stool. I turned around and saw a look of absolute amazement. She was silent for a few moments, just staring at me.

'Taji…' she managed to stutter, 'there has never been a more beautiful bride.' She stood before me, taking my left hand in hers and then the right; she gave them a reassuring squeeze as she brought them both up to chest level, her eyes locked in a gaze. I saw the water in her eyes. I'm going to miss you, Taji.' I held back my tears so that my makeup would not smudge.

A twenty-four-man wedding band arrived and lined the colony driveway. Uniformed in white trousers and jackets with red sash belts and traditional feathered helmets. Instruments were in position including the dholak, flute, khartaal and trumpets. We made our way outside where the car was waiting, coated in flowers and ribbons. The band began playing as they saw me come through the threshold, my final step from the family home as a single girl. Everybody stopped and a short prayer was read aloud by Abba, asking the Gurus to guide his daughter through her new life. I sat in the car with Ammi and Abba, and Nanni accompanied my siblings in the car behind as we all made our way to the gurdwara. Each of the men bowed in turn as we slowly passed along the line formed by the band, while they continued ceremoniously to play their piece.

The drive was a relatively short one as the ceremony was taking place at the local gurdwara where Ammi and Abba had got married nearly twenty years ago; a simple but large hall. Friends and family had already arrived, many of them outside waiting to catch a glimpse of the bride. Inside, guests were seated on the floor and turned to watch as I walked with my family to the front. There were many excited whispers and gasps, distant chatter, comments and happy laughter; my ears were ringing, my pulse increasing, but my gaze was firmly fixed on the ground as I took one nervous step at a time. From the corner of my eye I saw Abba holding his head high, my arm in his, proudly presenting his daughter. I walked up a few stairs to the raised platform where the holy book lay under a canopy. I bowed down and touched the floor as I approached, offering my respect and sat on the floor facing sideways to the guests.

The gurdwara was overflowing, the beige flooring covered in a sea of people. It certainly felt as if the five hundred guests had arrived. Given this was the first family wedding, Ammi and Abba had invited every family member, distant relative, neighbourhood friend and even work colleagues, nobody was missed out. My wedding was one of the most anticipated in Lahore, and now the guests, dressed in their prettiest saris and kurtas, waited for the formalities to begin.

The wedding band began playing again, signalling the arrival of the groom and his family. Many of the guests went outside where they greeted him while I waited onstage with Paal. Despite my encouraging her to go and enjoy the light-hearted customs, she remained with me for support. Nanni often said she was already an old soul at the age of fourteen; and certainly more mature than I was. Mohan came running back inside and tripped as he ran up the steps.

'He's come on a big white horse. I'm going to have a ride on it too.' Without stopping, he ran back outside.

I could hear roaring laughter and cheering in the entrance hall, as traditional wedding banter took place between the two families. The girls would be huddled together in the doorway with a glass of milk for the groom, which they would offer to him in exchange for rupees. This ancient tradition stemmed from centuries ago when grooms arrived on foot to collect their wives and would need an immediate thirst quencher.

As I waited for my groom to present himself, my stomach became tighter, my hands were shaking, I tried calming them by resting them on my knees, my mouth was dry. Paal told me that Gurpul was now in sight and heading towards the stage. The butterflies in my stomach were fluttering in anticipation, like a swarm of disturbed bees. My heart was racing, the palms of my hands moist; I was about to be married! I was filled with joyful energy, but at the same time wanted to hide away and pretend none of this was happening. From the corner of my eye I saw people walking up the staircase, and then finally caught a glimpse of him. His traditional knee-length, fitted coat revealed a slim silhouette and the Nehru style collars accentuated his long neck. I admired his simple, cream coloured sherwani. On approaching the Granth he bowed and touched the floor. His knee touched mine as he sat down, he looked at me, my eyes remained lowered; an electrical current shot through my body, awakening every sense. Ammi motioned for me to look at him, so that Abba could give the leader permission to begin the ceremony. I slowly turned my head and we made eye-contact. I looked into his almond-shaped, light brown eyes. His long, sweeping lashes blinked and opened again. He smiled and a soft dimple appeared on both cheeks; a kind and gentle smile, which oozed warmth. His face strong and defined by his prominent cheek bones and arched eyebrows. I was relieved he had the same skin colour as mine: I did not want to be darker than him and he fairer than me, that would make him even more striking and me less beautiful. He will be my husband soon I thought to myself, and this brought a smile to my face. The leader waited for the signal and Abba gave it without saying a word and then he told us to stand. Abba rose after us and placed one end of the groom's scarf, into my hand. As I took hold of it, I noticed the redness in Abba's eyes. The placing of the scarf in my hand signified Abba giving his daughter to the groom, letting go of his responsibilities as a father, and passing them to another man. On taking the scarf I agreed for him to take me into his care as his wife.

Passages from the Guru Granth Sahib were recited and in between my groom stood and led the way around the holy book, as I obediently followed with the end of his scarf in my hand. Once we'd completed the rituals, formally making us husband and wife, our families showered us with fresh flower petals and there was a cheer and loud applause from the guests and Balminder's voice was heard the loudest. My husband's family greeted and congratulated me and then my own immediate family followed; two very different emotions: the subdued faces of my parents in contrast to the ecstatic welcoming and delight of my in-laws, my new parents. Gurpul took my hand into his, his long fingers interlocked with my own, the softness of his skin gliding against mine. We walked down the staircase ready to begin a whole new life together.

Chapter 3

October 1978, Leicester, UK

Balminder lay in bed shivering, pulling the blanket over his shoulders and holding his arms tight inside. The broken springs in the single bed's mattress had squeaked through the entire night with each movement he made. Pulling out his arm, he felt his head almost frozen from the cold draught coming from the window behind. The bed squeaked again as he sat up and the floor creaked when he placed his feet on the wooden boards. The room was unprofessionally painted a yellow colour with drops of paint spilt around the edges. Patches of a darker shade were visible in some places on the wall where the double strokes had missed. A strange smell lingered in the small, tight room. Balminder tried to identify it and realised it was due to the dampness: the paint on the ceiling was peeling in the left-hand corner and a brown water stain surrounded it. Balminder changed out of Parwez's shalwar kameez and back into his own kurta and trousers, which he had placed neatly on the floor as there was nowhere to hang them. It was a relief to be in the warmth of his own clothes. He pulled back the brown curtains and looked out to see a block of back-to-back houses. No matter how far he looked, whether to the left or right, there were only houses; identical houses with tiny yards. There was condensation on the window and droplets of water fell down onto the sill leaving small puddles. Shaking his head in disbelief, he thought back to Taji's parent's house in Lahore. On many occasions he spent the weekend with them, and would wake in the morning to the smell of freshly cooked breakfast and cakes and biscuits baking. Taji's Ammi would send Masi to wake everybody and to clean the rooms. She would open the balcony doors first to let in the fresh morning breeze and they would all run out and play. The entire neighbourhood could be seen in the distance, along with the parks and bazaars. If Taji's Abba was to see the condition she was living in now, he would refuse to believe she was his daughter. To have a father as wealthy as him, living a peaceful life of ultimate comfort, and for Taji to be in such circumstances, was undeserved. Such things were only ever read about in books, nobody expects them to be real. He sat back down on the bed, still in a state of shock. Despite having been with Taji since the evening, Balminder was trying to convince himself that this was actually all true. He heard a key turn and caught a glimpse of Taji, Rasheed, whoever she was now, outside in the yard putting rubbish in a black bag. Taji would never have done such a job at home: that's what the servants were employed to do. From the window he watched her open the knotted black bag and place two small carrier bags in it, she knotted up the larger bag again and then shook the excess water from her hands.

Balminder pulled open the stiff bedroom door and made his way down the steep and narrow staircase. The staircase door opened out into the sitting room where they had been sitting the previous night: it had been cleaned and the air freshened with some floral spray. He took his final step down into the room and closed the door behind him. The kitchen was in the far left corner and Rasheed stood by the cooker frying some eggs.

'Ah, Balminder, you're up?'

'Yes. I could smell that lovely fresh food,' he lied, giving her a hug.

'Did you sleep well?'

'Yes.'

'You didn't, Balminder, you can't lie to me.' He remained quiet: he didn't want to upset her. 'I know this isn't what you're used to, or what we were both accustomed to, but things change.' He now watched Rasheed prepare breakfast; a pan of water boiled and she placed two tea bags in it, adding almost a quarter of a pint of milk as well.

'Asaff and Parwez at work?' Balminder enquired.

'They left early.' Rasheed replied, putting a plate with two fried eggs and a piece of toast on the table.

'Can I use the washroom quickly?' Balminder asked. Rasheed directed him out of the kitchen, towards the back of the house.

He tried turning the lock, but it was broken. There was an old brown bath suite and in the bathtub stood a bucket with a jug in it. Although scrupulously clean, the enamel of the bath was chipped, with a crack down the middle. Balminder decided not to get in, but just rinsed his mouth, washed his face and quickly returned to his breakfast. Rasheed poured the tea in two mugs and sat opposite him at the square kitchen table. Balminder cast his eye over the bare table: even when they were having snacks in Lahore the table was never so empty; and as for the main meals they were like feasts. They both tore a piece from the toast and dipped it into the egg yolk.

'I've heard of things changing and people moving on, but, Taji... this? How could your life change so much? If anybody saw the way you lived at your Ammi and Abba's house and saw you now, they would never believe it.'

'I don't believe it myself sometimes. When you've lived thirty-two years like this, and much worse at times, you become accustomed to it.' Rasheed quickly changed the subject not wanting to dwell on her state of living. 'You've told me so little about yourself, how's the singing coming along?'

'Work, life, everything's great, it's all coming along well. Folk singing has become my life now, I'm teaching at a college in Delhi too, training young boys and girls to sing and play the tabla. Concerts never seem to end, one after the other, I'm touring India in six weeks.'

'I wish I could see you perform.'

'Next time I'm in London, you will be there. Otherwise I'll refuse to perform.' From deep inside, through every cell in her body, Rasheed felt the warmth and love she had been deprived of for so long, because it was snatched from her prematurely and so cruelly. 'Shall we go inside? I'm getting cold in here,' Balminder said. He picked up both mugs and took them into the living room. He sat on the floor close to the fire.

'Why are you sitting on the floor? Here sit on this,' Rasheed said passing him a foot stool. She brought in another one from the front room and they both drank their tea.

'Can you believe we never met after your wedding, Taji?'

'Whenever I visited Lahore you were out of the city, or at work, or somewhere.'

'I always asked about you. I got up to date news of your pregnancy and Gurpul's business ventures.' Rasheed took a deep breath. The sound of his gentle voice, those intense eyes, images of life with her first husband flashed before her vividly, despite having been locked away in some dark corner of her memory.

'Can you believe I was so excited about getting married? I guess I was just a naive girl and didn't understand what marriage was about.'

'You were ecstatic.'

'Gurpul and his family treated me so well. I now realise just how lucky I was to have such a family.'

'You were very lucky.'

'Yes, I was lucky to have had that, but what about this? What about now? Do I deserve this too? To have been apart from my family, my own flesh and blood?'

'You don't deserve it, Taji, not in the slightest: but you've managed so well, and look now you've found us. I'm here sitting right in front of you!'

'I've found you, Balminder, and yes, you're the gateway to finding Ammi and Abba and Paal, Manju, Amardev, Mohan, but I've not found them yet. They still don't know where I am, they don't even know that I'm alive. They think I'm dead.'

Balminder knew very well that all she said was true: they did think she was dead, they had thought her dead for many years, many decades even. As to how they would take the news was worrying, unpredictable; Balminder contemplated how he would tell them. The whole burden of informing Taji's parents lay with him.

'Come on, don't be upset now.'

Rasheed obeyed and wore a fake smile.

'Tell me about Gurpul, I hardly knew him. You got married, moved to Mirpur and that was it. Come on, I want to know what went on,' he said teasingly trying to cheer her up.

'There's not a lot to tell.'

'You said it yourself: you had a wonderful married life, now I want to know everything.' Rasheed laughed and shook her head at him. 'From what the family said he treated you so well.'

'He was my friend, my best friend. And once Rajendar arrived our world become even more fulfilled with our daughter.'

'Rajendar?' he repeated, shocked. 'Where is she?'

'Married.'

'Married?'

'Yes.'

'So she was with you when all this happened?'

'Yes.'

'How?' Balminder asked, confused. 'How did you manage? Not only did you have your own life to save, but your daughter's as well.'

'It was difficult, more so because I was expecting our second child.'

'Second child?'

'Balminder, there's so much you still don't know.'

'You're telling me!'

'Let's take one step at a time, otherwise you will get confused,' Rasheed insisted. 'Rajendar remained with me, even after Gurpul,' her words trailed off before she even finished the sentence.

'Carry on,' Balminder said reassuringly.

'When I converted to Islam, Rajendar obviously converted with me. Although her name is now Zainub, not Rajendar.'

'Her name changed too?'

'We had no choice. She was only sixteen months. She doesn't remember anything, not even her Abba. At fifteen she married a relative of Asaff's and they lived next door.'

'You said you were expecting your second.'

Rasheed didn't respond. Thoughts of the baby circulated in her mind, how could she have done that to her child? No mother would, but she was forced to, she had no choice, it wasn't her fault. It was those people in the group, they were selfish, awful, only interested in saving their own lives, they didn't care about the baby. But they were punished, it didn't take long. The wound that had only been concealed, and never healed, opened ferociously as the anger raged within Rasheed. Tears streamed from her unblinking eyes, down her face and on to her chest. She held her hand to her chest, where she once felt the warmth of her baby.

'Oh Taji, my dearest cousin, I can't begin to imagine what horrors you have endured. I can't change any of it, I can only wish I could take us back to our childhood.' Balminder passed her a tissue and stroked her hair. She wiped away the tears and looked at the clock above the fireplace. 'It's one o'clock, I better get you some lunch before you leave.'

'I'm not hungry.'

'I'm not allowing you to leave on an empty stomach,' Rasheed ordered.

Balminder remained seated and listened to the water hitting the kitchen sink as his Taji, not the Rasheed she was now, washed her face. He heard her sigh out loud and then quieten. The sound of pans broke the silence as she prepared lunch.

'Please don't bother with lunch, we don't have much time left as it is,' he insisted, joining her.

'You take a seat here and I'll quickly put something together. Will daal do?'

'Anything, I don't mind. Your son went to a lot of effort to get in touch with your family.'

'I know,' she replied, expertly dicing the onions. They sizzled as she threw them in with the oil. 'It was such a bizarre coincidence.'

'What was?' Balminder asked.

'Finding you.'

Chapter 4

January 1975, Kashmir

Parwez sat on the charpai with a blanket wrapped around him. It was winter in Kashmir and without the heating he was used to in England, he felt even colder. A small portable heater was turned on but was not powerful enough to keep the room warm. The decoration had changed since Parwez had left home and emigrated to England: there were now settees and a matching unit, which held a complete dinner set and framed wedding photographs.

'Is your stomach any better, Parwez?' Rasheed asked.

'No,' he mumbled. 'I didn't think I would become this ill; I've not been in England that long.'

'Anybody who comes back home after spending even the shortest period in England, becomes ill. It's not just you. When your Abba came back he spent the whole two weeks lying on that charpai.'

'It's the unclean water and lack of hygiene,' Parwez complained.

The radio crackled in the background as they spoke.

'Is it raining outside, Ammi?'

'No.'

'Why is the signal so weak here?' Parwez asked, getting up to adjust the radio's aerial, which he had brought as a gift for his Ammi from England.

'"This is station Jalandhar," a voice clearly said.

'I'll bring you some tea with herbs, you need something to clear your system.' Rasheed put on her shoes to go across the yard into the kitchen.

'Leave it. It's cold outside.'

'I'm used to living like this,' she said, closing the door behind her.

Parwez sat by himself listening to the radio station which transmitted from neighbouring India.

'Here you go, drink this,' Rasheed instructed, giving him a cup filled with her own home remedies.

'What have you put in this, Ammi ji?'

She didn't respond to Parwez, her head turned towards the radio, listening attentively. Her eyes fixed on it, almost as if she could see into it, like one does with a television.

'Ammi, what's in this? You manage to find a remedy for everything.' She still didn't respond. 'What are you thinking?' Parwez asked raising his voice.

'Have you heard this before?'

'Heard what?'

'The song?'

'Yes. In England, everybody is listening to it, it's such a hit. He's a fantastic folksinger.'

'I know he is,' Rasheed replied.

'Really? Where have you heard him?'

'Parwez,' she said slowly, 'this is Balminder.' He remained quiet, perplexed at his Ammi's behaviour. 'This is Balminder Singh, isn't it?'

'Yes. Why do you ask?'

'He's my Abba's cousin.'

'What? Your Abba's cousin?'

'Yes. My Abba and Balminder are cousins.'

Parwez immediately sat up and leaned forward. He stared at his Ammi for a moment, confused.

'Ammi, he's a well-known folksinger. He's known all over India and I often listen to him in England. He's a presenter for Radio Jalandhar as well. He can't be your cousin.'

'Parwez, I might not talk about my family, but do you think I've forgotten them? Do you think I don't think about them every single day like they have never existed? I grew up with Balminder. He was like a brother to me.'

They both sat speechless. Parwez was dumbfounded at how passionately his mother spoke about her family. What she said was true, he accepted that. Within moments Parwez had mapped out how he would get in touch with Balminder and reach his Ammi's parents.

'Ammi, I will find your parents.'

'What?' Rasheed squealed, thinking Parwez had gone mad. How would he ever get in touch with her parents, it would not happen, he knew nothing about them.

'I'm going to visit Balminder.'

'You will never be allowed to visit the other side of the border.'

'You're right, the political situation probably won't allow that, but I can write to Radio Jalandhar. They can't stop me from doing that. I'm going to find out when he's next in England.'

Chapter 5

October 1978, Leicester, UK

Rasheed opened the fridge door and took out a golden coloured margarine box which held the dough for roti. Balminder watched her take some in her hands, cover it with dry flour and shape it into a small ball. She then flattened it with her fingers and rolled it out perfectly with a rolling pin. Tossing the chapatti between her hands, she shook off the excess flour and placed it on the flat pan to bake.

'You've become an expert.'

'No more servants or cooks, Balminder,' she laughed.

The lentils bubbled in the pan and she poured a plateful, sprinkled fresh green coriander and golden masaala on it.

'Sorry it's only daal, I would have made you some meat or chicken but...' Her sentence hung in the air unfinished.

'This is delicious,' he said.

The front door opened, bringing with it a gust of wind, which engulfed the inside of the house and closed the door with a loud bang on its way out.

'Sorry, that was the wind,' Parwez's voice came from the back room. 'Salaam, Ammi.' He greeted.

'Salaam.'

'I hope you've both managed to catch up a little, because we need to get going.'

'I'm done,' Balminder said getting up to wash his hands. 'That was wonderful, Rasheed.'

Rasheed smiled at him, he had remembered to call her by her Islamic name and not her Sikh name. Balminder took his coat and buttoned up.

'Right, Rasheed,' he said, preparing to leave.

'We're not going far, you may as well come too,' Parwez suggested, seeing the grief on his Ammi's face.

'I'll get my coat.' She ran upstairs, fetched her coat and changed her shoes.

They walked back down the route Balminder had taken the previous night, to the bus stop where they had alighted. The coach was already waiting.

Parwez walked ahead to buy a ticket from the coach driver. 'Single to Heathrow, please.'

A teenager walking past the bus stop shouted, 'this coach isn't going to wherever you people are from!'

'Watch your mouth!' Parwez shouted back in retaliation.

'No need for that, mate,' the driver defended, looking at the teenager with a can of beer in his hand.

'They don't belong here. That baseball head definitely doesn't belong here.'

Balminder remained quiet, thinking about Rasheed being subjected to such racist attacks.

'You arrived in our country long before we landed here and trust me you don't want me to go into the details of how the British left India when they were quite done with her!' Parwez responded. The young man walked away.

'We're ready to leave,' the bus driver shouted.

'Rasheed, take care of yourself,' Balminder said. Rasheed held back the water gathering in her eyes. He looked at Parwez, 'Look after your mother. I promise I'll be in touch, Rasheed.' He embraced her and stepped onto the coach, taking a window seat.

Rasheed stood still, inconsolable, not even returning his waves.

'Is that it? Am I alone again?' She muttered.

PART II

Chapter 1

September 1945, Mirpur, India

Taji's Story Continued

'Taji, I'll pick you up at four.'

'Where are we going?'

'Wait and see.'

'This better be worth it, Gurpul.'

'It will. I must go, there is a meeting at two.'

Before I had the chance to say goodbye the line cut out. I thought about the conversation, completely baffled.

'What's wrong, Taji? You look lost.'

'I am.'

'This is 13 Tucker Road, Mirpur, your in-laws' house. My name is Shashi Singh, your father-in-law and your name is Taji Kaur,' he mocked, while flicking through his regular morning read of The Hindustan Times.

'Abbu ji!' I exclaimed, laughing at his dry sense of humour.

Abbu was sitting in his usual leather armchair, by the window, with his feet up on the footstool. He was a healthy, slim man, who still dressed like a man of thirty, not fifty, especially when he was in his signature Nehru-style outfit or an English suit.

'What's happening here, are you teasing Taji again?' Ammi shouted from the dining room, after she had given Babu, the housekeeper, instructions for the evening meal.

'This wife of mine! I can't speak a word without being accused of something.'

'We're just playing, Ammi ji,' I said reassuringly. 'Gurpul called, he's taking me somewhere special.'

'Oh, I see,' Ammi said, looking at Abbu, who peeped over the top of his newspaper and gave a quick wink.

'What was that for? You know what's going on, don't you?' There was no reply. Abbu hid his face behind the paper.

'You've only been married a few months, you should be expecting surprises from your husband. It's the honeymoon period!' Ammi insisted.

'Yes, but he's never done this before.'

'Romance, my dear,' Abbu whispered, raising his bushy eyebrows.

'You should be excited, why are you getting so worked up?' Ammi asked, taking a seat beside me.

Although Ammi had remained slim most of her life, after turning forty she began gaining weight and was now rather plump, making her look even older than forty-seven. Her hair was rapidly turning white and despite the henna she applied, it was still visible when tied in fancy hair clips and bands.

'What are you going to wear?'

'I don't know. I don't even know where we're going.'

'Here we go again, women and clothes! I'm going to my office if anybody wants me.'

'Abbu ji?' I asked, waiting for him to look back, 'which office?'

'I've signed the business to Gurpul and now I don't even have permission to sit in my own office. I have no value in this house anymore!' he exclaimed, failing to see the funny side. 'Listen here, it's still my name on that office door.'

'Yes, Abbu ji,' I replied, laughing, as he strolled along dragging his slippers. 'That's what you think,' I giggled as he turned the corner.

'He's bored, now that he's retired. He likes having something to do,' Ammi observed, shaking her head.

Ammi and I walked through the downstairs corridor to the back of the house, where Gurpul and I had made our own private home. I opened the wooden door and felt the cool air from the fans sweep under my kameez. The mint green curtains had been drawn back and the netting underneath danced freely with the outdoor breeze. The rest of the doors within the bedroom remained open and I led Ammi to the dressing room on the far right side.

'I don't have much of a choice do I, Ammi ji?'

'Not at all, dear. If anybody saw this dressing room they would think you were deprived,' she said, raising her pencilled eyebrow.

We began looking through the three wall-length rails on each side of the room, overflowing with clothes. The white painted walls could barely be seen, only colourful reds, greens and orange garments caught the eye. Ammi began in one corner and I skimmed through the other.

'This sari?' she suggested, after a few minutes.

'Where did that come from?'

'It was with the clothes we gave you on your wedding. Here you go, have this pressed.'

Ammi made herself comfortable in the bay window and rang the bell for the servants' quarters. I opened the dressing table drawer and took out my jewellery: so many boxes of complete full sets, which comprised a necklace, earrings, bangles and a ring, all neatly stored. I began opening each box and passed them to Ammi for us to decide on the best match. There was a knock on the door and Dija entered.

'Take this and have all the creases taken out,' Ammi ordered. My maid obediently took it away. 'I like this, Taji, the sapphires match well with the blue in the sari. You have the perfect pair of courts to go with this.' Ammi went back into the dressing room and found the shoes she referred to, among the many pairs. 'Here you are. You have a perfectly matching outfit now. Start getting ready, it's past three already.'

I began applying my makeup, remembering the tips my Ammi gave before the wedding.

'Your sari is ready,' Dija said from the doorway.

'Just wait there one moment, I'm nearly done.' I looked in the mirror, pleased with my makeup skills.

'Come in,' I shouted, and Dija entered with the sari carefully draped over her arm. She was wearing an old mustard coloured shalwar kameez. 'How do I wrap this?' I asked, taking it from her.

'Put the underskirt on first, but not too tightly,' she said, looking at the slight bump on my stomach. 'How many months?'

'Three.' I pulled down my shalwar and stepped into the underskirt. 'Like this?' I asked, knotting the string. I had tied it too far over my waist and so Dija pulled it down, covering my ankles.

'Like this, Taji baji,' she said when she had finished.

'I've never worn a sari, this is my first time. Have you ever worn one?' I asked.

'No, Muslim women don't wear them.'

I didn't know she was Muslim, she did not cover her head like most girls, she usually tied her hair in a high ponytail.

'How did you learn to tie saris then?'

'I used to watch my neighbour: every morning she wrapped the sari around her waist, tucked it into the underskirt, put seven or eight pleats in the front, and then flicked it over her shoulder, leaving it to drape behind her back, it was quite a skilful performance.'

'Where does your family live?' I had never spoken to Dija at length previously and knew very little about her, despite her being my maid.

'I don't have any family. Ammi died three years ago from tuberculosis.'

'How old were you?'

'I was sixteen when Ammi died and when Abba died I was fourteen.'

She did not look nineteen: her face was clear and did not look as if it had matured since her early teens, she had a radiant complexion and soft skin. Her features were small, small squinting eyes and a chubby nose.

'I'm younger than you, Dija, so why do you call me baji?'

'Respect. I'm the servant girl and you're the daughter of this house, I'm not supposed to call you by your first name.' I remained still, feeling the sorrow in her voice. 'And, because I like you,' she added.

Dija continued with my sari, perfectly forming each pleat. After she had finished, I put on my shoes and took the necklace out of its box, tying the choker around my neck, and putting the earrings into my lobes. Dija combed my hair, carefully taking out the knots; she began from the bottom and made her way up, until the comb ran smoothly through. Taking three large strands, she plaited it, finishing off by placing two gold hair clips on either side of my ears, to keep it all neat.

'Taji, are you ready yet?' Ammi shouted from the corridor. 'Perfect,' she remarked inspecting me from the door.

'Dija baji helped me, she tied the sari.'

'Dija baji?'

'Yes, she used to watch her neighbour.'

'Yes, yes, but why are you calling the servant "baji"?' Dija made a quick exit.

'She's older than me and she calls me baji, plus she's a poor orphan, I felt bad when I found out,' I explained quietly.

'Yes, but Taji, she's our servant girl and I do not want you calling her "baji". Now, come on, Gurpul's waiting for you outside.' I obeyed Ammi's order and didn't question.

We walked out to the main gates, where Gurpul waited in Abbu's Chevrolet Sport Sedan. He got out of the driver's seat and opened the passenger side door.

'Where are we going?' I asked as we drove along Tucker Road.

'We're going for a drive.'

'A drive? How long will this drive take?'

'Twenty minutes.'

I changed the topic and remembered the morning episode.

'I think Abbu has found out that his name plaque has been replaced on the office door.'

'Replaced on the office door?' Gurpul repeated.

'Yes. The engraver came early in the morning and replaced it with your name.'

'What!'

'He told me that's what you had instructed.'

'Oh dear, Abbu ji isn't going to be impressed, is he?'

'Why not, if that's what you'd asked for?'

'Not at their house.'

'Where else then?'

'It will all be clear in a few minutes.' I looked at him, puzzled.

'You know today is the first time I actually spoke with Dija?'

'Who?'

'Dija, my maid.'

'And?' he asked, not very interested.

'She's a nice girl. You know, she's been calling me "baji" since I arrived a few months ago and only today have I realised that she's older than me.'

'Well, she is our servant.'

'Both her parents have died.'

'Yes, the mother used to work for us.' She became very ill one day and Ammi called for the doctor, but it was too late. She had a matter of days to live. Anyway, why are we talking about the servants?'

'Ok, so where are you taking me then? I've never seen this side of Mirpur.'

'But do you like it?' I looked out of the window and observed the surrounding area. There was more of a small town feel than what I was used to in Lahore. Men and women walking alongside the unstructured roads. Some relatively well presented, others visibly poor; barefoot, cradling babies in makeshift slings, baskets balanced well on their heads. Most had a cloth covering the bottom half of their face to protect against the clouds of dust lingering close, never too far. Street traders were in full swing with hoarse voices from all the hollering they do. Dotted around the town there was a mix of traditional family estates and many new developments of residential housing.

'How would you like a house here?' Gurpul asked but before my lips even parted, he continued, 'how about this house in particular?'

A guard opened the large iron gates and Gurpul drove up the tiled driveway. An immaculate white house was standing before us and I glared at it in astonishment, through the car windscreen.

'Is this our house?'

'Yes.'

We stepped out of the car and I looked around, staring at the top balcony and the front glass windows. Gurpul opened the obscured glass door which led into a large entrance hall. A grand staircase was directly opposite. I looked around speechless.

'Come in here,' Gurpul directed.

It was a room of over fifty feet in length. An archway split it in two; one was a drawing room with settees along all three walls and coffee tables in the centre, the other, further back, held an enormous mahogany dining table.

'When did you do all this, Gurpul?' I finally managed to ask.

'It's been an ongoing project, since before we got married.' He collapsed on the settee, taking me down with him. 'The long hours at the office...'

'You were sorting out the house. I could never have imagined such a surprise.'

'Our baby will be born in our own home.' He patted my stomach gently and I smiled at the thought.

'I can't wait to tell my Ammi and Abba. Come on, let's look at the rest of the house,' I insisted, pulling Gurpul back up.

There was an average size kitchen behind the staircase, a door from the dining area and one from the main entrance hall led into it. To the right of the house was Gurpul's office, already furnished with a desk, large leather armchair and filing cabinets.

'This is where you wanted the name plaque, isn't it?'

'Yes. The stupid man has replaced Abbu's plaque with mine for no reason. I'll call him later and ask him to put Abbu's back up.'

'I have my own bedroom don't I?' I teased as Gurpul chased me to the main bedroom, where an enormous bed lay in the centre of the right wall. There were two night-tables on either side of the bed, and wardrobes aligned beside them. The walls were the same mint colour as we had in our current home. The window looked down the driveway and onto the street.

'This is perfect,' I whispered to myself.

'Look in here,' Gurpul directed me to the ensuite.

There was a pink tiled bathroom, with a round bathtub, an English style flushing toilet and two basins. I caught a glimpse of him through the mirror above the sinks, a smile on his face, like I had never seen, not even on our wedding day.

'Let me show you the baby's nursery. He can play in here.'

'He?'

'He or she... it just slipped out,' Gurpul explained. He silenced and then continued, 'Although, it's important to have a boy in the family: they carry the family name; unlike a girl who takes her husband's name.'

'Well I do not choose the gender of the baby, I just carry it. If I could, I'd make you a whole cricket team.' Gurpul laughed.

'How about this as a baby room? This is for all the toys,' he said, examining the shelves.

The tour continued to the second level, onto the balcony which overlooked the whole of Mirpur.

'There is another room up here too, Taji. It will be useful in the summer, when it's humid in the house: we can sleep out here in the breeze.'

I felt my skin tingle as I imagined us spending a summer night together on the rooftop, a sweet breeze dancing between us, as our souls became one. I cared for him deeply, I longed for him to return from work so we could relax together, eat together, get to know each other. We laughed, we laughed every day; he made me laugh when I felt melancholy missing my family. He comforted me, he brought me food when I didn't want to eat, he held my hair back when I was sick with the pregnancy. Every time I looked into his eyes I saw a gentle soul. I hoped I was everything he wanted in a wife and that I loved him like all wives should love their husbands. Spending the rest of my life with him was all I longed for, just us, in our home, with our child.

'Is this really our home?' I asked again, trying to come to terms with the surprise.

'Yes, Taji, our home.'

'When do we move in?'

'Whenever you're ready. We can move either before the baby is born, or after.'

'I'll start packing tomorrow, and once everything is done, we'll move,' I suggested.

'Let's lock up for now then.'

When we returned home, dinner was ready to be served. Ammi was opening the double doors leading into the dining room and turning on the lamps around the room.

'The house is incredible!' I shouted as I skipped towards Ammi and Abbu, 'I can't believe this was all kept a secret from me. I feel so blessed with all I have: Gurpul as my husband, both of you as parents, the new house now, the baby on its way. I don't know what I've done to deserve all this.'

'Roopa and I,' Abbu began, taking his seat at the head of the table, 'have wanted Gurpul and you to have your own house, so that you can bring up your family as you like, and learn to take responsibilities. We don't want you to have to worry about us. Well, don't forget us altogether either,' he joked. They both had reassuring smiles on their faces. 'Now, come on, let's get eating.'

Abbu ji helped himself to the saag aaloo, making his usual comment as he poured two spoonfuls into his bowl,

'Saag is filled with vitamins, it's good for you. At our age we need to cut down on meat and have more vegetables.' He passed the dish to Ammi, who squinted as she took a quarter of a spoon.

'Look at her,' Abbu complained, as he reached out for the roti. 'She likes nothing but meat, no vegetables. Like her son she thinks vegetables are for poor people. She does not realise what the nutritional benefits are.' Ammi ignored him and pulled a face. His lecturing continued with,

'Taji, you on the other hand are about to be a mother; you should be eating well, so you have a healthy child. We don't want an underweight grandson, the healthier the better. It reflects badly on us if you have an underweight baby.'

We had all learned to nod and agree with Abbu when he was in lecture mode, because there was no reasoning at that point. But we still did as we pleased! I was also feeling the pressure of providing a grandson, because it was important for the next generation to start with a male head of the family.

'When are you going to begin packing?' Ammi asked.

'Before we begin, we're going to need lots of bags and boxes for our clothes,' I said.

'We?' Gurpul said, 'I have half a rail in the dressing room, the rest are all yours.'

'Yes, that's enough space for you.' I asserted.

'Tomorrow I'll call Babu and Dija and we'll have all your things packed; it won't take too long. You will be settled in your new home within the next few days,' Ammi reassured.

'I must call my parents and let them know,' I remembered.

'Ah, rasmalai,' Abbu commented, as Babu placed the crystal dessert plates down on the dining table, clearing the dinner dishes.

'Look at him,' Ammi teased, 'vegetables, saag, and now?'

'Here they go again,' Gurpul whispered under his breath. I thought about how much I would miss the evening drama at the dining table.

'There is nothing wrong with a little dessert, Roopa.'

'A little!' Ammi exclaimed. 'Your bowl is filled to the brim!'

'Oh, let me eat please,' Abbu whined. 'You know, Taji, rasmalai is my favourite dessert, even when I was a child.'

'Yes Abbu ji, I gathered it was your favourite. We've had it almost every night since I've been here.'

'And he talks about being healthy – it's all fresh cream and sugar cane.' Ammi pointed out.

'It's probably not good for you, but it tastes good, doesn't it, Gurpul?' Abbu asked, seeking some defence.

'Don't get me involved, I'm not here for long, I'd like to leave on a good note.'

'Stop sitting on the fence, is it a yes or a no?' Abbu asserted.

'I'm staying out,' Gurpul insisted.

'Look at him, he's still his Ammi's baby, defending her. He's going to be a father soon, but he's still a child at heart.'

'Father or not, he's always going to be my baby,' Ammi said.

'I'd better shut up, Taji, otherwise Roopa will throw me out of the house. At fifty, I'll be homeless.'

'You can come to our house if Ammi ever throws you out, but I'm sure she won't, she loves you far too much.'

'Roopa, love me? No, never. She married me because I was the son of a successful businessman. Good money you see?'

'So, Abbu ji, who did you really want to marry?' Gurpul teased.

'I wanted to marry my Roopa, of course. She was a beautiful young girl, slim, fashionable and she had short hair when we married. But look at her now, she's put on so much weight.'

'That's what happens when you get to our age.' Ammi defended, but Abbu wasn't going to agree.

'I worry about what's happening with the British Raj,' he commented, looking over at his newspaper.

'I have no interest in Britain's empires, we're living peacefully, that's all I want,' I said.

'But we're not living peacefully, the British have taken over our country,' Abbu began.

'I don't think she's very interested at the moment, she's tired,' Gurpul insisted. 'Come on, Taji, let's go,' he instructed before this turned into another political debate with Abbu.

Ammi and Abba went upstairs, to their bedroom, and Gurpul and I walked through the glass corridor to retire for the night.

Babu cleared the breakfast dishes, as Ammi and I took the final sips from our tea cups. He slowly piled the plates, with his hunched back and drooping shoulders. His dirty white coloured face was lifeless, with deep engraved wrinkles on his forehead and around his eyes, telling the story of hardship. But despite this, his heavy hooded eyes were still vibrant and those of a youthful man, as they shone through radiantly like the blue of the ocean. He lifted the tray and took it away. He had stains on his kameez from cooking and washing dishes, and it fell from his shoulders as if it were two sizes too big: his body barely visible, not even revealing an outline. His shalwar was too short, not reaching down to his feet as it should and leaving his skinny ankles exposed. The brown open-back slippers showed the cracking skin on his heel, with the outer material on the front of the slipper wearing away.

'What's the matter? What are you thinking about?' Ammi asked.

'Babu.'

'What about him?'

'He looks so frail, and look at the clothes he wears and the shoes he has.'

'He doesn't look after himself.'

'How old is he?'

'He has been with us so long, I can't remember.'

'He looks older than Abbu ji, doesn't he?'

'But the poor usually do look older, because of their lifestyle.'

That was not entirely true since Ammi looked older than she was because of her weight and thinning white hair.

'It's not a style Ammi, it's circumstance. They have no means of changing it,' I argued, as my gut clenched at the state of Babu. 'How long has he been with you?'

'Twenty years.'

'And how old was he then?'

'I'd say about forty.'

'It makes me uneasy that he's still working: he should be resting now, not serving us.' I thought about the staff my parents had, they were never seen in this state: they dressed well and looked healthy. Ammi looked after them, she had clothes tailored for them a few times a year, made to their own measurements; they were not glamorous or expensive, but they were still new and clean.

'We need to arrange for some servants at your house as well,' Ammi said.

'We don't need any living in with us, I'll just have a maid to clean and cook.'

'Every high society family has at least one servant with them.'

'I don't see the need, it'll only be Gurpul and me.'

'Things still get dirty, dust settles on furniture and it requires daily cleaning. And who will do the cooking and shopping?'

'The shopping I will do myself, that's not a problem, but the cooking...'

'Exactly, that's why you need at least one servant to look after the house.'

'Gurpul and I will sort that out later, once we've moved.'

'It's difficult finding good and trustworthy staff, Taji. You can't take anybody in, just like that. We need to find somebody, who has worked with a family for many years. If you take an unknown person, you don't know anything about their background and that's dangerous. Plus, staff today are very demanding.' I laughed at Ammi's observation.

'We can share with you, Ammi,' I suggested. 'Babu and Dija can rotate between the houses.'

'This Babu, we were lucky to get him.'

'Why is that?'

'He worked with a family for ten years and they were moving to Karachi and wanted Babu to move with them; but Babu didn't want to move away from his own family. He told the employer that he wasn't prepared to leave Mirpur, and they weren't pleased. They threatened him by saying he wouldn't find alternative work, because they would not reference him for his work.'

'How awful. So what happened?'

'Shashi was on his way to work one morning, when somebody got in the way of his car. He stopped and it was Babu. He had fallen from his bicycle and was trying to mend it. He had injured his leg, but he was not concerned about that, he needed his bicycle as it was his only means of transport. Shashi took him to the local cycle shop and on the way, Babu told of his dilemma. Shashi realised that he was clearly a good worker, which is why the family wanted him to move to Karachi with them. We had just bought this house and were looking for a servant.'

'So you picked him up from the street and brought him home?' I interrupted.

'Not quite. After the bike had been repaired, he drove Babu to the family's house. There he spoke with the master and told him of his worker's incident. The master was grateful and began speaking of Babu's commitment to work. Babu saw him out and Shashi left his business card and told Babu to come once the owners had left. A few weeks later he arrived.'

'Poor Babu.'

'Poor? He should be grateful, otherwise nobody would have employed him once his previous master had moved away.'

'You're lucky to have found somebody like him. I'm sure he has given you no trouble.'

'No trouble whatsoever,' she finally admitted, having difficulty allowing the words to part from her lips. 'Look at the time, it's eleven already. We've wasted so much time with all this nonsense servant talk.'

'I'll go and get started,' I said.

'Send Babu to get some boxes and I'll bring down any travelling bags I have upstairs.'

I went straight to the bedroom and found the door open. Babu and Dija were already packing. They had boxes and bags and were making neat piles of clothing.

'You've already started?'

'Yes, we waited for you and Bibi ji, but you were still having breakfast so we began,' Babu said as he neatly placed a pile of my clothes into a suitcase.

'How thoughtful.'

'This suitcase holds all the clothes from the rail near the door. Come, I'll show you,' Babu said, walking into my dressing room. 'We have emptied this rail, I'll label the suitcase "Rail 1" so you know where everything has come from.'

'That's a good idea. I'd never have thought of that.'

'That's the difference, choti Bibi,' he said, courteously addressing me as the younger lady of the house, 'old means wise.'

'I agree.'

'People think servants are stupid, but we're not.'

'I know, Babu, but I don't think like that.'

I was embarrassed at his comment as I knew he was referring to Ammi, for she did not respect him and dismissed everything he said. Since arriving at the house, I had not spoken to Babu much either, and he probably thought that I shared Ammi's views on servants, but he did not realise that we were of totally differing opinions.

'Taji, I don't know where that Babu has got to. I need his help,' I heard Ammi shouting as she walked down the corridor. Rushing out into the bedroom I tried to quieten her before she said anymore.

'He's here, don't worry, he's already got the boxes and they've started packing too.'

'Really? They've used their initiative.'

'Oh, Ammi ji, they're not as bad as you make out,' I whispered.

'What are they packing?'

'My clothes. They've already emptied one rail.'

'We'll start with your gold jewellery then. You need to keep it safe otherwise it will disappear in all this chaos.'

I opened the bottom drawer of my dressing table and took out the boxes holding my sets. All the jewellery from my wedding day was in red coloured boxes and the jewellery Gurpul had given was in blue boxes. I piled them in a bag that Ammi brought from upstairs, squeezing the smaller ones down the sides.

'I don't want to send this bag with all the other things,' Ammi said. 'We will take it once everything else has been moved. Dija, carry this upstairs with me.'

As they carried the jewellery upstairs to put away safely, I helped Babu fold the remaining clothes.

'You have a lot of clothes, choti Bibi,' Babu remarked.

'They are all from my wedding. I never had such a collection when I was with my parents.'

'It's all part of the wedding and the dowry isn't it?'

'Yes.'

'Dowry isn't a problem for the rich, but for a man like me, it's difficult. Your parents must have given thirty or forty suits in your dowry.'

'Yes, it was about that,' I replied, remembering that Ammi had actually given fifty suits. She could not pack them in two suitcases and sent Lala to buy another one from the bazaar.

'And Gurpul's parents gave you equally as many. I had the job of ironing and displaying them for the family to view.'

'That must have taken you a long time.'

'Two whole days. I couldn't straighten my back for days later.'

'Do you have any daughters?' I asked, thinking about his comment about dowries.

'I have two, but I feel blessed that I did not have any more: finding the dowry for Razia and Shazia was difficult. I worked day and night for Razia's dowry, I even begged for her in-laws to accept us the way we were.'

'What do you mean?'

'After visiting my home they realised how poor I was and refused to accept Razia's hand in marriage. I promised to give everything they asked for as part of her dowry; they accepted and gave a list of items which were to be delivered to their house one day before the wedding.' I listened attentively to Babu, who had stopped folding the clothes and was sitting on the floor with his feet tucked under his knees. 'They had asked for so much, I could not afford it.'

'What did they want?'

'Fifteen suits, a thirty-six piece dinner set, furniture for her bedroom, including a charpai for Razia to sleep on, and wedding jewellery. They asked for more, I can't remember exactly what, but I worked day and night to earn the money, and even then I didn't manage.'

'So what happened?'

'The day before the wedding they visited. The dowry had been displayed for them to view. The mother circled the room, scrutinising each item thoroughly, and noting exactly what there was. She took out a piece of paper and compared what she had asked for with what was in the room. It didn't match. I knew what she was going to say, so I spoke first and explained, "Baji, I have worked since the day you came for Razia's hand, and this is all I can afford. I have even borrowed money from the neighbours, but still I have not earned enough." She interrupted before I'd finished, "Ali, we agreed that you would provide the dowry I asked for and you have not, so this wedding will not take place." She stood up, ready to leave, but I got down on my hands and knees, blocking the doorway and begging for her to take Razia; to bring her son the next morning for the nikkah wedding ceremony, and to take my daughter. "Fine, I will take your daughter, but you must make up the dowry within one month of the marriage, otherwise I will bring her back." I agreed, and the nikkah took place.'

'It ended happily for you then?'

'No.'

'Why?' I asked, as Ammi entered the dressing room with a suitcase.

'Here is another case, pack the rest of the clothes in here,' she ordered.

Babu placed his pile of clothes in the case, and I thought about Razia, wondering what happened to her. For three months I had remained oblivious to Babu's circumstances, I had never thought anyone could live such a hard life.

'You're doing a lot of thinking today, Taji, why are you gazing?' I quickly got up and helped Babu with the clothes.

'I'm just thinking about all this moving, it's so hectic,' I lied unconvincingly, but Ammi did not question further.

Once the rails were empty, Babu zipped up the cases and tied the straps. He carried them out into the bedroom and lined them up against the wall. Ammi inspected the dressing room to ensure nothing had been left. Once she was satisfied, she ordered Babu to take the luggage out to the front hall. The furniture and household appliances which came in my dowry were still in the storage room, unopened.

'Look at the dust, Dija, clean these boxes,' Ammi said. Ammi waited for Dija to exit and then asked, 'What was Babu saying earlier?'

'He was telling me about his daughters and the difficulty he faced with their dowries.'

'Taji, it's important that you do not become so emotionally involved with the servants and their circumstances; this is what they want.'

'What do they want?'

'They want to trap you emotionally, so that they can take advantage of you.'

'Ammi, he's an old man, how will he take advantage?'

'In many ways; they are clever people, these servants.' I dismissed her warnings of servants and their so-called cunning behaviour. 'He will see that you have been moved by what he tells you, which I'll inform you is usually all made up, and then he will win your sympathies. Once he has that, he will start asking you for a nicer place to stay, more wages, new clothes, and in return you will suffer.'

Babu entered to take some more cases, he lifted two with great difficulty, one in each hand. I couldn't watch, I looked away.

'I am not one to get emotionally involved. I know where to keep servants and how to handle them,' I said assertively.

'OK, but be careful.'

'I'll go and see if the car is being loaded.'

I lifted a bag to take with me.

'Don't lift heavy things, Taji, leave it to Babu.'

Babu was in a worse state than me, so I carried the bag nonetheless. A red wagon was parked outside and Babu was loading it.

'Sahib sent this wagon, he said it would take too many visits in the car.'

'Did Gurpul say when he will be home?' I asked.

'Sahib was in a meeting, but he did say he will be home shortly.'

'Babu?' I asked, as he was picking up a box.

'Yes?'

'You didn't finish telling me what happened with Razia.'

'Choti Bibi, this is the life of a poor man, you should not worry yourself with it.'

'Did you pay the remaining dowry?'

'After one month I still had not made the money, so her mother-in-law sent her back.' Babu put the box down and leaned against the wagon, 'she came in ripped clothes and torn shoes and they had thrown her out of their house. It took her all day finding her way home: she'd never been out, she didn't know how to get from one end of Mirpur to the other. When she finally found the house, she ran inside and fell to my feet. I knew why she had come back. It was not her fault, it was mine. She told how they had taken the entire dowry and she was not given any of it. They confiscated all her new garments, leaving her with rags. She cleaned and cooked all day, while the others socialised. Her sisters-in-law wore her clothes and shoes, they would beat her and scold her.'

'Were you not relieved that she had escaped from them and returned home safely?'

'No, Bibi. Shazia not married and Razia already returned home? We would become the talk of the village, which would destroy Shazia's chances of marrying.'

'Could you not borrow any more money?'

'I sold the two goats and the little land I had on the farm. Once I had sold enough to make the money, I bought the remaining dowry items and took Razia back to her husband.'

'They took her back?'

'They got what they wanted. They were happy. They had new furniture for the house, new clothes and a servant.'

'You took a servant for them too?'

'Razia.' I gasped at the horror.

'Do you have no sons, Babu?'

'I had three, but they all died young. I thought I had been blessed with three sons and only two daughters, but I was not to know what fate awaited me. They were triplets and died when they were ten.'

'How?'

'Back then nobody knew why, they just died. And then my wife died a year later.'

'You raised the girls alone?'

'Yes.'

'What happened to Shazia?'

'She married my nephew, and because they're family, they didn't ask for a dowry.'

'People with sons are lucky. If I had three sons, I would not be so poor.'

'Because they would be working and helping you?' I clarified.

'Not only that, but because I would be entitled to three dowries when they married. That would bring me enough money.'

'Is this why sons are a blessing?' I asked, now understanding the true reasoning behind the highly acclaimed notion of sons.

'Taji?' I heard Ammi shouting from inside.

'I'm here, Ammi ji.'

Ammi climbed into the wagon and examined the loaded luggage. The Friday call for prayer was ringing in the background from the local masjid.

'Babu, there are a few more bags in Taji's room, fetch them and make sure nothing has been missed. There are sealed boxes in the storeroom, leave them for now.'

'Bibi ji, it's Jummah time, I'll run to the masjid, offer my prayers and be right back.'

'OK, be quick, we need you here today,' Ammi replied.

'Take your time, Babu, there's no rush,' I whispered. He smiled and ran down the driveway.

'Tell Dija to bring the remaining things from your room, there's nothing heavy,' Ammi said.

I returned to the room, where Dija was still cleaning the boxes.

'Are they not done yet?' I asked.

'No, there is a lot of dust, they've been locked up for a few months.'

'Just wipe the tops,' I told her.

'Bibi ji wanted them all clean, but the tops are done.'

'Wash your hands in the bathroom. I have some lotion on the sink, your hands will be dry after all that.'

I looked around at the remaining items. Gurpul's night stand was filled with papers and books. I had a family picture from our wedding on my stand, everything else had been cleared. The crystal flower vases in the bay windows still had flowers in them, they needed to be taken in the car. The small toiletries in the bathroom could also be taken later.

'My hands smell lovely and they feel so soft,' Dija said, smelling the perfumed lotion.

'You should put lotion on your hands after cleaning, it will stop them from drying out.'

'A bottle of lotion will cost one day's pay, I can't afford things like that,' she remarked casually.

I went into the bathroom and from the cupboard took out a spare bottle.

'Here you go, have this.'

'No, I can't take this from you.'

'I would like you to. Put it in your room otherwise it will disappear among all this moving.'

'I'll go straight away,' she said, almost running towards the door.

'Hang on, we may as well take all this as well, instead of coming all the way back.'

We both returned to the hall where Gurpul had arrived and was also inspecting the boxes in the wagon.

'Everybody is scrutinising poor Babu's work, he's done a good job,' I defended.

'Is Babu also your new friend now?' Gurpul teased.

'Why?'

'Well you're speaking in his defence, and in his absence.'

'Nothing wrong with sincerity.'

'Has Babu not returned yet, Taji?' Ammi asked.

'I don't think so. Jummah prayer is a long one.'

'But it's so inconvenient, we need him here,' Gurpul complained. Luckily he returned quickly and so they could take the first load.

*

Breakfast was being served in the garden the next morning. There was toast, fried and boiled eggs, omelettes, parathas, English cereal, a variety of jams, flavoured yogurts, melons and mangoes. Ammi had prepared a feast to mark our last day with them.

'This is the best breakfast I've ever had,' Gurpul said, astounded at the variety of food on the table.

As I took a seat on the cane chairs, a crisp morning breeze swept under the table, carrying with it the delicate aroma of lavender. I breathed deep into my stomach, sharing with my baby the sweet pleasures of the outside world. My eye caught the pink water lilies dancing proudly in the central pond, using the beautiful flat green pads to anchor themselves, as they came into full morning bloom. I imagined our baby playing around the pond, trying to reach for the petals, pulling them apart; this will be a mischievous child, I could sense it. Gurpul buttered his toast and sandwiched the yolky fried eggs, and upon his crunch I watched the yolk splatter all over his plate and shirt. We both giggled as we knew that would happen; another shirt change required. A plate of juicy ripe mangoes and perfectly red strawberries with their green foliage still perfectly attached called out to me. I felt content with the perfect summer breakfast, so romantically thought out by Ammi. The neighbour's cat was meandering along the rose walk, which Ammi had exquisitely created with reds and whites and pinks and yellows. She watered the roses every day, twice a day, during the summer months to prevent them from withering.

'I wish we could spend all day out here,' I said to Ammi.

'We will do it again, next time in your garden,' she promised. 'We have a busy day ahead, with unpacking. What are you going to do today, Shashi?'

'I'll be in my office reading these newspapers,' Abbu said, gathering his papers, folding them and securing them under his arm.

'There must be a lot of news if you're spending all day reading the papers,' Gurpul commented.

'A lot of news!' Abbu exclaimed. 'There has been a lot of news since the British arrived in India and now it looks like it's coming to an end.'

'Why is that?' I asked.

'The Indian National Congress and The All India Muslim League, both want Britain to quit.'

'That will cause anarchy,' Gurpul protested.

'Anarchy for a few months is better than having the British here for the remainder of my life. They have been here since the day I was born, they ought to go back home now. We don't want them here,' Abbu said furiously. 'We need independence, we're quite capable of looking after ourselves and we don't need the British to nurture us.'

'Calm down, Shashi, you'll have high blood pressure by the end of the morning,' Ammi said.

'I'll tell you one thing, my blood pressure will be normal forever when they leave.'

'Abbu ji, you're really not looking at this realistically,' Gurpul continued to argue.

'I am thinking of this realistically: since the 1857 War of Independence the British have made Hindustan their home, I ask why?'

'They have provided us with so much though: look at the rail network, there's nothing quite like it, we would never have managed such an orderly system on our own.'

'The rail network? Where did the labour come from? Our own men, our brothers have made that rail network, not the British. They are just good at ordering us about, we built the rail network ourselves. We have also fought in their wars, young men have died fighting their battles, many have also risked their lives for them.'

'All I'm saying is that you should think about your views practically and objectively: Britain leaving India will result in Hindustan collapsing.'

'It will not. We are not totally incapable.'

'Look what you've started now,' Ammi said, 'come on Gurpul, let's go.'

'I'll see you later, Abbu ji.' Gurpul said leaning forward to shake hands. 'And calm down, please.'

'I have a valid point, you know?'

'Yes, Abbu ji,' he said.

Out in the hall, Babu and Dija were sitting on the footstools, cooling their feet on the marble floor. They looked after each other and cared for one another like a father and daughter. I often saw Dija massaging Babu's feet at the end of the day, or taking dinner for him while he rested.

'Have you turned on the fans in the car, Babu?' Gurpul asked.

'Yes, Sahib.'

The car had been cooled; the leather seats were cold on my legs and back. Outside the driveway the same old man was sitting on his stool, carving some wood on his workbench. He wore no shoes, the shavings from the wood fell down to his feet, covering them like a blanket. His sharp knife tool was shaping the wood like scissors cutting paper.

'That man has been going for almost fifteen years,' Ammi commented as we came out of the drive and turned right, driving past him.

'What does he do?' I asked.

'Anything and everything. He's a talented man, he just needs somebody to hire him and allow him the opportunity to prove himself.'

'Have you had anything made from him?'

'Yes, the bedside tables in your bedroom.'

'He made those tables?' I asked surprised.

'Yes. He cuts the wood, makes whatever it is you want and then polishes them too.'

'Those tables are so perfectly crafted. I would never have imagined that he made them.'

'If you want anything for the new home, just go to him. He tries to double his rate when he sees he has a wealthy customer, but I never allow him to get away with it.'

'How much did he charge for the tables?'

'He wanted two hundred rupees, I gave one hundred. He was asking for twice the amount he charges other people. The poor think we have more money than brains.'

I didn't debate with Ammi. She was a kind and loving person, but only to those of her own class. She treated the poor like animals, she didn't even want to be near them, and Gurpul was occasionally of the same opinion.

The guard opened the gates as we approached; Gurpul drove to the top and Dija took in the view with awe, her mouth gaped open. She said something, I didn't hear, but I didn't need to hear because her face said all she was thinking. The doors and windows sparkled and the white paint was pristine. There were other similar houses on Maal Road, but none like mine: my house had been newly built.

The hallway was crammed: boxes and cases scattered around with the floor barely visible. Nothing had been placed in an orderly manner, just dumped wherever there was space. It took all day to unpack, but when we finished the house looked warm and felt like my home. Gurpul and I spent our first night there and it was almost like we were newly married once again.

Chapter 2

April 1946, Mirpur, India

The bright sunshine glared through the bedroom window piercing my eyes, so I carefully rolled over onto my left side forgetting that I no longer had an enormous stomach to take with me. My entire body was still aching with exhaustion. The midwife came in, lifted my nightie to my hips and massaged my legs. She dipped her fingers in a bowl of warm oil and rubbed it all over; her hands were warm and soft, and the touch of them making circular movements eased away some of the pain. Ammi had insisted Naseem was the best woman to deliver the baby and she was right: this woman must have delivered at least a third of the city's babies. With her husband now dead and her children married, she travelled all over Mirpur and stayed with pregnant women for the last week of their pregnancy, waiting to deliver the baby. Naseem was not like the other women who came to offer their services. As soon as Gurpul left for the office in the morning they would come in threes, in pairs or alone to offer advice and to explain their charging structures. Some said they would come and stay for ten days prior to the birth and ten days after, some arrived only a couple of days beforehand and those who lived close by insisted it was only necessary for them to come once the waters had broken. I would call Ammi and she would scold them for not allowing me to rest, insisting that she would humiliate them if they ever came when she was visiting; surprisingly, they were never in sight on such occasions. Ammi would only have the very best delivering her grandchild, and so she made her own enquiries and decided on Naseem. After finishing on my legs, Naseem took my hands and massaged them too, moving further up to my arms and shoulders as I lay on my back, relaxing. She was a humble woman and didn't speak much, just concentrated on her work, mentioning the name of Allah with every task she began. Dija quietly knocked on the double doors and came in, placing what looked like a tiny parcel in my arms and left again. My precious baby girl. Only hours earlier, she was curled up inside me, preparing to make her entry into our world; and now here she was. She freely kicked her small legs in the air as I loosened the blanket, like a bird freed from a cage, with so much to explore. She felt so light, she smelled so divine and her cries so angelic.

'A gift from Allah,' Naseem commented. I nodded in agreement, her Allah, my Guru.

My baby began whining, as I played with her cheeks, stroking her soft dark skin.

'She needs milk,' Naseem said. 'You ought to breastfeed her now.'

'Will it hurt?'

'Not for long,' she reassured, directing me to the correct position. My baby immediately stopped crying and suckled gently. I felt an overwhelming sense of contentment: my beautiful baby against my chest, healthy and well, fragile and tender to touch. I smelt her beautiful skin as I rubbed her back. Naseem took her away and I got out of bed, slipping into the pink cushioned slippers Gurpul had bought for me before the birth, and stood by the window.

On Maal Road, the same busy and lively neighbourhood attended to daily routines. Across the road, Shaista was standing by the blackboard, on the balcony of her house, teaching the local children. Although she held a cane she rarely used it to hit the children. It was her means of following the lesson on the board without having to use her fingers. Upraj was in his usual spot, with a hookah in his mouth, speaking to anybody who walked by. The poor man's wife eloped with his best friend thirty-five years ago. He still calls for her every morning when he brings out his stool and table and places them under the tree's shade in the street. He does not move until night falls and then he bids farewell to his wife, asking her to return soon. Abhi and Gita Gupta were returning from their weekly trip to the temple, offering thanks for the success they were experiencing after the opening of their textile mill in the city.

Dija entered with the breakfast tray and placed it on the round table beside the window.

'How are you feeling?' she asked.

'It was hard work!' I laughed, 'But when I held her in my arms, it was like the pain had instantly been erased from my mind. Who do you think she looks like?' I asked, folding the toast in half and dipping it in the tea. The front gates opened and I stood to see who had arrived; Gurpul's car drove up the driveway.

'I think I'll need to take another look before giving you my verdict. I'd better get back to work,' Dija said, taking a sharp exit before Ammi or Gurpul shouted at her for lounging around and not doing what she was paid for.

'How are you feeling, Taji?' Gurpul asked, entering the room.

'A little better, but still sore all over.'

'It's going to take some time,' Ammi commented, following behind.

'Where did you both go?'

'To the gurdwara and then we ordered some sweetmeats in celebration of the birth. This is my first grandchild and we're going to have a ceremony marking her arrival,' she said. 'But clearly if the baby was a boy, we would have had a ceremony matching the wedding,' she added quietly, but it was still loud enough for me to hear. I chose to ignore her comment.

'I guess you visited the gurdwara to set a date?' I asked, annoyed that they had not consulted me.

'No, we've not set a date yet, you need time to recover,' Ammi insisted. 'Although I can't wait, when do you think you'll be well enough for the ceremony?'

'I'm not feeling too bad, I don't mind if we have the naming ceremony in a couple of days.'

'Are you sure you'll be up to it then?' Gurpul asked.

'Well, it's Monday today and if I have until Wednesday to rest, then hopefully I'll be well enough for the ceremony that afternoon.'

The date was set, so Ammi called my parents and all the other guests to advise them of the time and location.

'I'll invite Junaid,' Gurpul said. 'He's been such a help over the past few months, with us settling in and keeping an eye on you while I've been in the office.'

'He's not only been looking after me,' I said.

'What do you mean?' Gurpul asked, confused.

'I think he has a personal motive for visiting us.'

'Such as?' he probed further, desperate to know what I was referring to.

'Dija.'

'Dija?'

'Yes.'

'Really?'

'I've watched his eye follow her every move, and her cheeks burning when he looks at her.'

'I wasn't aware of this.'

'And recently they've begun speaking too.'

'Now that you mention it, I do remember Junaid asking me about Dija.'

'What was he asking?'

'How old she was, whether she had any family, how long she had been with us...'

'There you go, he was doing his research.'

'You ought to speak to Dija, I'll consult Junaid, and who knows we may have a wedding to attend soon.'

Naseem left me for a few hours and then returned to prepare the bath with warm water and herbal salts. While she filled the bathtub I went to the baby's room and there she lay soundly asleep, breathing quietly. Her tiny hands were beside her head as she slept on the charpai that Naseem had been using. The chest of drawers remained empty and now needed filling with pretty clothes and the shelves with toys. Dija had the house in perfect order, she had been working extremely hard, not that Ammi would have allowed her to slack, while I was confined to my room over the past few days. There was a knock on the main door and I heard Shaista's voice. She ran straight upstairs and took me into her skinny arms.

'You're an Ammi now, congratulations,' she said, towering over me with her great height and emerald green eyes searching for the baby.

We both took a seat on the settee on the landing, opposite the nursery.

'When was she born?'

'Sunday morning. She's in the nursery sleeping; go through and take a look.'

Shaista tip-toed into the room and leaned over to examine her. Her back was covered by her brown hair, which was fashionably worn loose and crimped. She was a modern woman in many respects: fashion, thoughts and education. Being one of the very few female Bachelors of Sciences in the area, she was encouraging the education of girls as she believed they were being repressed by society. She was confident enough to stand up to the men in the local community and promote the opening of her own school. It was to be dedicated to educating young girls who would ordinarily not have had the opportunity to receive an education. Hearing her debate with a group of men was awe-inspiring for me, as I couldn't ever imagine what it must feel like to be so brave and intelligent. I sometimes struggled to understand what was being said but she'd always take the time to debrief me afterwards. Not only that but she was also effortlessly radiant, with a smooth, clear oval face and delicate features.

'I think she looks like Gurpul,' she said, returning to the settee. I couldn't comment as I wasn't sure who she looked like.

'I hope she has his intelligence!'

'Taji! You're an intelligent woman too. I was teaching mathematics today and some of those girls were so sharp, it makes me so hopeful about the future of our girls.'

Dija came upstairs with drinks and snacks for us, placing them on the table.

'Sit down and join us, you need a break.' I said. Like me, she too learned from Shaista.

'How old are you now, Dija?' Shaista asked.

'Twenty.'

'Are you looking to marry?'

'That would be my dream, but who will marry me? I have no family,' she replied.

'That doesn't matter,' Shaista protested.

'We can help you, Dija; Gurpul and I can look out for suitable bachelors.'

Dija's posture changed suddenly as she stopped slouching and sat upright.

'Really?' she asked.

'If you allow us to.'

'No one has ever offered to help me before,' she said. 'But,' she stuttered.

'Obviously we will look for a Musalmaan.' Re-energised, she skipped away, leaving Shaista and me alone again. 'Why do you not marry, Shaista?'

'Finding a suitor in Mirpur is difficult: it feels like all the local families have sons with little intellect, big egos and no initiative! I can't marry and just be a housewife.'

'So look further afield. Lahore, Karachi, Delhi, Bombay. Your Abba has land all over the country, such a wealthy zamindaar, he must come across so many eligible bachelors.'

'But none of them will be Michael will they?'

'He's gone back to England, you must forget him now, Shaista.'

'I can't forget him Taji. He's been a part of my life for five years. Abba might not agree to me marrying him because he's an Englishman, but I connect with him much more than I do with any of the Indian men here. In the summer months when we'd meet in Murree, we'd spend hours at a time talking about poetry, literature, the world economy, travel, horse riding.' For all of her independence and courage, Shaista was not able to bring her Abba around on this. He supported her, believed that women should have a part to play in society, but he was against her marrying an Englishman. Shaista believed the British Raj had left a sour taste in his mouth.

'Have you heard from him?'

'He still writes to me. He believes we'll be together again. Maybe one day he'll be posted back here, or I'll go to London.' I understood Shaista's dilemma; she was a woman ahead of her time and many of the men she met felt intimidated by her, or simply desired a wife who would raise the children and look after his family. For all the sorrows she carried with her, Shaista never let her guard drop. She spoke with me in confidence and I felt her pain, but there was nothing I could do to help.

'The naming ceremony is on Wednesday; you must come,' I said, changing the topic.

'Where will it take place?'

'At the local gurdwara at about three o'clock.'

'Taji, the bath is ready,' Naseem said, coming into the hall.

'You get bathed and I'll get going now,' Shaista said, 'if there's anything I can do to help just let me know.'

She left, lacking in energy, unlike when she arrived. I know the thought of Michael upset her and she missed him terribly.

I heard the bedroom door open and Gurpul walked in quietly. The tips of his fingers stroked my arm.

'Taji?' he whispered.

'I'm awake,' I managed to squeak from under the blanket.

'How are you feeling?' he asked, brushing the hair away from my face. 'Still tired?'

'A little, I need to catch up on sleep.'

'Dinner is ready downstairs, would you like me to bring it up?'

'No, I'll come down. I need to get out of this room.' He helped me up and out of bed and tied my night gown around my waist. 'Who closed the curtains?'

'I came up earlier to check on you and closed them, it was getting dark.'

'What's the time?'

'Eight o'clock.'

'Where's the baby?'

'She's downstairs. You've both been asleep for most of the day.'

Gurpul held my arm as we walked downstairs, I could see everybody through the glass doors seated at the table.

'Ah, Junaid's here as well?'

'Yes, he's been with me most of the day, helping in the office, so I invited him for dinner.'

'Taji, you've joined us,' Ammi said, as Gurpul opened the door.

'Hello, babhi,' Junaid's respect for Gurpul was such that he always greeted me as he would a real brother's wife. 'Congratulations on the baby.'

'Thank you.'

Abbu got up and came forward to give me his blessing.

'You've managed to come out of hibernation, Abbu ji,' I teased.

'I've only come for you. You know I'm comfortable in my own home, I don't like moving about too much.'

Gurpul sat at the head of the table and I beside him. Ammi and Abbu were sitting opposite one another as were Dija and Junaid, with Naseem on the end, probably feeling left out. I wondered how Ammi had allowed Dija to sit at the table, given she typically served us.

'Where's the baby?' I asked, looking around.

'Naseem's just put her on the sofa, while she eats dinner,' Ammi said. I looked behind me and there she lay, far away from the edge, so she didn't fall off. 'What would you like to eat, Taji? We've made all this for you, poor Dija has been in the kitchen most of the day.'

'I'll have some rice to start.' I glimpsed at Dija, but her head remained focussed on her plate, she didn't look up.

'Roasted chicken with chillies?' Gurpul asked putting the plate in front of me. I looked at the bright red artificial colouring and the large chicken legs which made me feel nauseous.

'I'll give it a miss for now.'

'How about chaat?' Abbu asked. 'There are chickpeas in this, salad and potatoes, mixed in yoghurt. Looks like Dija's made this spicy.'

'Just rice for now, Abbu ji.' I replied, becoming irritated at everybody's attempts to feed me. 'Junaid, how are your parents?' I needed to divert the attention.

'Ammi's knees are giving her problems and Abba is still fit and healthy, being out in the farms all day keeps him occupied.' Junaid always spoke gently and softly; unlike most men, he did not have a harsh voice.

'What are you doing these days?' Abbu asked him.

'Mainly mechanical work.' His hands did not look like they were in grease and oil for most of the day, they were clean and well kept.

'Are you married, Junaid?' Abbu asked, totally oblivious to the true reasoning of Junaid's presence.

'No.'

'You need a good wife to look after you, ask Gurpul, he loves every moment of it.'

'I'm waiting for the right girl to come along. Abba and Ammi would like me to marry soon.'

'You're a handsome boy, you won't have any problems finding somebody.'

'How about your friend across the road, Taji?' Ammi suggested.

Gurpul and I were taken aback at Ammi's inappropriate suggestion; neither of us was able to respond quickly enough. We both remained quiet, wondering what to say.

'I think she's much older than Junaid,' I replied, hoping that I was right, as I didn't know his age.

'How old are you?' Ammi asked him.

'Twenty-three.'

'Yes, he's far too young for Shaista, she's twenty-six,' I was relieved.

'Do you not know any other girls looking to marry? What about Babu's daughters?' Ammi asked, 'Are they both married?'

'Yes they are.' The table quietened again with poor Dija and Junaid still not daring to look up.

'I think everything has been sorted for Wednesday,' Gurpul interjected.

'Taji, you must wear your wedding lehenga on Wednesday.' Ammi said.

'It's not going to fit, I've gained so much weight: my waist and hips are a good few inches wider.'

'The weight would have come off by now,' Gurpul insisted.

'Does it look as if it's come off?' I snapped.

'Yes.' I ignored his observation.

'The lehenga was perfectly fitted to my size as I was on my wedding day; I won't get into it now,' I told Ammi.

'Try it on later and let me know.'

The baby was crying but quietened when I picked her up. I took her to the office and sat on Gurpul's swinging office chair. There were papers everywhere, but he would not allow either me or Dija to touch his things, just in case we misplaced something. The feeding was not as painful, but my breasts were still sensitive. When she had finished her feed I gently rocked back and forth; she was like a porcelain doll and I didn't want to break her.

'You're becoming an expert at this,' Naseem said, watching me. I was relieved that I had handled the feed without her having to correct me.

As we returned to the drawing room, I saw Dija and Junaid by the kitchen sink, where Dija was washing the dishes. Junaid was much taller and broader than her; she was a petite girl, desperately in need of a companion to share her life with.

'Is our princess back?' Ammi said. The table had been cleared and dessert was served on the coffee table in the drawing room. 'She's not difficult to feed is she?'

'Not at all.'

'Bring her here,' Abbu requested, leaning forward to take her in his arms. 'Isn't she beautiful? She looks just like her Abbu.'

'Do you think so?' I was still not sure who she resembled.

'She's got large, light brown eyes like Gurpul,' Abbu pointed out.

'The shape of her face is like Gurpul's as well: it's long, not round like Taji's,' Ammi commented, as she came to sit beside Abbu. They both played with her, stroking her hands and face. 'It's been so long since we've had a baby in the house.'

'They're only good to play with; staying up all night wasn't fun,' Abbu recalled. 'You both have the worst of it to come yet: many sleepless nights, having to wake up to give her milk, to change her, lots to come yet,' he warned.

'Nobody told us about that part of the arrangement,' Gurpul joked.

'Junaid's in the kitchen with Dija,' I told Gurpul, as Ammi and Abbu spoke among themselves.

'I know,' he replied cheekily.

'Did you speak to him?'

'I mentioned it, I said Dija was looking to get married. Did you speak to Dija?'

'I briefly spoke to her and she was delighted when I told her that we would help her find somebody.'

'I'm going to get going now,' Junaid said, coming back into the drawing room, Dija followed.

'Stay, Junaid, have some more dessert,' I offered.

'I've eaten enough. Ammi and Abba will be waiting for me, it's getting late. It's been nice meeting you again,' he told Ammi and Abbu.

'Good seeing you too, take care of yourself and salaam to your parents,' Abbu said, standing to shake his hand.

'And don't worry, Junaid, we'll find you a beautiful Musalmaan girl,' Ammi assured.

'I'm sure you won't have far to look,' Junaid commented, taking a glimpse at Dija. Ammi remained still, wondering whether she had heard correctly.

'See you soon, Taji babhi.'

'Bye, Junaid.'

Gurpul walked him to the door and Dija returned to the kitchen. Once the kitchen door had closed, Ammi quizzed. 'What's happening here? Junaid and Dija? When did it happen?'

I laughed at the sense of urgency in her voice.

'We think,' I began slowly, 'Junaid and Dija like each other, and it's just been confirmed.'

'Did you know this was going on?' Ammi began interrogating me.

'I noticed in passing and didn't really make much of it, but then Junaid's frequent visits convinced me.'

'What's going to happen now?'

'I don't know,' I replied as Gurpul re-entered. 'So what did he say?'

'Looks like we may have a nikkah as well as a naming ceremony. He's mentioned it to her and their feelings are mutual,' Gurpul reported.

'Well, who was going to ask us?' Ammi demanded.

'Ammi ji, we're Dija's employers, she works for us, we are not responsible for her private life, nor do we have a say in the matter,' I reminded her.

'But still,' she continued, 'Gurpul, where are you going to find another maid like her? This is such an inconvenience.'

'You're right,' he said, switching sides as he usually did when Ammi was angry.

'It's not going to be a problem, Gurpul,' I promised.

'Roopa, you do make silly comments sometimes,' Abbu said, also surprised at Ammi's remark.

'She has been with us for so long, her Ammi worked for us and died while she was in our service; I feel that we have a duty of care towards her,' Ammi said, trying to cover her tracks. 'What's to happen from here?' she asked in an altered tone.

'He's going to speak to his parents tonight and see what they say,' Gurpul informed.

'If Dija does get married, I'm going to have some suits made for her; it's the least we can do, she's been such a help,' I said, but there was no response from Gurpul or Ammi.

'Taji, I think you should get some rest,' Gurpul said. 'You need to recover by Wednesday. Abbu are you OK to stay here tonight, or do you want to be taken back home?'

'It's safer to stay. The papers are reporting more and more protestors are gathering in the evenings. It's best not to be on the roads late at night.'

'OK. Taji and I are going to bed. If you need anything, just let Dija know.'

'Good night, Taji.' Ammi said.

'Good night.'

*

I was in the office again the following morning, finishing the baby's feed, when there was an urgent knocking on the door. Gurpul opened it to allow Junaid in.

'It's Junaid with some news, have you finished?' he asked, peeping through.

'Yes, come in, I'm done.'

Junaid appeared from around the corner, his bright face and teeth on full show. He was dressed smartly in blue shalwar kameez, his hair in a side parting, combed back revealing a clear soft complexion, so rare for a man. His features were those of a woman, delicate and fine.

'Salaam, Junaid,' I said in greeting.

'I have some news for you, babhi.'

'Go ahead.'

'I spoke to Ammi and Abba about...', he stumbled, 'about Dija.' Gurpul and I could not help but smile at each other, 'They said if I approved then they have no objections.'

'Do they not want to meet her first?' I asked.

'They approve of my decision.'

'That's wonderful, Junaid,' I said. 'But we ought to ask Dija before we finalise anything.'

'I asked her yesterday, she accepts,' Junaid replied, without making eye contact.

'Still, we should make sure. I'll go and find her.'

I left the baby with Gurpul and went to get Dija from the kitchen.

'Taji baji, I'll bring you some breakfast,' she said, immediately getting up from the table where she was eating.

'No, no, I've not come for that.'

'Oh.'

'Somebody's here.'

'Shall I bring some tea?' she asked.

'No, it's Junaid.' In mid-flow she froze like a statue, but her mouth broke into a smile. 'He spoke to his parents and they are happy to accept you as his wife.' Her lips parted and the smile appeared. 'Do you want this to happen, Dija?' She nodded and looked at me sheepishly like a teenager in love. 'Come on, he's waiting for you.'

'What will I say to him?'

'You don't need to say anything.'

'But I've not even washed.' I laughed at the way she was panicking.

'OK, I'll tell him that you agree. Are you sure about this, Dija?'

'It would be my Ammi's wish that I married.'

'I'm sure you'll both be right for each other.'

I left her in the kitchen, probably at the happiest she had ever been since her parents passed away.

'Taji?' Ammi shouted as I walked along to the office, totally oblivious to her watching me.

'Yes, Ammi ji.'

'What are you smiling about?' she asked.

'I'll tell you in a minute,' I insisted, rushing along.

'What's going on?'

'Junaid's here.'

'I'll come and say hello.' That was the only excuse she could think of to join the discussion she felt she was missing out on.

'No, Ammi ji,' I persisted. 'Just give us a minute and then we'll join you for breakfast.' Without saying a word she returned to the dining area.

Typically being at the centre of all neighbourhood matters, she was finding it difficult to take a back seat.

'What did she say?' Gurpul asked when I finally reached the office, holding my side. 'Taji, you need to stop moving around so much, you're still recovering from birth.'

'You're right I do still feel sore,' I admitted, but quickly moved on to explain, 'It looks like we have a wedding ceremony to organise.'

'Thank you, babhi,' Junaid's joy was so explicit, I could see it rippling through him. He ran down the driveway, across the road and through the alleyway where he lived, to plan the nikkah ceremony.

'He looks like the happiest man in this world,' Gurpul said as we watched him from the front door.

'Dija's the same. Let's tell Ammi what's happening, she saw me talking to Dija and wanted to join the discussion in the office, but I told her to wait.'

'She'll be fuming now,' Gurpul said.

'And don't take your Ammi's side if she complains about Dija leaving,' I warned, but Gurpul did not respond.

'Is somebody going to tell me what's happening?' Ammi asked, before we had even fully entered the room. Abbu ji had no interest; he concentrated on reading his newspaper.

'Junaid and Dija are getting married,' Gurpul announced.

'What?' Ammi screeched.

'What's so surprising?' I asked.

'They're getting married? Junaid is such a good-looking young man, he could marry anybody.'

'Ammi ji!' Gurpul exclaimed. 'And so is Dija, they make a good match, you should be happy for them, they both deserve each other.' Gurpul had had a change of heart and Ammi was silenced.

'When is the ceremony? Dija needs to have some clothes made,' Ammi commented.

'He's going to arrange that,' I advised.

'It will be nice for Dija, to feel settled finally,' Ammi said.

'What do you think of all this, Abbu ji?' I asked.

'I'm delighted.'

'Let's worry about our own ceremony for now,' Gurpul said. 'I have some urgent business to attend to. Ammi will you go to the bazaar and pick up the sweetmeats and flowers?' Ammi nodded. 'Also, pick up any groceries we need for tomorrow evening's meal; Taji's family will be coming back here after the ceremony.'

After giving his orders, he departed.

'Taji, have you tried on the lehenga?' Ammi asked.

'I did last night, but the blouse would not zip up, and nor would the lehenga.'

'Leave all the outfits to me, I'll sort them out later today,' Ammi said.

I left the chaos downstairs and returned to my bedroom to get some rest. Dija had already made the bed and changed the plain mint green bed linen to the white and green with floral patterns. I took off my shoes at the door and changed into my slippers, so the exclusive cream coloured carpet we had in our bedroom did not get dirty. Gurpul had it especially ordered from Istanbul when we moved in, and it took five months to arrive. I slipped out of my night gown, pulled away the covers and got into bed feeling exhausted. The baby was crying, but Naseem quietened her fairly quickly, saving me from having to get up again. I thought about seeing my parents again: I couldn't wait. I wanted Wednesday to come quickly, but there were almost another twenty-four hours.

I dreamt of looking as graceful as a ballerina in the flamingo coloured outfit Ammi had left out for me; but I knew it was a dream when I looked down at my stomach which was now like a deflated balloon. A delicate pink sari with bursts of brighter pink petals all over; perfectly steamed and draped over the dressing room armchair. A pair of exquisite white pearl drop earrings were placed on the dressing table, reflecting shades of blue and pink as the light hit them. My baby's dress, a similar colour but with a ribbon of pearls to be tied around her waist.

'Ah, you're up from your rest?' I heard Ammi say. 'Do you like the clothes?'

'They're perfect.'

'Taji, the pearls I selected especially for this occasion: my Ammi gave them to me when Gurpul was born for good luck and to protect me and my child,' she explained, sitting down.

'Oh really? They're such charming pearls, I will always treasure them.' I said, gently touching her shoulder, and moved by the thoughtful gift.

'I've been to the bazaar three times today, but everything is under control. Flowers, sweetmeats, groceries, have all been collected. Babu is also here so he can begin making dinner for tomorrow night; it was all too much for Dija to do alone.'

'Babu is here now?' I asked, excited.

'Yes, he arrived a few of hours ago.'

I had not seen Babu for many weeks and he had not seen the baby yet. He spent the majority of his time at Ammi and Abbu's house, while Dija was here during the latter stages of my pregnancy, but I was thrilled he would finally get to meet my baby.

As Ammi left the room, I looked out of the window and saw Junaid crossing the road, lost in his own dreamy thoughts. I put on my gown, knowing that he was coming to talk about the ceremony. Dija let him in and they both joined me upstairs in the hall.

'My parents would like the nikkah to take place as soon as possible,' he announced. 'The mullah is available anytime.'

'Junaid, do your parents realise that Dija won't have a dowry, because she doesn't have anybody to provide one?' I clarified.

'Yes, they know she has no family.' Dija was clearly saddened by the directness of the dowry talk, but I needed to ensure this was clear and she wasn't going to end up in a situation like Babu's daughter. 'They would like to meet her before the nikkah. Would you mind them coming here?'

'Your parents are welcome to visit at any time.'

'Tonight?'

'It is busy here, but yes, they're welcome. We may not be able to spend much time with them, but they don't want to meet us, they want to meet Dija.'

'It won't be for long, just ten or fifteen minutes. Also, the nikkah could take place on Thursday, the day after the naming ceremony. What do you think?'

I looked over at Dija, who stood small and insignificant, gravity dragging her posture into the ground.

'Is Thursday OK with you, Dija?' I asked. She nodded.

'I will bring my parents after dinner tonight then,' Junaid said, preparing to leave.

'Junaid,' I called as he began walking away, 'I will arrange for Dija's wedding lehenga, a gift from us.'

'How very kind of you.' He took a glimpse at Dija, waiting for a smile or a wave, but she was totally oblivious to his leaving.

'Dija?' I said, once he had left. 'What are you thinking about?' She didn't reply, her eyes glazed. She tried speaking, but I couldn't understand her mumbling. I wrapped my arms around her and stroked her hair, trying to calm her. 'I'm here, I'll make sure you're OK. You've nothing to worry about, Gurpul and I will look after you, we're your family.'

'Even if I had one parent, just one parent, to be with me during my nikkah, to visit Junaid's family and tell me if they approved… But I have nobody, no family.'

'Dija, you have us. You're even going to be living across the road from us; we're still going to be here for you.'

'His parents are not coming here to ask for my hand: they're just going to take me like I'm somebody from the street.'

'How can you think that? Do you honestly believe that we would allow anybody to come and take you? Gurpul has known Junaid for many years, we know he is an honest, kind man, wanting to marry somebody like him so he can have a family of his own. He will look after you, Dija, we know he will.'

'Bibi ji said that Junaid could have anybody, why would he want me?'

Ammi always spoke her mind without stopping to consider who she could be hurting, or who could be listening.

'He wants you, he could marry anybody, but he wants to marry you. He has been asking Gurpul about you for a while.'

Her posture changed, she stood upright, 'is this true?' she asked, surprised.

'Yes. If I thought Junaid was not the right man for you, I would've told you. We all approve and we're all happy for you.' A small smile appeared on her face again.

'You're such a good person, Taji baji, Sahib is lucky to have found a wife like you.'

'Dija, I don't know how I'll cope without you.'

'I could still come here and help you,' she suggested, 'that's if Junaid agrees.'

'That would be great and I'm sure Junaid won't mind. Anyway, we have to get you a lehenga by Thursday so we'd better get going.' The mood had lifted and Dija was back to her excited self, as she was earlier in the day.

'I don't want anything too fancy, I can't afford it,' she said.

'You leave the lehenga to me, all you have to do is tell me which one you like.'

'You've done enough for me already, I can't accept any more from you.'

Although Ammi did not want me to visit the bazaar with Dija, especially since I'd just given birth, I still changed and left Naseem to look after the baby. Dija was ecstatic, she ran upstairs to the balcony bedroom where she had been staying and changed. Ammi tried calling Gurpul to tell him that I was going shopping with Dija, but he was busy in a meeting and was unable to come to the telephone. Dija and I escaped before anybody stopped us.

It was six o'clock by the time we arrived in the bazaar and the roads were snarled with traffic. We left the driver with the Chevrolet, where shoppers stopped in their tracks to admire the vehicle and enquire about who the owner was. I was still growing accustomed to the attention the car attracted from the locals here; given in Lahore it was more common to see such automobiles. People pushed past us as we walked along the narrow streets where stalls were set up along the roadside offering an abundance of fruit and vegetables, meat and fish, shoes and bags, lentils and spices, henna painting, shoe polishing, anything one could possibly need was found in this bazaar. Locals were prowling for bargains, stall owners howling prices; there was a cacophony of noise and pungent smells, all overwhelming. I rushed along the winding lanes into the clothes bazaar.

'Can we try this shop?' Dija asked. 'I've always wanted to buy something from here.' We stepped inside as the owner sat perfectly balanced and cross-legged on a small stool outside, reading his newspaper.

'Come in, come in,' he said invitingly when we were already in this Aladdin's cave of a shop. Brightly coloured fabrics were over-spilling on the shelves, a whole host of shoe styles piled up high, tied with elastic bands and black lanterns hanging from the ceiling. 'What would you like? What are you looking for today?' he asked.

'A wedding lehenga,' I said.

'For yourself?'

'No, for my friend.'

He looked through the piles of clothes behind him on the shelves and took out a few colourful packs.

'This is the variety of styles I have, they are available in many colours.' He opened each packet carefully and displayed the lehenga across the raised platform. 'Take a seat.'

'I love this heavy embroidery,' Dija said. 'But it will be costly.'

'Don't worry about the price, just let me know what you like,' I reassured her. 'Let's be quick so I can get back to feed the baby and rest.' She picked out two.

'This one has very heavy embroidery,' the shopkeeper said, stating the obvious. He opened the red lehenga, 'The gold work on it looks beautiful. Feel the weight,' he insisted, lifting it. It was heavy, I wondered how Dija would carry it, but I remembered that my lehenga was heavier and I managed.

'How about the gold one?' I asked.

'Yes, yes, here you go, this is lighter, it is of cheaper quality,' he said, trying to convince us to choose the dearer one. The platform was now flooded with a rainbow of colours and fabrics, shimmering and sparkling at us.

'Which one do you prefer, Dija?'

'How much are they?' she whispered to me.

'That doesn't matter.'

'Taji baji, you're very kind but we should still ask how much are they?'

'What are the prices?' I asked.

'This red one is tailored on the best quality material in the bazaar, you won't find it anywhere else, a good price, only one hundred rupees.' I wanted to laugh at him, 'And the gold one hundred and twenty.'

'Do you think I look stupid?' I snapped at the shopkeeper, annoyed at him for deliberately raising his prices.

'I'm making very little profit with the prices I am giving you. On the Lord's name, I'm making very little profit,' he insisted.

'Those prices are ridiculous. You know you would make so many more sales if your prices were honest and consistent. I don't have the time to bargain, come on Dija,' I threatened, standing up to leave.

'Please, sit down, why are you leaving so soon. I can reduce the prices especially for you. Look she really likes this style.'

'We're leaving.'

'OK, I'll reduce the price by thirty rupees, I'm making no profit by giving them to you at this price.'

He was still shouting from his shop as we walked further along the bazaar, other shopkeepers were laughing at his failed attempt at making maximum profit.

'I have exactly the same stock and I'll give you a good price,' another man claimed, stopping us outside his store.

'We don't want a "good price" like the ones he tried to give us,' I mocked.

'By Allah's name, I give all my customers good prices.'

'Let's see what this one does, Dija.'

He rushed along and took out the same stock we had just been viewing. This man had been standing at the door of the first shop, as most shopkeepers did, in order to get an idea of what sort of price range the customers are prepared to accept.

'Don't take them out of the packets, you'll be wasting your time, just tell us how much,' I told him, accustomed to the bargaining tricks. When I was in Lahore, I watched Nanni haggle with shopkeepers almost every week, she was an expert.

'Let me show you the quality, they are very good quality.'

'We've seen the quality, thank you. Just tell us the prices.'

'This red one is more expensive, because it is heavier in embroidery; it has gold stitching all over the lehenga and on the dubatta, but the kameez is plain because it gets covered.'

'Tell us the price,' I insisted, fed up with the marketing techniques.

'I'll charge you ninety rupees.'

'Sorry, no,' I said purposefully, although this was a lower starting price. 'I have sixty rupees with me and that is all I'm spending.'

'No, Bibi ji, please, I have to make some profit to take home to my children.'

'Listen,' I said to the old man, 'this girl is a Musalmaan orphan, and she's getting married on Thursday,'

'Mubaarak,' he said to Dija, interrupting me.

'I, her employer, am purchasing a lehenga because she cannot afford to buy one, so why don't you perform a good deed as well and give a good price? Take it as zakaat, your compulsory charity, for this orphan.' He stopped to think, staring at Dija's face, probably trying to work out if I was lying.

'Sixty rupees.' I placed the money on the table.

'No, Bibi ji, this is too little.'

'Listen, if I, a Sikh woman, have the heart to buy this Musalmaan a lehenga for her nikkah, then you should have more compassion.' He quietened again, as he thought about what I said and then began packing the lehenga. I looked at Dija and smiled, 'It requires practice to do business with these people. Look around and see if you like anything else.' Dija picked out another two outfits, a shawl and some sandals with the money Ammi had given her. After a little more negotiating we left with the wedding shopping done.

Dija took the bags from me and we walked along towards the gold bazaar. She was swinging the bags, pleased with the purchases.

'I've never spent this much money,' she noted. 'I've always wished that I could, I've dreamt of walking into clothes shops and buying whatever

I wanted, but then I would think I was being silly because it would never happen. If only my parents were here to see me as a bride, in my lehenga.' I wished I could take away the grief in her voice and the emptiness I saw on her face. I couldn't imagine not having my family, who loved me so dearly, who shared all my happy times with me.

'They will be watching over, Dija, they'll be proud of how you've looked after yourself.'

'Yes, they will be, but they will also be thinking that I've gone mad, spending so much money on clothes.'

Dija looked into the window of a jeweller's, the sparkling gold twinkling in her eyes. If only I could buy her a gold necklace to match the lehenga, but Gurpul and Ammi would never approve.

'I'm extremely tired now,' I said, exhausted by the trip, so soon after giving birth.

'You stay here and I will tell the driver to bring the car.'

She ran down the narrow street, dodging the crowds of people like an expert; her carefree movements told me she was buzzing with gratitude. It was nearly eight o'clock and the sun was beginning to set, leaving an orange surface on the horizon. Candles were being lit in the shops to save electricity. The keepers did turn on the lights when potential customers entered, but otherwise the calming candles flickered into the night until the day's duty was done. My legs felt tired and I missed my baby, it was the first time I had been away from her. Naseem would have taken care of her, but she still needed feeding. I began panicking thinking about her, but Dija appeared from around the corner where the driver was waiting.

As we approached the driveway, Junaid and his parents were walking through the alleyway towards the main road. His Ammi walked precariously with a stick, following her husband who took long strides, racing ahead.

'What good timing, there come Junaid's parents.'

'What do I say to them?' Dija asked nervously.

'Don't worry, let them do the talking.'

As the car came to a stop at the main door and we got out, I asked the driver to go back down and drive Junaid and his parents up the hill. I opened the front door and things were havoc in the house with Ammi yelling orders to Babu and the baby crying.

'Taji, the baby needs feeding,' Ammi shouted.

'OK, I'm back now.'

'Where's the driver gone? He needs to pick up Gurpul.'

'Yes, he's left,' I said reassuringly. 'Junaid's parents are here, is the drawing room clean?'

'The entire house is, they can sit wherever they please,' Ammi replied flippantly, still irritated she would be losing her live-in maid with Dija marrying.

'Please quieten everybody; we don't want to scare them away,' I said.

I turned on all the lights and closed the windows in the room. Dija followed me in.

'They're here, they're getting out of the car,' she announced.

'Keep your dubatta on your head, most families like that in a girl.' As she covered her head with the scarf around her neck, they knocked on the door. Dija stood still, staring at me, 'Go on, it's for you,' I said encouragingly. 'I'll be down in a moment to say hello.'

I quickly walked through the dining area into the kitchen, where Babu was busy preparing dinner for the following evening.

'Babu!'

'Mubaarak, Taji. I wanted to come earlier to see the baby but they needed me at the other house.' He wiped his hands on the towel which was draped over his shoulder and came forward to greet me.

'Have you seen the baby?' I asked.

'No.'

'I'll bring her down.'

'Don't bring her in here, all these spices will hurt her eyes.'

'OK, you come upstairs.'

'Now?'

'Yes.' He quickly walked back to the stove and turned down the heat under the pans and then he washed his hands in the sink and cleaned them with a fresh towel.

'I bought something for her.'

'You shouldn't have, Babu.'

'I wanted to.' Towards the back of the kitchen, he opened a drawer and took out a small paper bag. 'This is for the baby.'

I was taken aback because he didn't have enough money to feed himself, let alone buy presents for my baby. We both went upstairs where Naseem was playing with her.

'I'll take her, Naseem.' Babu was beaming, he wanted to hold her, but he was shaking, 'Sit down, Babu,' I said. He took a seat on the settee and I placed her in his arms. He rocked from side to side and spoke to her, laughing and smiling and stroking her face.

'Mashallah,' he said, 'she's beautiful, just like you.' I let out a short, shallow laugh for I knew I wasn't so beautiful and Babu was generous with his words. 'Open her present,' he reminded me. I opened up the bag to reveal a colourful plastic baby rattle with a carousel painted around it.

'She will love this, Babu.'

'Give it to her when she cries, she'll quieten as she shakes it.' I rattled the egg-shaped toy and held it in front of her as she listened to the sounds of the balls.

'She likes it,' Babu decided, happily watching her. 'I wanted to buy you something as well, but I didn't have enough money.'

'Babu, you do enough for us, please don't spend your money on us as well. This is a very special toy.'

'Babu?' Ammi shouted angrily from the stairs.

'Ammi ji, he's coming,' I responded, taking the baby from him. 'Will you send some drinks into the drawing room?'

'How many people?'

'Four, Junaid's parents have come for Dija's hand in marriage.'

'What wonderful news!' he said and quickly exited before Ammi shouted again.

After feeding the baby and putting her to sleep, I finally returned downstairs where Junaid's parents were already preparing to leave.

'You're leaving so soon?' I asked.

'Yes, we've taken so much time, I'm sure you must be preparing for dinner,' Junaid said.

The old woman stood up with Dija's help and used her walking stick to keep her balance. She was rather oversized but of average height; I wondered how Dija had managed to help her onto her feet. Junaid had no resemblance to his Ammi; she had very dark skin and black moles on her cheek and chin, the one on the chin featured distinctive stray hairs. He definitely had a likeness to his Abba though, with his strong proud torso and light eyes. As they left, Junaid glanced back at Dija, he caught her eye but she looked away shyly, because I happened to catch their romantic exchange. I could feel the fireworks going off around me and loved being a part of this joyful energy that charged any room they were in.

We watched them walk down the well-lit driveway out onto the rather dark street.

I asked her how she was feeling, her grin said it all: her love for his parents was blossoming quickly, but only because she was longing for parental love again.

'Go and tell Babu. I mentioned it to him earlier and he's delighted.' She ran to the kitchen where Babu was waiting for news and there they both laughed and joked.

Chapter 3

April 1946, Mirpur, India

I twirled around as Dija tucked the sari into the petticoat. My waist was not as small as it used to be, but that was a small price to pay for the elation I felt when I looked at my baby. I escaped to a euphoric place whenever I held her in my arms and felt her soft skin against mine; in that moment we were in a special world, just me and her. Dija was already washed and changed, running from one room to another trying to keep things in order. She was in high spirits, probably because she was going to see Junaid at the gurdwara. Her hair was combed back neatly in a bun and she had moisturised her delicate face leaving it glowing; even her clothes had been perfectly steamed. Junaid was already at the gurdwara welcoming early guests; he had called to say people had begun arriving. I felt no pain or fatigue, today my body felt like it was filled with helium, effortlessly floating, waiting to see my family and to give my baby a name.

The downstairs hallway was cluttered with sweetmeat boxes to distribute to the guests after the ceremony. All the tidying Dija had been doing looked as if it had gone to waste, and we were all running late.

'Gurpul, I thought these boxes were going to the gurdwara, what are they still doing here?' I asked as he walked through the front door. He was wearing a gold turban to match the sherwani Ammi had bought for him. He looked handsome, although I did not tell him because I was far too irritated at his lack of organisation; despite his insistence that everything was under control.

'You look beautiful.' I ignored his compliment and went to see what Babu was doing in the kitchen.

'The wife's not pleased, I think you should get moving.' I heard Abbu warn Gurpul.

Babu was hard at work. He was not attending the ceremony, for Ammi insisted he stayed at home to ensure the house was presentable upon our return. I had wanted him there, but nobody had the authority to override Ammi's commands. Dishes from lunch were still on the dining table as nobody had had the time to move them, and so Babu would have to do that too once we had left. I stopped and gazed at the wedding portrait on the wall. Gurpul and I were standing in the centre with both our parents on either side, and my siblings kneeling on the floor. Gurpul had taken the smaller version of the photograph, which I had framed on my night table, to an artist and commissioned an oil painting in colour. Here we were less than a year later with an addition to our family. Ammi finally made an appearance and we were ready to leave.

Most of the sweetmeats and flowers had been loaded into the van and the driver was taking the last few boxes.

Children were playing outside the gurdwara with my younger siblings Manju and Mohan among them.

'My Ammi and Abba are here!' I shouted, I could not wait to see them. Gurpul parked amid the muddy gravel along the roadside which made it difficult for me to get out, but I didn't want to be stuck in the car waiting for him to find another spot, so I wasn't going to complain. Manju and Mohan came running over.

'Taji didi, Taji didi!' they yelled. Gurpul held the baby while I greeted them; they had grown up so much. Despite being only eight Manju's hair had grown so long, like she always wanted, and was perfectly braided in a French plait. Mohan on the other hand had stained trousers from playing on the floor with his marbles.

'Come on, your parents will be waiting inside,' Ammi said hurrying me along.

The gurdwara was filled with guests, some already sitting on the floor, others talking among themselves. My parents were at the front speaking to friends and they turned to look as we entered. They watched us acknowledge the guests one at a time. Everybody wanted to see the baby, stroking her head and hands, kissing her forehead, commenting on whether she had Gurpul's nose or mine, his eyes or mine. It was becoming boring because everybody thought she looked like her Abba. Gurpul's parents stopped to talk to some friends and I was losing my patience: I wanted my parents to meet their first grandchild. Politely ignoring any attempts to converse, by broadly smiling and swiftly moving on, I finally reached the front.

'Congratulations, my dear.' Abba said, stepping forward to embrace me.

'Mubaarak, Taji,' Ammi said. 'My first grandchild! Taji, she's so beautiful.'

'We've all missed you very much,' Abba admitted.

Amardev and Paal looked like young adults, both waiting quietly beside Ammi and Abba.

'Amardev, you look so handsome in a turban.' I patted his head and kissed his cheek.

'Taji didi, I'm not a child anymore, don't kiss me in front of all these people.' He had a deep voice, no longer a childish one.

'Ammi, how have they all grown up and changed so much? I feel like I've missed out.'

'Take it from me you're lucky to have missed out.' We all laughed at Ammi shaking her head.

'Have you all been a handful for Ammi?' I asked the children.

'No, we're good,' Paal protested, looking more womanly now with a defined chest. Her tall, slender figure was perfect for a classical dancer.

The children wanted to play with the baby and Manju was pulling at my sari, asking me to kneel down.

'You can play with her at home, she'll start crying here. We can't have tears on her naming ceremony,' I tried explaining. She sat back once Ammi told her to stop pestering.

'Go and take a seat on the platform, guests have been waiting for a while, they're becoming restless now,' Abba said to Gurpul and me.

'Gurpul's parents are too busy talking,' I said looking around for them.

'I'll go and get them,' Abba said.

Gurpul and I took our seats on the platform where the granthi was stroking his long white beard, waiting to begin the ceremony; Ammi and Abbu quickly followed. The elderly religious leader began with a prayer from the Guru Granth Sahib. The hall quietened as we listened to the book being recited, even the baby remained quiet as the holy words worshipped by Sikhs echoed in her ears for the first time. He was praying for her good health and Sikh way of life, like the Gurus had lived. Granthi finished reading his initial prayer, closed the sacred scripture and then opened it again randomly, approximately one quarter of the way into the book. Lifting his head, he acknowledged Gurpul and me before continuing to read the hymn on that particular page. There was so much anticipation because the initial letter of the first word was to influence the name we were to choose for our baby. I listened attentively, holding my breath, as he began reading and it was a letter 'R'. I thought of names beginning with 'R' and my favourites were, Raushan and Rupinder. On completion of the hymn he announced that the first letter was 'R'. There was a murmuring among the guests as everybody suggested names.

'She's got the first letter of my name,' Ammi said proudly.

'Think of a name, Roopa,' Abbu instructed. 'Do you have any names, Taji?'

'Raushan and Rupinder. They have lovely meanings.'

'What do they mean?' Gurpul asked.

'Raushan is a famous person and Rupinder is the God of beauty; she is beautiful after all.'

'No, no, you need a strong name, nothing superficial,' Ammi insisted.

'Such as?' prompted Abbu.

'Rajendar.'

'Rajendar?' I repeated, not too keen on the harsh sounding consonant.

'Yes, it has an extremely strong meaning,' she insisted, 'The King God of Gods.'

'I like it,' Gurpul said, without even thinking. Abbu remained quiet.

'Any others, Ammi?' I asked, hoping she would suggest another.

'No, that's all. I think it should be Rajendar. A child's name influences their character and we want her to be a strong Sikh girl, not somebody who is interested in being famous or beautiful,' Ammi said boldly.

'Have you decided?' the granthi asked.

'Rajendar,' I advised him.

'Rajendar Kaur,' he shouted to the guests, who were all waiting to hear the final choice.

There was a cheer as they all shouted, 'Sat Siri Akal, God is great!'

Everybody stood and Junaid brought forward the sweetmeats for Ammi to distribute and Dija brought the flowers. Ammi placed the marigold and jasmine garlands around my neck, thanking me for bringing her family a grandchild. We stood by the stage as the photographer took pictures and we were congratulated by the guests as they collected their sweetmeats.

Outside even more well-wishers waited. Although the tradition was to distribute sweetmeats to the entire neighbourhood for the birth of a boy, Abbu and Ammi insisted we did so for the arrival of our girl. The rich, the poor, the Hindus, the Christians, the Musalmaans, were all invited to collect celebratory gifts.

*

After looking around the entire house and scrutinising each item of furniture, Ammi and Abba, came back to the drawing room delighted that Gurpul had built me such a wonderful home.

'You've done a good job, son,' Abba said.

'No wonder Taji doesn't miss us, what else could she ask for?' Ammi said accusingly.

'I miss you all very much,' I protested. 'Shall we serve drinks first, or would you like dinner?'

'I think dinner, it's nearly six o'clock and we need to go back to Jhelum tonight,' Abba said.

'Are you not going to stay?'

'No, work waits in Lahore and the children have school.'

I didn't insist that they stayed because I knew it was a long drive back; not only in the heat, but the route was difficult as well. They'd spend the night in Jhelum, which was no more than ninety minutes away, with Nanni, and then leave for Lahore in the morning. It was easier breaking up the journey so the children didn't become irritated in the car.

'I'll go and tell Babu to begin serving.'

Babu was outside in the garden relaxing, after spending so long preparing dinner.

'You're back?' he said, sitting up. 'What name did you choose?'

'I didn't, Ammi did. It's Rajendar.'

'This is baby Rajendar?' He stroked her cheek.

'Yes, Rajendar Kaur, now she's officially a Sikh girl. My parents are here, they want to leave soon, so will you serve dinner? I'll call Dija to help you.'

'Are they going back to Lahore? It's not safe to drive so late at night in the current political climate.'

'They're going to spend the night in Jhelum with my Ammi's relatives and leave for Lahore tomorrow morning.'

Babu got straight to work; he had all the serving dishes and spoons ready, laid out across the kitchen worktops. I left Rajendar with Paal so she could play with her, and went to find Dija. She was outside with Junaid, saying farewell for the evening.

'Junaid,' I called, 'stay for dinner, Babu has prepared so much.'

'Another time, we have a busy day tomorrow.'

'Such an exciting day! What time would you like us to bring Dija over?'

'Just before midday.' Junaid confirmed.

'OK. Dija, will you help Babu with dinner.' She got straight back to work leaving me and Junaid. 'It's going to be difficult not having Dija here to rely on, she's such a help.'

'She can still come and work for you, I'm sure she would love to.'

'Well it will save me from having to find another maid. I'd better get inside, my parents will be wondering where I've got to.'

'We shall meet tomorrow, then,' he said, turning to leave.

The drawing room looked like a jovial party scene: with the children playing, both Ammis speaking in one corner and both Abbus and Gurpul huddled together in another. I watched them from the doorway, all happily celebrating; if only every day was like this, but tomorrow everybody will be back in their own homes. I joined the men to see what they were talking about; they were all leaning forwards in their seats, their heads so closely joined that they looked glued together.

'When Gandhi called for Britain to leave India in the 1920s, they found an easy way to get rid of him: imprisonment.' Gurpul's Abbu was saying as I approached.

'But that didn't quieten the civilians: the Congress still called for complete independence,' Abba stated.

They were talking about politics and when it came to politics I just switched off. I watched Dija bring the dinner plates in and set them on the table. The Wedgewood china formed part of my dowry and this was the first time I was appreciating the elegant white floral crockery and the crystal tumblers Ammi had ordered because a girl's dinner set said a lot about the family she came from. Gurpul's hand hitting the table drew my attention back to their conversation.

'Well, they've given in. On March 14th they washed their hands and declared independence,' Gurpul said. 'But now the question is whether or not we can handle independence and get back onto our feet.'

'Of course we will,' his Abbu protested, 'remember, Mahatma Gandhi said, "Leave India to God. If that is too much, then leave her to anarchy." Once we've got rid of the British, we can pick up the pieces.'

'That's the easy solution, Shashi, but what will happen to people like us? I'm settled in Lahore, I have my house and my business there, and your house and business in Mirpur, both these areas may fall within the Pakistan side of the border, what will we do?'

I went to both Ammis, who were sitting back on the settee sipping their cold drinks.

'She's had her first child, I think she should have her second soon,' Gurpul's Ammi said.

That's all she talked about, so I left them too before the lecturing began.

I joined my siblings, who were all sitting around the rug; I squeezed in between Manju and Amardev, it felt like being back at home.

'Are you all getting top marks in school?' I asked.

'I came first in the class in mathematics and English,' Paal boasted.

'Very clever, what did Ammi and Abbu give you?'

'Why do you call Abba, Abbu now?' Mohan asked.

'Gurpul says Abbu, so I do too, it means the same thing, doesn't really make a difference.'

'I got a gold necklace. Ammi said I could wear it on my wedding,' Paal continued.

'Oh.' I was surprised that Ammi had already begun preparing for her wedding.

'I want a pink dress like Rajendar's,' Manju whined, pulling the ribbon on the dress.

'Don't pull, you'll hurt the baby.' But it was too late, Rajendar had already begun crying.

'Taji, go and feed her and change her out of that dress, I think she needs to be in something more comfortable,' Gurpul's Ammi said, shouting from the other side of the room.

'You kids stay here and I'll be back in a moment.'

Naseem was coming down the staircase with her bag, as I came out of the drawing room; she had not brought much with her for ten days, but I guessed she was a seasoned traveller.

'Taji, I must leave now.'

'Will you not stay for dinner?'

'No, it's getting late.'

'Wait here, I'll call Ammi.'

I went back into the drawing room and called her out. Ammi collected the suits she had bought for Naseem.

'There are two suits in here and fifty rupees.' Naseem was delighted. She looked in the bag and examined the material.

'You're very kind people, may Allah keep you this way.' She put the clothes back into the bag.

I was sad to see her go, she was an old woman, so caring and had helped with the baby so much. I understood why she was in such demand.

'I'd better get back to the guests,' Ammi said, 'hopefully we'll see you again.'

'Yes, Inshallah, if God wills.'

'Not too soon, please, I need a break,' I protested.

'That's what they all say, but it happens in no time. Look after yourself, and if you need anything just let me know,' Naseem said. 'Salaam,' she walked away closing the front door behind her.

Almost all the chairs at the dining table had been taken. Babu and Dija joined us too, as I had invited them in celebration of the naming ceremony and also marking Dija's last night with us. The groupings from the drawing room had transferred to the table, everybody catching up on news from the past nine months. The table top could barely be seen with all the mats and dishes covering the wood. The men were still exchanging views about Gandhi and Jinnah; I presumed both Ammis would still be discussing babies. Adopting the role of elder sister again, I sat between my siblings, ensuring they ate dinner properly without making a mess. After laughing and joking with them and answering all their questions about my married life, I came to realise how much I actually missed them. I missed playing and chasing around the fountain and skipping in the back garden. I felt like I had been forced to grow up. Marriage required me to mature considerably and had deprived me of all the childhood pleasures. Motherhood will take it further and soon I will be sitting among both Ammis, discussing family life and children.

'Why do you live far away, didi?' Mohan asked, with his mouth filled with rice.

'Because she's now married and she must live with her husband,' Amardev explained.

'Why did you get married then?'

'Because Ammi and Abba wanted to get rid of her, they had too many children,' Amardev teased, confusing poor Mohan.

'Were you naughty?' he asked innocently.

I listened while feeling left out: my life differed from theirs now, they were all still innocent children, and I didn't feel like I was any longer, although Gurpul's Ammi believed I was.

'Kulgeet, I think we should make a move,' Abba said to Ammi, rising from his chair. 'Taji, it's been wonderful finally coming to your house and seeing all that you speak about on the telephone. Gurpul, Shashi and Roopa, have clearly accepted you into their family and I know you will definitely live happily with them for the rest of your life.'

'Kishin, had you ever doubted how we would treat her?' Gurpul's Abbu asked.

'Not even the slightest, but now that I've seen it with my very eyes, my heart has settled. I'll never worry about the state my Taji is living in and whether she's happy; those fears have been put to rest.'

Abba walked around the table and stood behind my chair, his arms rested on my shoulders as he leaned in, a lump formed in my throat: I did not want them to leave. I wanted Abba to lift me by my waist and twirl me in the air, like he used to do when I returned from Nanni's house; but I did not get the twirl, I did not get to cuddle up to him on the settee and fall asleep, leaving him to carry me to bed. I was his favourite when I was at home, I wondered who would be now. Pulling the chair back, I stood beside him, my arms tightly wrapped around his waist, his arm around my shoulder, he lovingly squeezed and pecked me on the head.

'Kishin, the gifts are still in the car,' Ammi said. 'Amardev, will you fetch them?'

'There was no need to bring gifts, your visit has been the best gift I could ask for,' I said.

Amardev returned with a large bag, holding it in front of him with both hands while his legs kicked it as he walked.

'Do you need a hand there?' Gurpul teased.

'There are clothes in here for you all, they've been labelled so you can look at them later,' Ammi said, opening the side pocket of the bag. 'These are for you, Taji.'

I opened a square box to reveal glistening sapphire stones set in four gold bangles.

My fingers glided over the deep blue stones, my eyes hypnotised by the starry reflection deep in the cut. I felt an instant attachment to them; because they were a symbol of Rajendar's birth. 'Ammi, these are stunning.'

'Try them on,' she insisted, helping me take them out of the box. 'I told the goldsmith to use the size he had from your wedding, I hope they fit.'

'They fit fine,' I reassured, sliding two on one arm and two on the other. 'But you've given me so much gold already.'

'A girl can never have too much gold,' said Abba. 'So your Ammi tells me.' The men all howled with laughter and of course the Ammis nodded in absolute agreement. I circled the room showing everybody my new bangles, gleaning as I heard all the amazed sounds.

'We must leave now, it's late,' Abba ushered everyone along whilst bidding farewell to Gurpul and Abbu.

'Take care of yourself, Taji,' Ammi ordered.

'And be happy always, my child,' Abba stated. 'Bye, everybody, Sat Siri Akal,' Abba shouted from the window and drove away while the children waved from the back seat.

*

I went up to the balcony room where Dija had spent her last night. The overhanging tree branches were swaying from side to side in a slow rhythmic movement. My eyes focussed on the calming motion as I listened to the koels calling from near and far, creating their own orchestral symphony. The doors had been opened out onto the balcony and the thin linen curtains danced with the morning breeze on this special day.

'Dija?' I called from outside, seeing her outline through the curtains.

'Come in, Taji baji.'

Her bags were packed. She did not have much, but everything she did possess was in a small rectangular travelling bag. I looked around. The room was now totally empty with the drawers and dressing table cleared and the bed made. It looked like a guest room again, another empty room in the house.

'Bring your lehenga down to my room, get ready in there,' I suggested. 'I'll help you.' She picked up the lehenga and shoes and I carried her bag, it did not weigh much.

I gave Dija a towel and showed her to my bathroom, leaving her soap and moisturisers so she could pamper herself, while I fed the baby. Ammi and Abbu were preparing to leave; packing their bags and searching the house for any belongings lying around. The car was waiting for them outside to take them back home. Ammi had been here for almost one week and Abbu had just about survived three days. He was relieved to be returning home.

'Taji, we're ready to leave now,' Ammi announced from the hall.

'Do you have everything?' I asked.

'We think so, but not to worry, I'm sure we'll be seeing you in a couple of days.'

'Of course.'

'What time is the nikkah?'

'Midday.'

'We'll send the driver straight back. Look after Rajendar and if you need any help, call me,' said Ammi. 'And get some rest, the last few days have been chaotic.'

'Don't worry, I have nothing else to do.'

'And if you get bored, ask Gurpul to drop you off at our house in the mornings when he leaves for the office,' Abbu suggested.

'Give our best wishes to Dija,' Ammi said, 'and don't eat anything at the nikkah, you don't know where the food has been prepared.'

'Ammi,' I exclaimed, concerned that Dija might have heard.

'Bye, we'll see you soon.' Ammi and Abbu picked up their bags and left, closing the door behind them.

'Taji baji?' I heard Dija shouting from my room.

'I'm coming.' I checked Rajendar and she was sleeping peacefully. Dija was wrapped in a towel, the water from her hair dripping onto her bare shoulders.

I pulled out the dressing table stool for her to sit on, combed her hair, and then towel-dried it. Once I had finished, she took the lehenga into the bathroom and changed. The lehenga suited her well, although I could not imagine wearing anything like it. Such outfits were mass produced in factories, not originals, like my wedding lehenga. For Dija it was a dream come true: she was twirling around in it, the bottom flaring out, revealing half her legs.

'I love it, Taji baji, it's just what I wanted. This is the best lehenga I've ever seen.'

'Come on, sit back down here, let's get some makeup on you.'

'I've never worn makeup,' she said reluctantly.

'There's nothing to worry about, trust me.' I matched the colours with the red and gold shades in the lehenga, outlining her eyes, cheeks and lips. 'What do you think?' I asked once finished.

'You've transformed me,' she replied, staring in the mirror.

'I've not transformed you, I've just highlighted your features.'

'Just my hair left now.'

'Well you're better at hair than I am, you just need to put it in a bun now.' I could see that Dija was enjoying the pampering. Her hair was being flicked over her shoulder and then in front of her shoulder, she was watching herself in the mirror, carefully examining all my cosmetics. I knew how she felt as I was the same when I was a child, watching Ammi getting ready.

I went to check on the baby since there was no Naseem or Dija to do that for me now. The front door opened as I came out of the nursery and I heard Gurpul's footsteps coming up the stairs.

'Are you not changed yet?' Gurpul asked.

'I'm helping Dija get ready.'

'Have you bought Babu's shalwar kameez?'

'Yes, it's here,' he said, passing me the bag.

Babu did not have any appropriate clothes to wear to Dija's nikkah, he said he would attend in the clothes he wore every day, so I'd sent Gurpul to buy him a new pair. I felt it my responsibility to look after him, since he had no family to do so.

'Will you give this to Babu and tell him we'll be leaving in twenty minutes?' I said passing the bag back. 'Your shalwar kameez has been ironed. I'll leave it in the hall.'

'I'll go like this; I'm not going to come back after the nikkah and change again for the meeting.'

'You can't go to Junaid's nikkah in an English suit, you'll be overdressed.'

'OK, OK, as you say,' he said, walking off.

'Is this all right?' Dija asked, showing me her neatly twisted bun.

'Perfect.' I took Gurpul's clothes and put them on the settee in the hall.

'How do I put this dubatta on?' she asked, holding it out in front of her.

With both hands I lifted it over her back and onto her head, letting it drape in front and covering most of her plain blouse. 'You make a pretty bride, Dija.'

'Do you think so?'

'Definitely. Wait until Junaid sees you, he'll barely recognise you.' She blushed, her mouth ready to break into a shy smile. 'I'll quickly get changed, you put on your shoes and help yourself to some perfume.'

After changing into some plain clothes, I moisturised my face and combed my hair back. I didn't wear any makeup because I didn't want Junaid's family to think badly of me for dressing up. Dija was sitting on the bed waiting, still taking a glimpse in the mirror every so often.

'I'm done, let's go,' I said. I picked up Rajendar and we went downstairs where Gurpul and Babu were waiting.

'What a doll,' Babu commented, and Gurpul agreed. Babu looked at her proudly; he was the closest person she had found to a father. He was wearing his new beige shalwar kameez, perfectly starched and ironed without a single stain. It was almost a transformation compared to what we usually saw him in. He had even washed and shaved and neatly combed the little hair he had around his temple area.

'Thank you for the shalwar kameez.' Babu said, watching me admire what I saw.

'It really suits you, Babu,' I said.

Gurpul opened the car doors, Dija and I got into the back, and Babu sat in the front.

Gurpul parked outside Junaid's house in the narrow alleyway. Their house was quiet, almost like there wasn't a wedding taking place; Gurpul looked back at me doubtfully.

'I'll go and tell them we're here.'

He opened the creaky, black metal gate and stepped inside; the gate closed behind him. We couldn't see in because the stone walls were high and enclosed the house from the dirty alleyway. Gurpul returned and told us they were ready. He held Rajendar while I helped Dija out, lifting her lehenga so she didn't trip on it. We stepped into a yard, no more than three square feet in size. There was a door directly in front of us and a few women stood huddled together, supposedly there to greet us: they threw small leaves, which they had picked from the trees outside, not roses or colourful confetti. Gurpul left the baby with me and was led into another room with Babu. I went with Dija into what looked like the sitting area. There was a charpai and a few cushions on the floor. It was a smallish room, but I guess not too small, probably the size of my bathroom. Two cupboards were lined up against the wall with small ornaments placed on top. Junaid's Ammi was sitting on a stool beside the charpai.

'Salaam, Dija, welcome to your new home.' Dija leaned down and hugged her while she remained seated, probably due to her knee problems. 'Look at my daughter-in-law,' she proudly boasted to a woman who was sitting on the floor beside her. 'Take a seat on the charpai, Dija.'

There were five other women, I didn't know who they were, but they stared at us both, Dija kept her eyes lowered and I smiled back at them awkwardly. They were trying to whisper to one another, but I could hear everything they said.

'Look at the lehenga, I've never seen anything like it.'

'How much do you think it cost?' Another woman asked.

'Over one hundred rupees.'

'One hundred? We could feed our families for six months with that money.'

'She's silly for buying a lehenga at that price, she should return it and give the money to Junaid.'

I couldn't believe what these women were saying; but they were poor and money was clearly not readily available. I would not allow Dija to sell her lehenga, it was a present from me and she would keep it. There was a murmuring at the door, I looked up and saw the mullah in the doorway with the rest of the men behind him.

'Nikkah,' he announced.

The women began getting themselves in order, those whose scarves had fallen from their heads covered themselves and they made room for the men to stand. The mullah entered with Junaid's Abba, Gurpul and Babu, Junaid was not with them. Babu and Gurpul were Dija's witnesses and they were there to say that they agreed and gave permission for the nikkah to take place. The bride's family were usually the witnesses, but Dija had nobody else. Gurpul looked as uncomfortable as I did. The woman who was sitting beside Junaid's Ammi got up and covered Dija's face with the dubatta, she pulled it forward, probably ruining her hairstyle. The mullah began reading something from the Quran.

Rajendar started crying and I tried quietening her, but she screeched louder as the mullah read faster. The women looked at me in disgust, so I took her into the yard, but she still continued crying. I didn't know why, it may have been the change in surroundings.

'Babhi, are you ok?' I turned around and Junaid was walking out of the room where the men had been sitting.

'What a handsome groom you make!' He was wearing a white shalwar kameez with a red waistcoat. 'Why are you not in there with the men?'

'I'm not supposed to be there: the mullah will always ask the bride first and if she agrees to the marriage, he will ask the groom. We remain separate until the nikkah has been completed.'

'Now that she's finally quietened, I'd better go back inside.' As I reached the doorway, the men were coming out. The women were around Dija congratulating her. I had missed the nikkah. I had broken my promise. Dija's face was covered by her dubatta, I sat beside her and stroked her hand, 'Congratulations, Dija.' She did not utter a word, I heard her sniffling. My chest was throbbing. 'What's wrong, Dija? I asked.

'I was alone, there was nobody here with me; no parents, no family, not even you.'

'Forgive me, please, forgive me,' I begged. 'Rajendar was crying, she wouldn't stop, she was distracting the mullah.'

'It is not your fault, Taji baji, this is my fate. I'm always going to be alone. Whenever I've needed a friend most in my life, there has been nobody there.'

'Dija, you should be thinking positively, this is the beginning of a new life. You will have a blessed life with Junaid, he will look after you and he will cherish you like a precious stone.' She turned to face me and I lifted the scarf away from her face. Leaning forward, she hugged me tightly. The women stared, but we ignored them. I took a tissue from my handbag and wiped away her tears. 'Look, the kohl in your eyes has all smudged!' We burst into laughter. 'Let's reapply it before Junaid sees his wife with black eyes.' The women still watched us, but I didn't care. I brushed her hair and pulled the dubatta back so her face could be seen. Junaid entered, his eyes respectfully lowered as were Dija's. The women were whispering again. Gurpul was standing beside Junaid and brought him to the charpai where Dija and I were seated.

'Come on, Taji, let him be seated beside his wife,' Gurpul said.

'It's tradition for the groom to give the bride's sister or friend something, to allow him to sit next to her.'

'Babhi, come on, don't make me wait any longer,' Junaid pleaded.

'Sorry, you don't get this seat so easily.' He put his hand in the inside breast pocket of his waistcoat and took out a yellow rose.

'Here you go,' he said, giving me the garden-picked rose.

'You've come prepared?' I was surprised. I got up. He sat close to her, his arm touching hers, but they did not look at one another. There was a sense of unease in the atmosphere, except for Gurpul and me making conversation with the bride and groom. I scanned the room and everybody's lips were sealed, but they all stared intently.

Gurpul held Rajendar and I kneeled down beside Dija and asked Junaid, 'What do you think, doesn't she look stunning?' He remained silent, raising his eyes slightly to look at me, 'Come on, take a look, I want an answer.' He turned his head, I could see Dija blushing, not daring to meet his eye. 'Come on, Dija, I want an answer from you too.' Her tight lips couldn't help but part, their eyes met and they both gazed. Not a single word was uttered and nor was it needed, because at that moment their hearts spoke, and they were paralysed with happiness.

'We wish you every success in your marriage,' Gurpul said to them.

'I hope we're as happy as you and babhi.' Junaid said.

Babu took out small rupee notes from his pocket, giving Junaid one and Dija the other.

'You look after Dija,' he said to Junaid, 'She has no real family, but I'm here for her as long as I'm alive.'

'You're the Abba I lost all those years ago.' I heard her whisper as he embraced her.

'And I always will be.'

Chapter 4

January 1947, Mirpur, India

There was an unexpected neighbourhood meeting happening in Gurpul's office. Shaista's Abba, Abdul uncle, her brother Ajman, and Abhi Gupta from next door were all gathered around the desk. I joined to ask how Shaista was doing, given I hadn't seen her since I'd found out I was expecting our second child, but they were deep in conversation.

'It's our job to remain prepared, this is an extremely unpredictable situation,' Abdul uncle was saying.

'It's just transfer of power,' Abhi insisted.

'You're mistaken, this is going to be the worst transfer of power you have ever witnessed: the British leaving will result in bloodshed and a loss of lives.' Abdul uncle replied.

'But it will be a steady move, it's not going to occur overnight,' Gurpul argued.

'Date for independence has not even been set yet, but bloodbaths around the country have already begun. Just five or six weeks ago, thousands of Muslims were slaughtered during the Great Bihar Killing.' Abdul uncle, like Abbu kept note of all the events relating to independence and partition. 'There was a heading in Dawn newspaper, "No Muslim left alive within 300 square miles". Just look around this table,' he said, leaning forward. 'I'm a Musalmaan; you're a Sikh,' he looks at Gurpul, 'Abhi, our Hindu friend. We eat together, celebrate together, yes we worship different gods, but beyond that I see no difference; and here we are turning on each other now.'

'It's difficult to imagine that such atrocities are occurring around the country while we live peacefully in Mirpur,' Ajman noted.

'You're right Ajman, we might be ok for now, but such incidents have been taking place for many months now. Take the Calcutta blood bath, five days of slaughter and arson attacks which took five thousand lives.' Abdul uncle said, heated and red in the cheeks.

'Who was to blame for the attacks?' I asked, joining the conversation.

'Who knows?' Abdul uncle replied, 'it takes one person to say something out of line and that's it; this is how volatile the situation is. It's safer to remain quiet than to speak your mind. One small remark could hold you responsible for thousands of murders and killings. I've called us all together because we must look out for each other.' They all nodded in absolute agreement. 'We all have businesses in the area, our families, we have a duty to this neighbourhood. We must remain vigilant.'

I could see Junaid walking up the driveway with a huge grin. He knocked on the door and Babu answered. I stepped into the hallway.

'Boy or girl?' Babu asked.

'It's a baby boy,' Junaid shouted, his smile reaching from ear to ear.

'Mubaarak, mubaarak,' Babu said. A roaring cheer was heard as the neighbourhood committee joined us in the hall from the office and a chorus of congratulations followed.

'When was he born?' I asked.

'Seven o'clock this morning. I would have come sooner, but we've had our hands full.'

'Tell Dija I will come in an hour to see her,' Babu said, returning to the kitchen to finish preparing breakfast.

'Who does he look like?' Abhi asked.

'That is all Ammi and Abba have been talking about.'

'And?' Abdul uncle prompted.

'They say he looks like me. I must get back home, there's a lot to do.'

'And this is just the start,' Abhi teased. 'I must get going too. Tell Dija, Gita and I send our regards.'

'We'll see you later on, Junaid.' Gurpul said, whilst seeing the neighbours to the door too.

Babu joined me at the table and had some tea with biscuits. When it was just the two of us, we were both able to catch up on the goings on of the two houses and neighbourhoods. He missed his daughters and I was gladly a surrogate to that father-daughter bond. He cared dearly for me and Rajendar.

'Before I head back to Bibi ji's, I'll cycle to the bazaar to buy Dija some gifts. I can't wait to see her baby,' he said.

'I'm sure he's beautiful. After Gurpul has finished his paperwork this morning, we'll also drive in. Don't be too long Babu, I know Ammi is waiting for you this morning.'

'I just want to get some sweetmeats and flowers for her and I'll be straight back.' He left for the bazaar.

Rajendar was lying on my bed rolling about, babbling to herself, shaking the rattle Babu gave her and giggled every time it made a noise.

'Let's get you changed, Rajendar,' I said; she looked at me and smiled. The office door opened and closed. 'Here comes Abba,' and she jumped up and down wanting to be let off the bed. I placed her down and she stumbled towards the door. 'There's my little angel,' Gurpul said, watching her from the hall. She laughed and jumped around waiting for him to pick her up.

'We ought to go pick up gifts for Dija and Junaid too. Babu has already left for the bazaar.' I said to Gurpul.

'Let's go now then as I need to head into the office for meetings later.' Gurpul picked up Rajendar and we left for the bazaar.

After the previous night's thunderstorms locals were back to their usual businesses, out on the streets selling something or the other, whether it was food, furniture or their services. Gutters were overflowing from the downpour, leaving roads wet and muddy, requiring people to hold up their trousers and shalwars. Towards the bazaar the road was busy with crowds of people huddled together.

'I wonder what's happening here,' Gurpul said. I tried looking but couldn't see anything. 'Someone's display has probably been knocked over and they'll be causing a commotion.' I sat quietly and listened to Gurpul complaining as he did whenever there was some unexplained waiting. 'How ridiculous causing all this havoc? Who tells them to trade on the roads anyway?'

'They're making a living.'

Gurpul weaved his way through some of the traffic, manoeuvring awkwardly trying to avoid the potholes. He thought he would escape the congestion, but there was a bus blocking the entire road. Crowds had gathered and the piercing sound of the emergency services' sirens could be heard in the distance but getting closer.

'You should get out and see what's happened,' I told him, knowing that it was not something as small as a dispute.

He left the car in the middle of the road and approached the swarm of people, trying to push his way to the front. I was feeling anxious and couldn't understand why. The pulse was pounding in my temples, I took deep breaths trying to get more oxygen to my lungs. Watching the crowds, I was trying to understand what might be happening, but couldn't make much sense of it. Then somebody pulled out a crushed bicycle and threw it near the bus. It looked familiar. Very similar to Babu's cycle, the one he'd used for over twenty years. I couldn't just sit in the car waiting, doing nothing. Leaving Rajendar safe in the locked car, I also pushed my way through the crowd.

'This is not the place for you, stay back,' a man said.

'My husband's there,' I said assertively and pushed passed him.

There were people kneeling on the floor, Gurpul was among them. They were shouting and screaming at each other, giving orders. Somebody was lying on the road, all I could see was a pair of legs.

'Gurpul, Gurpul!' I tried to get his attention.

He looked up, his eyes bloodshot, 'go back to the car, Taji!' He ordered.

'Who is it?'

'Just go back to the car, now!' He repeated.

The ambulance and police arrived and dispersed the audience that had gathered so quickly. A pool of blood engulfed the back of the man's head, his face turned; one arm awkwardly pulled behind his back, clearly broken. His sleeve torn, revealing his bare skin; wounded like a chunk of his arm was missing. I felt my stomach somersaulting, the pounding in my chest was uncontrollable, I couldn't breathe and broke out in sweat. "Babu!" I saw the sweetmeats all over the road, many of them had been trampled on and the flowers torn, leaving crushed petals. Near the bus wheel was a broken rattle, he had bought Dija's baby a rattle as well, but the plastic had been shattered.

'What are you doing? Get him to the hospital!' Gurpul shouted to the paramedic.

'He's-' The man began, I knew what he was going to say. The noise around me became fuzzy, everything slowed down and felt distant, as if I was dreaming.

They put him onto a stretcher and covered his body with a white sheet. The ambulance doors closed and they drove away, leaving the red staining and yellow sweetmeats all over the road. The bunch of flowers, torn to shreds, but just one white carnation lay whole. That was all that was left of Babu.

'What happened?' Gurpul asked a man who was also watching.

'The old man was cycling along and then this bus…' he said pointing to it, 'Turned right and hit the cycle, knocking the old man off. The bus's wheel drove over him.' Gurpul's head dropped, he looked limp and floundered towards the car, without saying a word or acknowledging what the man had just said.

'Is he your relative?' the man shouted out.

'You could say that.'

In the car Rajendar was crying. Gurpul held her and we sat frozen. The police were talking to the crowds, taking statements to find out what had happened. The bus driver was still talking to the police; I saw his exaggerated hand movements as he tried to explain what had occurred. They lifted what was left of the crushed cycle and put it into their jeep. A policeman approached us with a notebook in his hand. Gurpul rolled down the window.

'Sahib, I'm told you're related to the victim.'

'He worked with our family.'

'Could I take your address details, we'll contact you once the body has been examined.'

Gurpul wrote down our details on the paper and handed it back. He reversed and drove back home. As we approached the driveway he said, 'We ought to let Dija and Junaid know. They will know how to arrange his funeral.' I didn't want to think about it, it was too soon. 'Shall we go to see them?' I nodded, unable to speak, and he turned down the alleyway and parked outside their house. 'Put on a smile somehow, Taji. Let's congratulate them first.' I tried to remove any evidence of what I'd just witnessed and wiped my face with a tissue. Rajendar had fallen asleep, the crying had exhausted her.

Junaid stood up as we opened the gate to see who had arrived, he came to the door.

'Come on in,' he said. 'We were expecting Babu.' None of us would see Babu again. He had been taken from us in such an awful way. Rajendar would never know him and he would never meet my second baby. I didn't know how Dija would cope.

'Congratulations, Junaid,' Gurpul said. 'Where is he?'

'Go through into the sitting area.'

Dija was lying on the charpai with the baby in her arms, wrapped in a blanket.

'Mubaarak Dija. Let's have a look at him,' I said, as Gurpul and Junaid sat on the chairs beside the door.

She unwrapped the blanket and moved the hat away from his face. He was as fair as Junaid and had his features; they were very much alike, there was no debating about it.

'Who does he look like?' Dija asked. 'Not that I don't know the answer, I'm just hoping somebody will think he looks like me.'

'Sorry to disappoint you, but he looks just like Junaid.'

'Can I get you a drink?' Junaid offered.

'I'm fine,' I replied and Gurpul asked for some water.

'Where has Babu got to?' Junaid asked. 'He said he would be here within an hour, that was over two hours ago. Do you know where he is?' Junaid asked, catching us glancing at one another. We didn't answer.

'Taji baji, is everything OK?' Dija asked when she saw a tear escape and fall onto my hand. 'What's happened? Where's Babu?'

'Calm down, Dija, he'll be here soon.' Junaid reassured.

'No, something's happened to him. Is he not well? Is he ill?'

'I saw him this morning and he was absolutely fine, he was thrilled that we'd had a boy.'

'Tell us, Taji baji, please.'

I looked back at Gurpul and mouthed for him to tell them. Junaid sat back down on the chair beside Gurpul waiting for him to speak.

'Tell us, Gurpul bhai,' he begged, now also realising that something was wrong.

'Babu went to the bazaar to buy you some gifts,' Gurpul began.

'And?' Junaid pressed.

'On his way back… he was knocked over by a bus.'

'Is he OK? Is he hurt?' Dija asked, taking the covers from her legs and sitting up.

'No, he's not,' Gurpul said.

'Is he injured?' Junaid prompted.

'He died at the scene of the accident.'

Dija looked from Gurpul to Junaid and then me. I watched her eyes circle the room, back and forth; internally questioning what had just been said and then digesting what she had just heard. Her posture stiffened, her face drained of all colour. There was silence and then a hysterical scream.

'Why does this always happen to me? It's me, I'm bad luck, aren't I?' I tried holding her, calming her, her body was cold, her hands blue. Her head shaking, refusing to accept the news, in denial. She finally looked me in the eyes. We both loved him. We both understood the pain each of us felt. 'Taji baji,' she mumbled, like a small child needing comfort. She embraced me tightly as we consoled each other.

'He didn't even see my baby. I was waiting for him. Junaid said he would be here shortly. I knew he would be going back to Bibi ji's house today. Why didn't he just come here? Why did he go to the bazaar to buy gifts?'

Gurpul and Junaid went outside into the yard. Both their heads were lowered as they discussed the funeral arrangements. Babu would need to be buried by a mullah, at a masjid, but Junaid would have to sort that out. At the gurdwara we would cremate the body and dispose of the ashes in the nearest river, but Musalmaans didn't do that. Tears were still pouring from Dija's eyes, I didn't know what to say… How could I make her feel better? I went outside to find out what was happening.

'Taji, where do Babu's daughters live?' Gurpul asked.

'I don't know, they live around Mirpur somewhere, but he never said where.'

'The body will probably be released by the hospital this afternoon,' Junaid said, 'we need to bury him as soon as possible, the sooner the better.'

'Will you sort things out at the masjid?' Gurpul asked Junaid.

'Of course.'

'I will see to the costs of the funeral, you don't have to worry about that,' Gurpul said reassuringly.

'Shall we go now and see what the mullah says?' Junaid suggested. Gurpul nodded.

'I'll keep an eye on Dija and the baby,' I offered, as they both prepared to leave.

I went back into the drawing room and Dija was lying down again with the baby by her side. I tried taking her mind from Babu and asked her about the birth, but she was not responding, she didn't want to talk, so I let her rest.

Gurpul and Junaid returned within half an hour, having made all necessary arrangements. They had called at the hospital and they were ready to release the body immediately.

'Babu's grave is being dug up in the graveyard next to the masjid,' Gurpul informed us.

'When will they bury him?'

'After prayer time, around three o'clock.'

'How are you feeling, Dija?' Junaid asked, kneeling down beside the charpai.

'People come and go in this world so quickly, it's not fair, why does it always happen to me?'

'You have me, I'll look after you,' Junaid vowed. 'And now we have this little one, we're a family, all we need is one another. And I'm not going anywhere.'

'Come on, Taji, let's go home, we'll call Ammi and Abbu and let them know. Junaid, come to the house for 2:30 and we'll drive to the masjid.'

'Dija, at least he's gone to a better place, there was very little left for him in this world,' I said.

'I want to call the baby, Ali,' Dija immediately protested, ignoring what I had said. Junaid and Gurpul looked at her. How poignant I thought; Babu's first name. Now his memories would live on for us through this baby, especially for Dija given he was the closest thing she had to family.

'Ali Junaid,' Junaid said, 'I like it.'

The house was empty when we returned: there was no Babu to make me tea or to look after Rajendar. I went upstairs into his room; he did not have much, even less than Dija. There was only one pair of shalwar kameez draped on the chair. He had worn the pair I bought him on Dija's nikkah, he only wore it on special occasions.

'Taji,' Gurpul said, standing in the doorway watching me.

'Yes?'

'I've spoken to Abbu, he will come to the masjid for the funeral. They don't know where his daughters live either.'

'Can you not postpone the funeral and try to find out? They will want to be at their father's funeral.'

'Junaid and the mullah said Musalmaans should be buried as soon as possible: they believe the soul doesn't leave the body until they're buried and so we can't delay. I need to find a white shalwar kameez to wear.'

Gurpul looked though the wardrobe and found his white shalwar kameez; it had been ironed and folded neatly. He changed and then looked after Rajendar while I rested. A knock on the door woke me, it was already 2:30.

'Taji, we're going now,' Gurpul said. 'Rajendar's sleeping, I've already given her something to eat. Call Shaista and ask her to come, or go and see Dija. I don't want you to be alone.'

'I'll be OK, you'd better leave.'

I watched them drive away. Junaid was also all in white, with his head covered in a white hat too. It was the first time Gurpul had attended a funeral.

I strolled around the house thinking about Babu, I felt lonely and miserable. The kitchen even smelt of him. He had prepared so much food, all in boxes piled up neatly in the refrigerator. He had washed the dirty laundry, it was drying out in the garden. It almost felt like he left the house knowing he was not going to return: everything was in perfect order. I wasn't hungry, I just felt sick. I looked at the clock, it was four o'clock. I watched the drawing room window but there was no sign of them returning.

Children were playing, chasing one another. I wanted to be as happy as they were. There was still no sign of the car driving up the road. I checked on Rajendar and she was sleeping with the rattle beside her. She enjoyed playing with it, but she would never remember the man who bought it for her. He didn't even live to tell her stories like the ones he told me. I finally heard the car doors close and the main house door open. Gurpul and Junaid silently walked up the stairs. An air of emptiness engulfed them; lowered heads, limp shoulders, dragging of the feet and puffy eyes.

'We've laid him to rest,' Gurpul uttered, looking at his soiled hands.

Chapter 5

August 1947, Mirpur, India

An orange flame erupted and engulfed the north of the city. Thick black smoke covered the Indian summer skyline, like English fog on a cold winter's day, making it difficult to witness the escapade. The sound of sirens reverberated through the city, warning all of dangers ahead. Neighbouring residents ran frantically through the streets and alleyways, in and out of their homes, arms waving in blind panic and terror. Across the road, Shaista threw items from the first floor terrace. She leaned over the red painted balcony, placing her feet between the pillars and the rest of her body far over the low wall, passing a travelling bag to Ajman bhai who reached up from the ground, snatching everything she sent. Abdul uncle was in the driveway loading a carriage and one of his cars, running back and forth without stopping for breath.

'The papers from my desk too, Shaista,' he shouted as she turned to go back into the house.

'How much do you want me to get?' She screamed back, irritated and clearly tired.

'Come on, please, keep up. If I have my paperwork I'll have evidence to claim back all the land we have.'

'We'll be back, Abba,' she insisted. 'Things will calm down and then we'll return.'

'Get everything from my desk, empty the side drawers too. Quickly, we're running out of time.'

'Abdul uncle? Abdul uncle!' I shouted from the balcony trying to attract his attention, but he didn't turn to look, he didn't hear me.

Walking closer to the left of the balcony I shouted, 'Shaista? Ajman bhai?' But they did not hear either, so focussed they were on their escape.

What felt like only a few moments later, the centre of the city blew up in flames. Red and orange fires burned wildly, tremors shook the whole of Mirpur City as a result of the collapsing buildings and houses. Thick black smoke and dust choked the clear blue sky, making it impossible to see but a mile ahead; all that could be heard were cries for help. I tried to understand what was happening, as I contemplated the answers, I remembered all those political discussions and talks of the volatile situation. A racing horse cried loudly in the streets below: a Hindu man on horseback galloped through the opposite alleyway shouting.

'The Musalmaans are attacking, run! Escape from here! Get your children and run, leave your homes!'

He held the reins with one hand and a whip in the other, attempting to increase speed. Musalmaans had already entered surrounding villages. In groups of five or six they attacked by setting alight houses, and shooting and stabbing anybody in sight, their clothing covered in bloodstains. Some of them wore scarves on their heads, while others used them to cover their faces, only showing their eyes. From the balcony bedroom I picked up Rajendar and struggled downstairs. At the double doors I stopped for a breath and then bolted them and closed the shutters. I was alone. Gurpul was at work and it was not safe for me to be in the house. I picked up the telephone receiver but the operator line was dead. A loud thudding on the main entrance doors caused me to drop the telephone and wake Rajendar. The banging became louder: the Musalmaans had come to get me. They were going to kill me. I heard somebody shouting my name and hurried downstairs, leaving Rajendar upstairs.

'Open the door!' a voice shouted from outside. The banging continued. I paused petrified. I wanted to ask who it was, but no sound came from my mouth. 'Taji babhi, open the door, it's me. Quickly, open the door.'

'Junaid!' I cried in relief. 'What's happening? What shall I do?'

'You need to get out of here now. Where's Rajendar?' he asked, desperately scanning the room. 'We have no time, come on, babhi, get yourself together.'

'She's upstairs.'

Junaid ran upstairs taking two steps at a time. He wrapped Rajendar in a blanket and covered her head with a hat. From the chest of drawers in the nursery he gathered some of her things and put them in a bag. I rushed into the bedroom and unlocked the safe holding all my wedding gold and placed it in a jewellery bag. Securely tying a knot, I put it into the pocket attached to the vest under my kameez. I was wearing the gold Gurpul gave me after the wedding, and the bangles Ammi bought me for Rajendar's naming ceremony.

'Come on, babhi, we must leave.' He ordered.

I hurried back to the landing where Junaid was waiting, holding Rajendar.

'What shall I bring, Junaid? What do I need? Where's Gurpul?'

'You have no time to get anything. Saving your life is much more important right now.' While holding Rajendar in one arm, he used his other to help me downstairs. The front doors were wide open. Noise levels were still rising with villagers in uproar, firing rifles, shooting arrows, clanking of swords and howling horses galloping through alleyways and streets. The turmoil had intensified tenfold since coming down from the balcony. My heart was racing and I could feel pains in my stomach. I recited stanzas from the Guru Granth Sahib, trying to put all my faith in the Gurus to guide me and my family to safety.

'Taji! Thank goodness, you're safe!' I heard Gurpul's voice. He ran to help me with the last few steps. I wrapped my arms around him, not uttering a word, just relieved that he was with me. 'Musalmaans have entered the village, targeting Sikhs and Hindus, we must flee immediately,' he insisted. 'Junaid, I cannot thank you enough. You must help your family; there will soon be counterattacks. I'll take care of things here. Ammi and Abbu are still in Delhi with friends, please get hold of them and tell them we'll be in touch when we're safe.' Gurpul took Rajendar as we briskly walked to the door, and then Gurpul and Junaid shook hands firmly. 'Run Junaid, get to Dija and Ali.' In what felt like a long second, they embraced and their eyes locked. Why did this feel so final? They were like brothers, he was like family. Before I had a chance to say anything, Junaid made a sharp exit.

On hearing the sound of rifles firing so close, Gurpul and I ran from the house towards the main gates. Rajendar wailed as her innocent ears became exposed to the clamour of the rioting. Gurpul pulled the pink hat further over her ears and held her tightly. There was total chaos and disorder. Villagers were running in all directions with heavily loaded wagons, carriages and horses, travelling at full speed. Houses were in flames along Maal Road, and bloodstains spattered across the ground. Possessions had been discarded along the road, outside doorways, people's lives and belongings strewn across muddy paths. Junaid was running down the alleyway towards his house, when a turbaned Sikh man on horseback came face to face with him, and ruthlessly fired a gunshot into his left arm. He faltered but retained balance by leaning against the wall. Another man on foot appeared from around the corner and stabbed him. The perpetrator and wall were sprayed in molten red as Junaid lay face down with both hands by his head, fingers wide apart. A second gunshot and he was dead. Gurpul held me up in a firm embrace, preventing me from falling, as I lost all feeling in my legs. The metallic taste of blood in my mouth. The rage in Gurpul's eyes, I felt in the pressure of him holding me. His chin involuntarily dropped on my head and I felt his silent tears falling in my hair.

Leaving our home, we ran with no sense of direction, just anywhere away from the riot. This was the house Gurpul and I had lived in after our marriage, where Rajendar was born sixteen months earlier and where

I had conceived our second child, almost nine months ago; everything I possessed was in that home. How could we just leave it? My ears could not take the noise anymore, my body was immobilised in shock. I felt like I had no control over anything. My ears were ringing, my eyes burning, my brain a cloud of haze. I held my hands to my ears to block out Rajendar's high pitched, distraught, screeching. I closed my eyes tightly, blocking out what was happening around me. It could not be real; this nightmare would be over when I opened my eyes again. Along the road a mother cradled her teenage son, like one does a new born; she repeatedly kissed his forehead, gently ran her fingers through his thick curly hair, called his name, but he lay peacefully asleep, never to awake again. Beyond them, a young girl of five was sitting alone by the roadside, pretty in her orange party dress. Her gentle hands making a hypnotic, repetitive movement, twirling and twisting her pigtails. Her gaze locked with big wide eyes that did not blink. The once familiar streets now seemed alien: buildings charred, smoke rising to the sky. Bodies were scattered on the ground with people running and tripping over them, desperately trying to escape from the attackers. Monsters on horseback galloped down the road, torches held high in one hand still setting alight houses. The nauseating taste in my mouth showed no signs of easing. I wondered if my home had been destroyed. We walked past the masjid where Babu had been buried and Musalmaans had gathered there, some of them praying to Allah for protection, others attempting to hide. I could see his grave across the road, fresh flower petals had been scattered all over it: his daughters must have visited. Masses of people were running with us and past us, some directing and others following, but everyone at a loss. An elderly lady; clutching the hands of a young boy and girl, approached us.

'Sahib, have you seen my Abba and Ammi? I can't find them. Have you seen them?' The young boy of about six stopped to ask. Gurpul was voiceless, affected by his innocence.

'No, son,' he eventually answered, ruffling the boy's hair, 'I've not seen your Abba.' It was all he could do and say. The young boy moved on to the woman behind us.

'Madam, have you seen Abba and Ammi? We can't find them and my little sister wants Ammi.'

'You're a brave boy, aren't you?' she said.

'Abba said I must be a brave boy and look after my sister and give her everything she wants, because she's younger than me. So I have to find her dolly and find Abba and Ammi so I can tell them that I gave her what she wanted.' The young girl quietly stood by her brother whilst watching the elderly woman with them, turning over corpses like they were children's dolls, littering the streets; but these were real life dolls and their bodies had been dismembered. These cruel people were our neighbours, friends and fellow villagers, who all believed in good and worshipped a God, even if that God was given a different name by us. All she wanted was to find family members, dead or alive.

Clothes shops and grocery stores were left open, stock remained outside on the streets, while owners fled in fear of their lives. Tables and stools overturned, tins and jars swept off shelves, brightly patterned sari's, shalwar kameez in rich colours, next to black burkas. Our lives had been woven together over hundreds of years, but every thread was now being violently dissected and separated.

The sun began setting; we had left the house at midday and had been running since. My feet had lost all sensation, I could no longer feel the soles. A small prick would cause them to burst, leaving a sea of water. A cool sea that I would happily immerse myself into to escape everything around me, and float in the gentle waves. The skin around my stomach, felt tighter and although Ammi had always told me not to scratch the stomach during pregnancy, I used my muddied nails to dig deep into the skin and relieve the itching. I collapsed and fell to the ground unable to stand.

'Gurpul!' I shouted as he walked along, concentrating on the road ahead. He disappeared among the crowds and I sat on the ground lacking the energy to shout again.

'Have you lost your family?' A man asked kneeling down.

'Yes, my husband, Gurpul, he's in that crowd,' I said, pointing straight ahead. 'He's holding my daughter, please find him.' The man quickly pushed ahead, leaving me with his family, a Musalmaan family.

'We're trying to find our way to the Muslim area,' his wife said, sitting down beside me. 'We all lived so happily; the Muslims, Sikhs, Hindus, Christians, why have they destroyed our land?' She was right, no one differentiated between the religions, so why were we all escaping? Who was responsible for this? Why was this allowed to happen? I wanted to ask so many questions but the sheer pressure of the baby's head trying to lock into position, distracted me.

'Taji, what happened?' Gurpul asked, frightened at the thought that he had almost lost me.

'Best of luck, Mr Gurpul, I hope you reach safety soon,' the man said, resting his hand on Gurpul's shoulder as he prepared to carry on with his journey. His wife looked down at my stomach and smiled weakly.

'I will pray to Allah for you.' She walked away with her two children.

'I can't walk anymore, Gurpul, I'm exhausted. I can't carry this weight.' I explained, holding onto my stomach. 'I don't have the energy to move,' I protested.

'Try to get up, Taji, we need to carry on, we must get out from here.'

Rajendar was still in Gurpul's arms, her eyes frightened, taking in the unfamiliar surroundings. Gurpul put Rajendar down and helped me up. I couldn't feel the ground beneath my swollen feet. With continued firing the sky wasn't getting any clearer. There seemed to be no sign of any calm, no hope of returning home, no chance of peace. Although still in pain, I continued walking and we caught up with the group ahead. Blood dripped down my leg and I silently prayed that my baby was safe.

At sunset we reached the Courts of Mirpur: over half the courtyard was filled with people standing and lying in all corners of the open space. I sat down beside a wall as Gurpul tried to find out what was happening. I pulled up my kameez and cradled Rajendar in my arms, covering my bare skin with the dubatta. Rajendar drank without stopping for a breath, she was hungry, having not eaten for over seven hours. Troops of police officers and soldiers made their presence known when the sound of their heels hit the ground and reverberated through the courts. They may have been taking long, confident strides in their perfectly starched and pressed military uniform, but many of them still held a look of nervousness. This disturbed me, given these were the personnel we were to rely on to take us to safety.

'I've spoken with one of the military officers, he says instructions will be announced shortly,' Gurpul informed me when he returned. Rajendar fell asleep after having her milk and lay soundly on the ground with her pink blanket placed under her.

'I'm Colonel Singh, heading the army and police force here,' a loud voice emerged through a speaker. Hundreds of people shuffled and positioned themselves so they could see him. He was a large man, at least six feet tall and probably weighing eighteen stone. His green turban added a few inches onto his height. 'Mirpur has come under attack because the Indian Independence Act 1947, has suggested it be placed in the boundaries of Pakistan. Although the partition is not due to take effect until August 15th, another ten days, there has been uproar around the country and this has resulted in Mirpur being attacked too.' He rushed on without stopping. 'Numerous lives have already been taken and we must prevent this number from rising, by directing you to safety as soon as possible. We aim to take you, into the confines and the grounds of India, out of the Pakistan region.'

The court grounds were overflowing with citizens still arriving every minute; desperately trying to enter, to reach safety, to understand what was happening. Every centimetre of floor space was taken: some standing, others sitting, there was no sight of the marble floor beneath us. Soldiers gathered large groups of people and escorted them out. Gurpul and I remained further back, relieving my lower back and feet from carrying the baby weight. The area was becoming less crowded with people leaving to cross the border through the night. Eventually a soldier approached us.

'Are you together?'

'Yes,' Gurpul replied.

'In this group,' he said, pointing to a group of around fifteen people.

The soldier moved on to a young woman and her son, sitting a few yards away. Everybody remained quiet, waiting for further instructions. I looked around acquainting myself with the faces of those in the group.

'Taji, take off the necklace and bangles, it's not safe to be wearing gold jewellery,' Gurpul said after his eye caught a glimpse of them. He unhooked the necklace and with some difficulty I pulled the bangles off my swollen hands. I parted with my wedding ring too, I had never taken it off in the two years we had been married. Without jewellery I felt bare. Gurpul carefully placed them in his trouser pockets.

'We are ready to depart,' the soldier announced, directing us to the exit.

In pairs, members of the police force stood armed with rifles guarding the grounds, questioning all who entered and left. On departure we were stopped by Colonel Singh.

'I am taking the name of each person in the group, so there is a record of those who have departed to cross the border. On reaching Jammu, the same will be done: you will be registered again.'

The Colonel held a clipboard and gave orders to his men in an authoritative voice while stroking his coarse black beard, which was as thorny as a rosebush. After attending to the people ahead, he came to Gurpul and me.

'Family or couple?' he asked, without looking up.

'Family,' Gurpul replied.

'Names. Husband's first and ages,' he ordered.

'Gurpul Singh, 22; my wife, Taji Kaur, 18; and my daughter Rajendar Kaur, 16 months.' He scribbled away in what I thought was illegible writing. 'My wife is pregnant, almost at full term.'

'Thank you, sir,' he said hurriedly, moving along to the remainder of the group, having taken no notice of what Gurpul had said.

'This is group number twenty-five,' the Colonel announced, returning to the front. 'Jagdesh Taran, Anand Bachan and Hari Devindar are guiding you to the border, with Major Taran heading the group. His Lance Corporals, Bachan and Devindar will assist. These men are your protectors and defenders, they will fight for you. Women with children should remain within the centre of the group and men towards the front and back.'

At last we left the court having been there for hours.

Night had fallen on what began as a perfectly calm and normal day. Gunfire continued to sound in the distance, though less frequently. The streets had quietened with not as many people in sight, but murdered bodies mounted along roadsides. Unlit streets made it difficult to assess the damage and the sky remained misty. The group huddled together, careful not to stray. Walking out of the city should have been a relatively straightforward task for the soldiers, but due to the lack of lighting and the extent of damage, we made several wrong turnings, adding almost an hour to our journey time. Mirpur had become home for me and now leaving the city felt so final. We were not choosing to leave in the quest for a better life or opportunity, but we were all being forced out. How that was even possible I couldn't comprehend. Late into the night we arrived at the foot of the hills which were to take us to the Zaskar Mountains. The group looked around, heads turned in shock, frightened at the thought of having to cross such large hills and then the enormous mountains behind. Slowly kneeling down, still staring at the vastness of nature, I sat on the rocky ground hoping to relieve the muscle spasms in my back whilst trying to come to terms with the day's events.

'I intend to stop here for a few hours, as it would not be wise to begin crossing at this time. I will inspect and finalise the planned routes and between us we will successfully cross the mountains and arrive in Jammu safely,' Major Taran said.

He left the group to rest, while his Lance Corporals scrutinised the surrounding area. Flashing torches followed the paths through the hills and over. Everybody remained quiet with only the cries of wild animals or movements made by the soldiers to be heard.

'They shouldn't have taken so long, Gurpul,' I said.

'Who?' he asked lost in his own thought.

'Major Taran and the Lance Corporals.'

'Checking the initial stage of the journey could take a while.'

'They must have left a few hours ago,' I guessed.

'Excuse me, do you know how long we are spending here?' An old man of at least sixty asked Gurpul. 'I'm deaf, so I didn't hear any of the Major's instructions.'

'He didn't specify how long,' Gurpul replied, sitting up.

'They've been gone a long time,' his wife interrupted.

'Yes, my wife was saying the same.'

'Is this your wife and daughter?' The old woman asked, leaning forward to look at us.

'Yes.'

'Where have you come from?'

'Mirpur, we live just outside the main city.'

'We managed to escape from the North before the attacks began,' the old man informed. 'Apparently it all began in the North, I don't know why. There must have been some conflict.' He coughed heavily and spat out the phlegm. Removing his glasses, he wiped his face.

'Are you OK?' Gurpul asked. I listened to their conversation, still lying down, unable to get up.

'I'm old,' he laughed. 'I'm old and this is what my life has come to.' He looked around shaking his head. 'My entire life I've lived here and now I'm being thrown out of my own city.'

'Do you have any family?'

'Plenty, my son, plenty.' He stopped for a breath. Gurpul waited for him to continue. 'Five sons,' he said boastfully. 'My first five were all boys; we had been blessed by God. My father was proud of me. He told me I must have done a good deed at some point in my life to have received such a blessing.'

'Absolutely.' Gurpul replied with all seriousness, even though he thought such values held no weight in today's world.

'Then five daughters followed. My father said I must have committed a serious sin.' Gurpul laughed, but the old man remained seriously quiet, contemplating the thought.

'Where are your children?' Gurpul wondered.

'All grown up, married with children. Six of them moved away from Mirpur, the others stayed. The rioting warnings left us with no time to contact them, we abandoned everything and ran. Now look where I am: in the middle of some mountains.' He dropped his head. 'Are there just the three of you?'

'Yes.' He didn't ask any more questions; he probably knew the answers, there was no time to stop and contact relatives. I thought about my family in Lahore and Gurpul's parents being in Delhi. The woman looked at me sitting up with difficulty.

'You're expecting,' she said. 'You shouldn't be sitting like that. Did your mother-in-law never tell you?' She came by my side, leaving the men to converse.

'She did, but how else am I supposed to sit here?' I remained in the same position, with my knees to the side.

She took my arms and helped me lie down on my back, placing Rajendar's bag under my head. 'If you lie like this the baby will have room to move as he wants.'

'As he wants?' I asked, surprised. I felt the baby moving and kicking more than it usually did, awake at this time of night, also feeling the unease of the outside world. She examined my stomach with her eyes, although I was sure she couldn't see anything in the darkness. But then she felt the entire shape, slowly moving her rough hands over my stomach.

'You'll have a boy.' I looked at her and then at Gurpul; he smiled. Perfect, I thought; a little brother to Rajendar. My son.

Major and the Lance Corporals eventually returned after a few hours of investigations.

'We have inspected the initial ten-mile route and it is safe from obstruction and danger. We will not encounter any major difficulties, but it will require effort. This stage will be completed by sunrise and the further journey will be much easier in daylight.'

Everybody prepared to leave. The rest had not made us feel any better, or any less exhausted, but we continued, having many days of crossing ahead.

'It's going to be difficult carrying Rajendar and walking through the hills at the same time,' Gurpul said. He was right, but I didn't know what to suggest. 'I need some cloth.'

'Why?' I asked.

'I'll tie it around my neck and place Rajendar in it, like a harness.'

'Use my dubatta, it's big enough.'

He tied the two ends of the scarf above his right shoulder and secured it with a number of smaller knots. I lifted and placed Rajendar into the harness, with her legs on either side. She was strapped close to Gurpul. Once she had settled and the others ready, we began the journey.

A path followed the hill to the peak, which Major Taran showed us by flashing his torch. It wasn't secure, so I walked far back from the edge, scared that I might fall or trip. The ground was uneven and rocky, and each step we took needed to be placed carefully so we didn't trip or fall. For hours we ascended these vast hills, which stood silently, appearing so grand and confident in their presence, and we so vulnerable. We passed wild trees, bushes, thistles and hawthorns. The sleeve of my kameez tore while walking past some thorns, cutting my arm and causing it to bleed, but I walked on, unable to stop and tend to the wound. I could feel my stomach churning due to the altitude. The old man was ahead of us shaking as he walked up the steep path with his walking stick.

'I need to stop for a break, I'll lose my balance if I carry on,' he told his wife. 'Ask the Major to stop.'

'When do we stop, Major? My husband needs to rest.'

'Tired already? We have many days ahead of us yet. Continue,' he commanded without even glancing back.

'He said we must continue,' his wife repeated. They both spoke and complained among themselves, irritated with the manner of the Major.

All of a sudden his walking stick became stuck in a wide ground crack. He stumbled trying to regain balance and his wife reached for his hand, but she fell back unable to take his weight. Just as Gurpul stepped forward to pull the shouting couple back from the edge, they fell forward, face down. Everybody stopped, but nobody looked over the dark edge. A few moments later the sound of two loud thuds came from the bottom of the hill. Nobody moved.

'I can't see anything,' Gurpul said, looking over. The walking stick lay over the crack.

'We don't have time to stop. Accidents will happen in such conditions.' Major marched along.

The long walk continued, two members short. The drop flashed through my mind: before I even had the chance to blink, the couple had tripped and fallen to their deaths. If only the Major had stopped and given him a break; if only Gurpul had reached out sooner. The sound of the bodies hitting the ground reverberated in my ears, along with the cold words of the Major. Lost in these thoughts I walked on, failing to see long branches hanging from a tree until they scraped my face.

'Be careful, Taji, watch what you're doing!' Gurpul exclaimed, pulling me back.

'I didn't see them,' I murmured, tired and wounded again. I felt cuts and scratches on my forehead. Gurpul attempted to wipe the blood away, but a deep cut above my eyebrow would not stop bleeding.

'Leave it, I'll be OK. We must catch up,' I insisted, watching the group disappear in the distance.

The entire night had passed by without a break, but the sign of dawn raised our spirits.

'This point marks the end of the upward journey,' Major Taran announced, stopping ahead of us at the peak of the hill. 'It has been a difficult crossing and we're all tired, but we must keep going, so we reach the other side by sunrise.' He walked on like an iron man showing no sign of fatigue, but instead wearing a look of determination.

'Can we stop to recover a little and to feed our children? Look at them, they're frightened, they're hungry, they need rest,' a man protested, looking around at the toddlers and babies in the group, his arm around a weak-looking boy.

'This is a matter of life or death. If you want to make it to Jammu alive then I suggest you continue. By daylight you will hear the violence escalating yet again. This will continue for many days or weeks, there are no signs of any ease in tension. We need to make it to the border as soon as we can,' a terse response came from Major Taran, who was infuriated with the demands for rest. 'I will continue down this path, if you feel you need a break then you may stop. Follow on when you are ready, but we will not wait.'

He resumed walking, not turning back to see who followed; neither of the Lance Corporals remained behind either. Almost half the group stopped, but the others continued. Rajendar's eyes were puffy, her chin quivering, but little sound coming from her mouth now. Her neck was injured from rocking back and forth. Gurpul took her out and placed her in my arms as I leaned against a tree to feed her. Although relieved to be off my feet, I was frightened at the thought of being isolated on the peak, with no help in sight.

'Ammi, I'm hungry,' a young boy pleaded, 'I want something to eat. Ammi, please give me something to eat, I'm so hungry.'

'Jaan, we have no food here, we must reach the other side before we can get some.'

'But, Ammi, I can't wait, I want to eat. I'm hungry, I can't wait. Why do I have to wait?' he complained, holding onto his mother's leg pulling her down.

'When we reach the other side you will be able to eat whatever you want,' she tried convincing the child, but he refused to listen. He sat down on the ground, creeping towards the edge of the hill. 'What are you doing? Come away.'

'No! I want to eat, I'm hungry and tired,' he protested.

'Move away now,' she shouted, pulling him back. He cried, stomping his hands and feet. 'Stop being so naughty!'

'I want Abba, where's Abba? Abba will give me something to eat.' The mother's eyes filled with sorrow as the boy cried for his father, kneeling down on the ground she tried to cuddle him, but he pushed her away.

'Come to Ammi, Jaan. I'll give you everything you want to eat when we reach the bottom.'

'No! I want Abba now!'

'He's dead! I can't bring him back. Abba's gone, they've taken him away from us.' She buried her head in her knees and her frightened son sat beside her.

After feeding Rajendar we caught up with the rest of the group. Many of those who stopped had already begun the steep descending journey. From the peak I could see people scattered around at different points, a few were already close to the bottom. Although walking down was easier, the steepness prevented a steady paced walk, making it strenuous and dangerous. Midway, the path divided in two; one was a sharp bend to the right, and the other a straightforward path. Both directions were taken, with people incorrectly following the bend.

'Come back up, you're taking the wrong path,' Gurpul shouted down. A few heads turned back, but they continued, probably unsure of what he said.

'There's nothing we can do, Gurpul, let's carry on.'

In the daylight the end of the path could be seen, it was a sign of hope which made me determined to continue, despite the agonising pain in my stomach. I looked at the crystal clear water in the little river running between the mountains and hills, sparkling where the sun's rays hit it. I thought of being able to quench my thirst, having remained without food or drink for over a day. I continued, trying to block out the pain.

A blood curdling sound of a scream echoed through the air, and then in a flash a huge ball of fire erupted from the bottom of the hill and belched high up towards us like a volcanic eruption. A whirlpool of fire;

my eyes were burning with the intense heat, orange flames and black ashes. As I removed my hands from my ears, I had a split second of panic, before I calmed when I felt Gurpul and Rajendar. Those people who had reached the bottom circled my mind. They were probably relieved to have completed the hill crossing successfully, but unaware of what fate awaited them. We tried walking forward but with the smoke so thick we were unable to move.

'Let's stay here until the smoke clears, Taji. I don't want to risk walking any further.'

Nobody was in sight, not a single person. I sat back and listened to the firing of rifles sounding again. Major Taran was correct: an escalation in violence accompanied the daylight. The air began clearing and we commenced our remaining journey walking quickly through the lingering smoke. We reached the bottom where a raw site awaited us: the journey of our fellow group members and our defenders, as we were told, had come to an abrupt end. Both by and in the riverbank, ruptured limbs and defeated carcases floated away to another world. No mullah or priest or guru to utter a prayer for them or ask for forgiveness. No loved ones to clean them and wrap them in a soft white cloth before setting them free. Alone they arrived and alone they depart.

'Their determination to reach the bottom resulted in their death.' The rioting intensified and became louder. 'Who is firing here?' I asked, confused as to where we were.

'This is the Muslim region, we are still on their grounds and they must have been informed that this route is being used by Hindus and Sikhs to reach the other side.'

'We need to get out,' I panicked.

Before Gurpul even had the opportunity to reply another explosion hit. I was thrown into the air and landed with a thud on some heavy rocks. My lower abdomen and back felt the impact of the landing, causing a circuiting stabbing pain

'Gurpul, where are you? Gurpul!' I screamed out, but there was no sign of him. I couldn't hear or see him. I couldn't move.

'Abba, Abba!'

The cries of a child shouting for his father echoed in my ears. Raising my head from the rocks I looked around. A young boy was huddled beside the mountain edge, with his head between his knees. A pain sheared through my groin and then my abdomen; the contractions became stronger until I couldn't bear it. Eyes closed, fists clenched, I called out. Light footsteps approached and the young boy was standing before me. I struggled to my feet realising that my waters had broken. The boy pulled at the bottom of my kameez.

'Will you help me find my Abba?' He wiped the blood from a cut on his arm.

'Come on, come with me. We'll find your Abba and Gurpul and Rajendar,' I finally managed to answer.

We walked slowly, his quivering hand clenched mine, searching for all that we had left in the world. The smoke blurred our vision and made it difficult to breathe. After five minutes I no longer had the energy to continue. I sat down again by the river.

'Go find somebody to help us. I will wait here for you. Go on, good boy.' I encouraged and he ran off shouting for help.

The shouts faded, but I was not left in silence, for the rifles were firing. Breathing deeply, I wondered whether the Musalmaans would kill me if they discovered me on their land. The baby wriggled uncomfortably low in my abdomen, clearly as confused and disturbed as I was. A new born baby should only ever know love and protection, but my baby was being introduced to a world where hate and conflict was rife. The pains eased: I got up and followed the young boy. Like litter in the bazaars, they were scattered everywhere: men, women and children alike, nobody was spared. Some appeared fully intact, but covered in blood, others limbless.

Children were floating in the river, some lying peacefully on their backs with their eyes guiding them to the heavens; the rest faced down, drowning in the horrors of the world. I walked along a narrow path with a river flowing gently on my left; being by water had always calmed me, until I noticed the once clear waters were slowly turning red. Straight ahead the mountains proudly stood dominating the landscape, fearlessly reaching high. The morning sun broke above their peaks, its gentle yellow rays shining in the cloudless sky. I stopped in wonder, admiring what I saw, while realising that here below nothing was beautiful, it was brutal.

'Taji!'

A familiar voice interrupted my thoughts. Gurpul was approaching with Rajendar. The side of his face was wounded, his shirt torn, limping towards me.

'Gurpul! What happened? Where were you?' I asked, desperately. 'You're hurt, your head is bleeding.' He stepped closer and kissed my forehead.

'I was knocked unconscious, Rajendar's cries woke me.' She held onto her Abba petrified, her head buried into his shoulder.

'My contractions have begun, they are becoming more and more frequent. What do we do?'

Rajendar began crying, I reached out for her and she opened her arms weakly, my starving baby. Despite my pains I cradled her.

'Sit down, you need to rest, and Rajendar needs feeding. I'll try to find some help.'

My feet dragged as I walked. Gurpul took Rajendar from me, while she screeched, her arms tightly gripping my neck, not wanting to let go. Despite our attempts at calming her she continued screaming. The mother and son we saw at the top of the hill approached us and asked for directions; her hand attempted to cover a deep cut in her upper arm, but a red eruption was still showing between the slightly parted fingers.

'We're just walking,' Gurpul said. 'My wife is in labour.'

The labour contractions in my lower back, racked to and fro.

'It's getting worse,' I managed to mumble between the breaths.

'Sit her down, here,' the woman pointed towards some flat ground. Gurpul helped me towards the spot. 'No, wait.' She unwound her scarf and laid it on the sand, before easing me onto it.

'Taji, I'm going to find help, I'll be back soon,' Gurpul said, taking Rajendar with him.

'How old is your daughter?' The woman asked, trying to take my attention from the pain.

'Sixteen months.'

'And another baby already on the way,' she said.

'I don't even know your name.'

'Kareena,' she replied, 'and my son is Aman.' She looked over to where he was playing in the sand, using two small stones as cars, crashing them into each other.

'What about your husband?' I asked reluctantly.

'Our home was set alight,' she started slowly. This already sounded like a familiar tale. 'Hari was on the rooftop when he saw a gang heading towards our grounds. He shouted for Aman and me to leave. I heard him coming down the staircase as we were running for the back doors; I knew he would be right behind,' she insisted. She looked over at Aman before continuing. 'A few moments later the house was up in flames. Three gunshots followed. I knew he had been killed.'

I listened, not mentioning that the pain had returned. I trembled and had hot and cold flushes, despite the morning sun. I was ready to give birth, so Kareena took off my shalwar and soaked it in the river to wipe the sweat from my face. She guided me and showed me how to breathe, and all I could think about was how my child was being born into this. She carried on talking, but I couldn't tell what she was saying. I saw Gurpul returning with some other people who looked familiar: the young boy who had lost his father was among them. Realising I was in labour, they stayed back, squatting on the sandy ground, with their backs to us.

I could no longer see the bright shining sun, or the cloudless blue sky, only mist and fog. Kareena's voice came from the distance as she wiped my forehead and face with a cloth, cooling me in the rising heat. My fingernails bit into the palms of my hands and there were sickening white flashes on my closed eyelids; burning homes up in flames before me again. A baby was burning in the flames and I tried to rescue it but I couldn't. There was silence in the outside world; no firing, no eruptions, nobody spoke; but my own screams reverberated in my ears as if they came from a long distance and didn't belong to me. My body racked with convulsions running from the top of my abdomen to my pelvis and then into my back. My legs shook and I felt nauseated and faint all at the same time, whilst tasting salty drops of sweat and tears on my lips. Then the contractions would come and I'd become aware of Kareena's attempts at soothing and cajoling me, not managing to hide her urgency in willing me to let this baby come into this terrible world.

Finally, the strong urge to push the baby overcame every other emotion and thought in my mind. Every ounce of my being was used to push this life out from the safety of my womb. My body went limp with the momentary relief. The force of the contraction eased whilst I felt the fluids seep out from me, I rested my head back. I opened my eyes to see once again the midday sun, far up in the sky, bringing with it the innocent cries of a new born baby.

'It's a boy! Mubaarak, Taji,' Kareena shouted out, and the crowd cheered.

He was so healthy and full of life; unaware that he had arrived into a space of death. Gurpul stroked his head as I held him, not wanting to let go. My utter elation was short-lived as I saw Gurpul dry his wet cheeks with the back of his hand. His eyes were heavy with sorrow, his face drawn, not even a smile; this was not the Gurpul I had seen at Rajendar's birth. There was no excitement, no beaming smile, no loving words. My abdomen was already sore from birth but the agony on Gurpul's face hit me like a further blow to my stomach.

I looked at Gurpul, 'she was right…' I mumbled, remembering the old woman who had told me I would have a son. He nodded. Gurpul and Kareena took the baby to the river and washed him. Before they returned the sound of rifles began again, no longer sporadic, more like an approaching army. I tried getting up but couldn't.

'Gurpul! Come back. Come back!'

The men huddled together, staring wildly, not knowing what to do.

'Where do we go? In which direction?' One of them protested. 'We don't know what's safe and what's not.'

Before anybody could reply, an explosion erupted from the hills we had just crossed; causing the ground beneath us to shake like thunder in the sky. Sand and rubble were sucked up with the force and then rained upon us falling back to the ground. A cloud of black ash smothered the hills; whilst the nauseating smell of charcoaled carcases surrounded us.

A voice shouted from behind us. 'Run!'

I tried to stand, but the immense pain prevented me from doing so. Gurpul and Kareena helped me to my feet and I leaned against a large rock for support. Gurpul placed Rajendar in the harness he had made and Kareena wrapped my baby in the same cloth on which I had delivered him. She left him on the ground and picked up Aman. I was in agony, realising that I must have torn myself with the last push.

'I'll carry you, Taji. I can carry you on my back,' Gurpul said.

'What about our baby? Give him to me.'

'You can't carry him as well.'

Lying on the ground the baby's cries did not quieten.

'Give him to me, Gurpul, he needs me.' I tried to bend down, but although my arms reached forward my legs didn't move and the pain intensified when I bent my knees. 'He's my baby, he needs me. Give him to me!' As my cries became louder, the gathered group frantically looked around.

'You must quieten your wife, she'll get us all caught,' demanded an older man.

'Taji, please, stop this.' Gurpul wrapped his arms around me and I buried my face into his shoulders. When I quietened, he pulled back and picked up our baby, but he didn't manage to calm him. Kareena and Aman stared, Aman's arms around his mother's neck.

'Give him to me,' I pleaded, reaching out again. Gurpul placed him in my arms and I held him securely against my chest. I sighed in relief, 'all I want is my baby.'

There was still no sign of any visible danger, but some disturbance was drawing closer.

'Taji, get on my back,' Gurpul instructed, panicking.

'I'll walk and carry my baby too.'

'You're in no fit state to walk.'

'I'll manage.'

Determined to do so, I took a step forward, dragging my feet and taking deep breaths. I persisted. My breathing became louder and deeper, my heartbeat in overdrive, every muscle shutting down, as I carried my own dead weight. I wouldn't give in. Gurpul with Rajendar, and Kareena with Aman, they all walked behind me. After no more than ten steps I collapsed to the ground, dropping my child. We screamed. Kareena reached for the baby, rubbing his head. Gurpul remained motionless, a look of despair in his eyes.

'I told you not to carry him, didn't I?' he shouted. I stared at him, not knowing what to say. Nobody understood, all I wanted was to be with my baby.

'What's happened now? This is no time to be having a family conference. The fighting is coming closer and all this commotion will draw attention to us. Can you not stop that child from crying?' The same man shouted again. He was a large Sikh man, as tall as Gurpul, but he had no family with him.

'Everything's OK. Don't worry, Satbir. I'm sorry.' Gurpul was trying to reassure the man and himself. The others were standing some distance away.

'Come on, Taji, I'll carry you.' He kneeled down and I climbed up with the help of Satbir. Kareena held the baby, with his continued cries.

We walked on. Aman now started crying because he felt scared and wanted to know why the men were shouting. Kareena tried reassuring him, telling him that they were making sure we were OK, but he continued sobbing. Again, the others looked back and told us to hush.

'Why are you carrying him, Ammi? Carry me, I don't want to walk, carry me.'

'Aman, you can walk because you're a big boy, but this baby can't walk, can he? I need to carry the baby. Come on, we're nearly there.'

'I don't want to.' He stamped his feet and refused to go any further. Kareena looked back at Gurpul and me, hoping for a solution.

'Pick him up, Kareena. Put the baby down,' Gurpul brought himself to say, putting me down at the same time.

'If this continues it's a matter of moments before we are all caught. Leave the baby here. You can come back for him when we find safety.' I didn't even look up to see who spoke, I knew it was that self-centred, insensitive Satbir. 'You may not want to get out of here alive, but the rest of us do. We're drawing attention to ourselves with this noise. We can't all risk our lives for one baby.' Rajendar and Aman both remained quiet, but the baby refused to, despite our efforts to calm him.

'I've just given birth, my baby has entered this hellish environment, where houses and villages are being set alight, rifles are firing and seeing brutally murdered people is now the norm. How can you expect him to be quiet? How can you expect me to leave him here? You haven't carried

158

him for nine months. I will not leave him. He is coming with me whether you like it or not, and if we get killed along the way then so be it!' I shouted with all my might.

'Do as you please, but we are not waiting here any longer.' Satbir continued walking.

'Taji, calm down,' Gurpul said. 'We need to remain with these people, otherwise we will be totally lost and we'll never make it to the other side. We must leave our baby until we reach safety, until we know where we are at least; for Rajendar's sake, for this young boy's sake. We cannot risk everybody's life, it isn't fair. He's wrapped up in the scarf, we will return once the coast is clear,' he promised.

Leave him? Leave the baby I had just given birth to? The baby I had not even fed yet, not yet held close to my breast? My mouth could not utter a single word. I had lost all feeling in my lips and tongue, not even a tingling; like the nerves had been cut. I opened it but no sound emerged. Gurpul picked up our baby, kissed him on the cheek and brought him forward to me, but I couldn't even look at him. I was a terrible mother, I had brought him into this. No mother leaves a child to save her own life. I watched Gurpul place him beside a large rock.

'Don't put him there,' Kareena asserted. 'Leave him by the river, at least there will be some breeze.'

Gurpul ran to the bank, a few metres away and put him down, his lips touching the soft skin of our baby's forehead.

'Come on,' Gurpul ordered. I stood motionless. 'Come on, Taji.'

'No!' I shouted. 'Leave me, take the baby. I will be fine here, come back for me. Just take the baby, please, Gurpul. Don't leave my baby.'

'Taji, don't do this. He is our baby. We will be a family, the four of us.'

He came and stood close to me, his hands cupped my face and he gently lifted my head so my eyes met his. I felt his sorrow, as I watched his lower lip quiver and my face vibrate in his shaking hands. The confident, carefree Gurpul was not standing before me; I saw a numb and helpless man who'd lost his fight. His eyes began glazing over, as he lost focus and a salty drop of water fell to my cheek. His shaking hands released my face and he embraced me tightly, he held me close to his chest and I felt his heart beating rapidly. He stroked my hair, and by doing so was silently longing for me to trust him. I placed one foot on the side of a rock and used it to help me get onto Gurpul's back. I tried not to separate my legs, but I had to. I made the sudden movement, telling myself that no pain could be greater than leaving my newly born baby. An electric current shot through every vein in my body as I felt the wound tear like an envelope being torn apart. I wanted to scream out, but I bit deep into my tongue instead, which sprayed the inside of my mouth and left a coppery taste. Gurpul began walking in the direction the other five men had taken. He shouted for them to slow down, and they did. My heart had been butchered; being stabbed one hundred times would not come close to what I felt as we walked away. I did not know myself any longer. I could not understand how I was allowing this to happen. My soul had been snatched from me; a part of my body had been left behind.

'I will come back.' I pledged to my boy, as I turned to look at the riverbank, where a tiny parcel lay.

We reached some mountains but we didn't know whether they were the ones we needed to cross. Everybody stood frightened, not knowing what to say.

'Standing here is not going to get us anywhere, is it?' A young man said and walked on.

We all followed. Instead of the mountain he led us up a hill, which had a steady, unobstructed path. We faced another mountain, but not as steep as the previous one. Gurpul carried both Rajendar and me: precariously balancing us both, his knees and back hunched over, almost like they were ready to snap, but he didn't utter a sound.

'I'll walk, Gurpul, put me down.'

'No, you've just given birth, Taji!'

We reached the top of the mountain without being attacked. Below us was a small village. We began our descent.

The place looked peaceful, undisturbed by the devastations of our home city. It was obviously a poor village; crude huts no bigger than kennels clustered together. Most had only a single storey, but a few had stairs leading to the roof. There was nobody in sight, it was hard to tell if anybody was living there: no washing on the rooftops, no children playing, no sign of habitation. The villagers might have fled, but there were no signs of disturbance either. As we stepped from the foot of the mountain onto flat ground, three Musalmaans emerged. They stood perfectly lined, white scarves shading their heads from the heat, rifles casually hanging from their shoulders like squash rackets. We instinctively fell back in complete shock. Gurpul gently lowered me. The men scrutinised us from head to toe. I looked behind, three others were blocking the path: they'd boxed us in, like bullies in a playground, leaving no hope of escape. One of them, with a thick brown moustache covering his upper lip, took a few steps forward. There was a sinister smirk on his face.

'Are you Sikhs and Hindus lost?'

'Brother, we don't want any trouble, we're just trying to get to the other side,' Satbir protested.

'Nobody wants any trouble?' He exclaimed. 'So why is it that thousands of Musalmaans are being murdered by you and your friends?' We remained quiet, terrified. 'How long have you been on the run? Haven't you heard about the massacres all over the country? Sikhs and Hindus are killing every Musalmaan man or woman found. It's headline news in every Hindustani newspaper. So whilst you all try to escape and save your own lives your people are killing my people! Now since you have honoured our village with your presence, maybe we should do the same.'

He didn't stop to allow anybody to speak. Evil was written all over his dark scarred face. His gaze was that of a predator waiting to jump on his prey; as he slowly ran his hand over the sleeked back hair. He crossed his arms, so they rested on his stomach, as he stepped back to think. I watched his nostrils flare as he took deep breaths. The very sight of him sickened me.

'Brother, we have not killed anybody. We are all family people. All we ask of you is to direct us towards the Zaskar Mountains and we'll leave your village.'

'Oh no, my dear brother,' he cruelly ridiculed, 'you may not have killed anybody, but your people have. Come this way, you're guests of our village now.'

We looked around for an escape route, but there wasn't one. A young teenager towards the front of the group jumped at the man who had been speaking, trying to seize his rifle, but the man was much too quick and experienced. He used his elbow to clip the teenager under his chin and almost simultaneously punched him in the ribs, causing him to lose his balance and fall to the ground. A shot in the leg made sure he wasn't able to get up.

'That wasn't a good move. Any more of that and each one of you will get a bullet through your head. Follow me.'

Someone lifted the young man to his feet and he stumbled along with difficulty leaving a trail of blood behind. We followed, not knowing what would happen; the six Musalmaans ushered us along. The village women could now be seen, peeping out through their doors and windows. Would they help us? No, they couldn't. These men were their husbands, sons and brothers; if they did anything they would be killed too.

Behind the smaller huts was a large house surrounded by tall gates. This was the home of a rich man. The door stood above five marble entrance steps with pillars on either side of the veranda. We were taken around the back to a hut, like the ones in the main village. Perhaps the servants lived there, but in such a large house, servant quarters should not have been so small.

'Women and children downstairs,' one of the men said. 'Men upstairs. And silence!'

Gurpul took Rajendar out of the harness and gave her to me; as our captors stood close to ensure we did not speak or touch. My husband walked up the stone staircase without saying a word. I entered the room, where there were women already seated on the hard cement floor. The room had no furniture, only solid mud walls and no windows, just a small frame for the door. We were not their first captives: a total of ten women were sitting along the walls, frightened, holding on to one another. It felt damp and cramped in the small, airless space, which was overcrowded even for animals, let alone humans. Kareena and Aman and Rajendar and I sat in the middle of the floor. The door was slammed shut and locked from the outside. We were left in darkness and complete silence. Finding it too painful to remain seated, I stood again, putting Rajendar down.

'Can't you sit on the floor?' Kareena asked, looking up with Aman in her lap.

'No, my wound hasn't healed.'

'What's wrong, my child?' An elderly woman asked.

'Maa, I gave birth only a few hours ago.'

'This isn't the child,' she said. 'Where's your baby?' She looked around.

'I had to leave him. I left him by the river. They forced me to. I didn't want to leave my son!'

His cries echoed in my ears; I smelt his sweet, milky scent and I saw his olive coloured skin as he lay in my arms. My beautiful baby. Maa did not move for a few seconds, and the other women gasped; she struggled to stand, but eventually came to me and consoled me. She told me to take her seat, on a small haystack, against the wall.

'No, I cannot take your seat.'

'Sit down, my child,' she insisted.

Despite its muskiness, the hay was easier to sit on than the cement floor; and although Maa was frail and elderly, she massaged my feet and legs.

'Is your husband upstairs or...?'

'Yes, he's upstairs, Maa,' I interrupted before such words tripped off her tongue and made me contemplate my worst nightmare. My pulse beat in harmony with his; my life was only complete with him by my side. I barely remembered life without Gurpul; he'd always been a part of me and always would be.

'My husband is also upstairs. We've been here for three days,' she explained. 'Five whole days it took us to reach the Zaskar Mountains from Jhelum, but we got no further.' She let out a loud sigh before continuing. 'There they were waiting for us, and for three days they have kept us here, giving us only dried berries to eat.' Everybody in the claustrophobic hut listened to her gruesome tale which could have been fictional; but each of us was living this, it was our reality, our tale. We just hadn't stopped for long enough to acknowledge what had happened so far; we had lived through the nightmare she described.

'Maa,' I asked hesitantly, 'Are the men still alive? You haven't seen them for three days.'

'We're sure that they are: sometimes voices can be heard, although we can't make out what they are saying. They've treated us so terribly, should we need the toilet, we must wait for somebody to come to the door, or try knocking on the door to get their attention. They then take us to the side of the hut, "There are leaves on the trees if you need them," they say. They don't even turn their backs, no! They look, they take a good look.'

Maa talked to us for the rest of the day. Night fell, but we were given neither food nor water. All they needed to do was draw water from the wells, but we didn't even get one bucket. The rays of light which came through the cracks in the door during the day disappeared, and we were lost in complete darkness. Aman, Rajendar and a young boy who was with his mother when we arrived, stopped crying for food and finally fell asleep. We waited, hoping they would at least bring us some berries, but they didn't. They brought us nothing.

If we had slept at all, the morning birds and village cows would have woken us up early. There was a loud bang and the squeaky door opened. One of the men who had captured us threw in a bag. His head moved in a stiff semicircle to look at each of us in turn; I lowered my gaze when his eyes met mine. He closed and locked the door again. The berries were passed around and we took a handful each. These could be poisonous, I thought, and ate no more. The footsteps ascended and then stamped heavily around the room above. Only one voice was heard, but what it said was not clear. Then a shuffling began, as if the men were moving about.

'What's happening up there?' Maa asked, looking concerned. Nobody spoke, we listened quietly. The footsteps descended, not just those of one man, but a whole group of them. After a couple of minutes, the last reached the bottom and then there was silence. The door opened again. It was a different man this time. I tried to see if Gurpul was there, but the bulky figure in the small doorway blocked the view.

'Any young boys in here? This way,' he commanded.

The boy with his mother next to the doorway was dragged out. Aman tried to hide but the man walked into the room and pulled him out from behind Kareena.

'Come with me.'

'I don't want to go. Ammi, I don't want to go. Please, Ammi, please!' He cried and screamed holding onto Kareena's arm as the man snatched him away.

'Don't take my son, he's all I have. Leave him, please, leave my son. Don't take him away from me. He's just a child!'

'Shut up!'

Aman was dragged across the room, not letting go of his mother until they reached the threshold, where the man gave a final pull and slammed the door shut.

'Ammi, come with me, don't leave me. I want to stay here with you.' Aman's cries became fainter as he was taken away, until they stopped altogether.

We strained to listen for sounds outside, but heard nothing. No footsteps, nor voices; even the birds had stopped singing. There was complete silence. I wondered what was going to happen. Why had they dragged Aman and the men away? Nobody dared speak their thoughts aloud, or acknowledge the impending doom we all felt. Kareena was sitting in a corner, an air of absolute desolation surrounded her, she couldn't speak or move. Her soiled and dusty hands wiped away the tears, leaving smudges on her pale face.

'We can only pray,' Maa said, after what seemed like many hours.

Prayers would not make a difference, I thought; prayers will not change the fate that awaits us. Despite the lack of response, she continued trying to raise our spirits, to prevent us from losing hope. Maa was a small and weak woman, but she was stronger than the rest of us and courage was something she would never lack.

'They have probably taken them to do some work. They will be back tonight. We are worrying for no reason. They will be back.'

'Maa, that man dragged Aman across the floor. Why would they do that if all they wanted was to use him as a labourer? Why would they take a five year old child for labour? This doesn't make sense,' Kareena protested.

Once again the sun's rays penetrated the gaps in the heavy wooden door, slowly filling the dark, damp hut with light and heat, allowing us to see each other, reminding us that what we were enduring was not a dream, but reality. The sound of footsteps startled us again, we gazed at each other in hope and all simultaneously leaned towards the door.

'Are the men back?' One of the women whispered.

Nobody answered. We listened to the footsteps approaching, the shuffling of boots in the gravel, the murmuring of voices, but not the voices of our men. And then again, silence. Shadows were visible under the bottom of the door. All of a sudden a key turned in the lock and the door creaked open. Three men stood on the threshold. A medium height, white-bearded man, with a brown scar covering his right cheek, stood in front of the others. He looked so ordinary to me, he reminded me of Babu. How could somebody like Babu be capable of holding us captive like this? His two guards on either side of him were larger in size and held rifles across their chests.

'Stand. Follow me. Quickly, don't just sit there gawping.'

For a small man his voice projected loud and far. From the doorway he watched us gather the few poor items we still possessed. I had been sitting in the same position for two days, unable to stretch my legs. I struggled onto my knees and by wedging myself against the wall finally stood upright. My legs felt lifeless and numb. Shaking, I watched the others rise. Maa had difficulty standing too, but Kareena helped her up and kept hold of her. I kneeled back down to pick up Rajendar, her head was tilted back, staring. I suddenly remembered her bag; we had left it somewhere, along with the rattle Babu bought her. It was her favourite play thing, but it was long gone. Rajendar was weak, having not eaten for many days. Her large brown eyes looked as if they would pop out of their sockets: she had dark circles around them. Her thick black hair was lying wildly around her face, uncombed and unwashed, stuck in clumps with blood and mud. Her skin was scathed over her arms and legs. I was transported back to just a few short weeks before when I took pride in dressing my daughter in beautiful dresses and combed her hair with sweet smelling hair oil to make it grow long and thick. I lifted her, feeling so light, no longer the healthy, chubby child I had known. Her arms clasped my neck and I began walking out of the hut. Nobody spoke.

Fresh air. Daylight. Warmth. It was as if I had not seen the outside world for many months. Every hour locked in the hut had felt like a day. But now we were out, we felt more afraid than ever. In single file, we followed the white-bearded man. One armed guard was on my right and another further back. Above the mountains a radiant yellow sun beat down like a glowing medallion in the sky, trying in vain to restore colour to our faded skin, smiles to our dull, starved faces. I looked in awe at her beauty; so unaffected by the ravages that we were being subjected to. To be the sun I imagined, and bring light, heat and joy to the world each day; and then, take rest when the day's work was done, handing over to the moon, never leaving the sky empty. If only I could be the enchanting star that is the sun. Ahead lay the imposing white house we had seen upon entering the village. No one was around to help us. By following the overgrown path we finally reached a small door at the side of the house. The guard opened it and with a curse ushered us inside. The last man to enter slammed the glass door behind him, startling us. We were in the kitchen. Each of the three doors that led out of it, were closed. It looked as if it had not been used for many months, dust had settled on the surfaces and cobwebs draped in every corner. For a house of its size, the kitchen was small and old-fashioned. An open plan clay oven for baking roti was at its centre with a small stool for the cook. She would have had to sit up against the burning heat to ensure each side cooked properly, with no window or door to admit air to keep her eyes from burning. A plank of wood, a metre in width, had been placed where the roti would be rolled out. The rolling pin still remained in position. Tired looking, heavy duty steel pots and pans were hung on hooks and told the story of many banquets and dinners.

'You're to follow right behind and not make any noise. Do not touch anything,' the white-bearded man said loudly, standing in front of a door, opposite the one we'd entered.

It opened out into a dimly-lit corridor, narrow and unadorned; the servants' quarters. The corridor led into a large square entrance hall, with marble flooring, a chandelier hung in the centre of the ceiling and a staircase opposite the main doorway led upstairs. We looked around in amazement at this opulent house still in perfect condition, unlike our houses which had been taken from us and burnt to the ground. This house stood so peacefully, so confidently and safely. Through some double glass doors, I noticed a library which held volumes of legal books. This was the residence of an educated and influential family. I couldn't comprehend why our captors would bring us here. As we were escorted up the staircase, I caught a glimpse of myself in the mirror; dried blood on my forehead and cheek, my face covered in scratches, skin filthy with mud and hair tangled and dishevelled. I felt ashamed at my appearance. Even my clothes were torn. My body was still swollen from the pregnancy although the lack of food and water caused a rapid shrinkage of my abdomen. My brain was playing tricks on me, for this reflection couldn't belong to me. The girl who looked back at me was not Taji. I couldn't even recall how all the injuries were inflicted.

'Quickly, I said!' the man shouted, interrupting my thoughts.

My hand hit something under my kameez, the gold! I still had my gold. I could sell it for food. I could give it to that man in return for bringing Gurpul back and allowing us to escape. The gold would be enough for him to feed his family for years to come. Gurpul, Rajendar and I could then return to pick up our baby and forget all of this. There was now hope; everything would be ok. My plan was almost formulated, I just needed to work out when to give him the gold. We were taken into an empty room on the first storey of the house. It had no furniture: bare walls but a large rug still covered most of the wooden floor. I could see this was once a stunning master bedroom. There was a large window with nothing obstructing the most breath-taking views of nature: the scenic hills and surrounding mountains. Even this very sight of nature was tarnished with the ghastly events we'd gone through, everything we'd lost.

'Is my papa here too?' The young girl asked the man who had guided us to the room.

'Keep watching that window. You will see your papa soon,' he replied with a smirk. 'That is why we have brought you here. We knew you would all want to see them again.'

He closed the door behind him. Locked it. He tried the handle again to ensure that it had locked. His footsteps faded away and my stomach began to churn.

'Why have they brought us here? Why would they take us from the hut and bring us to this spacious and beautiful room?' Kareena said. She looked around for somebody to put her mind at ease. 'Maa, what is going to happen?'

'I don't know what to think.'

'That man said I could see papa out of the window, but he's not there,' the young girl protested.

Lowering her voice, turning away from the girl, Kareena asked,

'Where can we possibly see them? Mountains and hills face us, nothing else. What would they be doing there? How will Aman climb the hills?'

Two days in a windowless, cold, damp room; then, wall-size windows, a dazzling view, bright warm sunlight. Sitting on a rug felt like ultimate luxury. Rajendar lay on her right side, facing the window, her hand under her ear, cuddled up with her knees touching her chest, fast asleep. Peace and sleep was what she had been denied. After watching at the window for over half an hour, Kareena and the girl joined everybody on the rug.

170

I lay down and stretched my back. Although my body was easing, my mind remained in turmoil. Thoughts of Gurpul and of what they might be doing to him, prevented me from resting. Other than Rajendar nobody slept, but lay on the rug, all eyes on the window.

'Look, look, there they are. There's papa.' The girl banged on the window waking Rajendar.

Jumping to our feet, we saw a line of men climbing the hill: backs bent, hands tied, heads bowed, they dragged their feet, single file.

'What's happening?' the young girl asked. 'Why are they walking like that?'

Her mind, which was unpolluted and pure, could not conceive the tragedy that lay ahead. Armed men with spears and swords held upright followed on each side. At the top of the hill, the tall man who first captured us was waiting. He stood with his hands on his hips, looking down at them. Next to him was a waist-high horizontal wooden plank, with a round hole in its middle.

'That plank, why is it there?' I asked, dreading any confirmation of my fear. Rajendar's intermittent whimpering became louder as she longed for me to comfort her and provide her with regular milk and food. At last I could see Gurpul, walking beside a guard. We all remained silent, knowing the men would never return to us. We couldn't comfort one another for each of us was dumbstruck with what we were about to lose.

Twenty men faced us with their heads up, arms still tied back. They were motionless, like statues, as we watched in anguished despair. Gurpul was fourth in the line. He saw me, our eyes were locked, but there was no reaction. It was as if they had beaten out his soul leaving behind a hollow shell. I didn't know whether to show Rajendar her Abba for the last time. It would mean little to her, but I knew Gurpul would want to see her. I took her to the window. She stared out. Pulling her hand forward, I moved it back and forth to wave. He nodded ever so slightly, acknowledging us. He couldn't wave back, all he could offer was that rigid nodding of his head that showed us how little of his spirit remained. I kneeled to place Rajendar on the rug and as I did, felt faint and dropped down with her. She crawled closer towards me and tried to play with my face and hair. I took her hand, she was all I had left.

'No!' I heard Maa scream and ran to the window to see a fleshy decapitated head come bouncing down the hill until it hit the rocky bottom. The sword was still in the perpetrator's hand, dripping with blood. Maa hit the palms of her hands against the window, screaming. It was the bodiless face of her husband. Kareena pulled Maa away to stop her from hurting herself. Looking back to the top of the hill, I saw Aman standing by the plank, too small to reach the top. I held my breath and looked around at Kareena, she was sitting with Maa, vainly attempting to console her. I gasped out loud but didn't know whether to call her or not. Not him, I whispered, biting my nails, please not him, he's just an innocent boy, not Aman. But then Aman was pulled back and the next in line was shouted for. Was he spared and shown some mercy for being a child or simply given some time for more torture in this living hell? Still with Maa, Kareena had no idea that Aman was next. She joined me back at the window; we both looked out at the same time and saw Gurpul standing at the plank. This time it was Kareena who gasped. My nails ripped into the skin of the palm of my hands, as my knuckles turned white. My love, father of my children, I couldn't live without him. Gurpul, run, don't just stand there, run away. But he couldn't hear me, nobody could hear me, because nothing was coming out of my mouth, my throat had tightened and I felt like I was being strangled. As they forced his head down into the hole, he resisted and looked up one last time. He lowered his neck and his head hung over the hill, with the plank obscuring his body. Two men battled to pin him down, while a third swiftly raised a sword and brutally slashed his head off. I felt every inch of the sword going through his neck, I felt the bone break, I heard the crack of his spine. Slaughtered like an animal, a stream flowed down the hill like muddied water from a waterfall. With clenched jaws, eyes protruding from their sockets and every vein in my neck pulsing, I screamed out; removing the blockage in my throat. Kareena and some of the other women held me back to stop me from breaking the window.

Chapter 6

August 1947, Kashmir

Two days later we were still in the same room, but they had begun feeding us better, providing bread and milk, rather than berries; as if that was a replacement for the barbaric acts we'd witnessed. My husband couldn't be replaced with some basic food. My voice was still hoarse and the ringing in my ears hadn't stopped. The food didn't matter to me because I had no appetite. The scrutiny we were subjected to relaxed and the door was now left unlocked, allowing access to a bathroom next door. The water in the sink taps was not clean, it was dirty brown and left a stain in the basin; but some of the women were relieved to be able to wash. I didn't risk it. Out in the hallway, the room was guarded by men on a shift basis, but during the night we came together to plan escape routes. I tried to work with the other women, but I hadn't stopped shaking and weakness prevented me from standing for too long and I wasn't sure I'd be able to escape. It would be difficult, but Maa insisted that a mere thirty yards away there was a road that led to Jhelum. She said there was a police station along that road and it was vital that whoever escaped reported the barbarity occurring in the village.

Noor, the young girl, was only twelve years old and spent most of the day weeping. She rarely slept through the night, she was a girl still in need of nurturing, but despite our attempts to comfort and befriend her, we could not replace her Abba or Ammi. She briefly slept with her head resting on my knee one afternoon and I stroked her black silky hair, which shone like the moon hitting the sea on a dark night. It was her birthday on 11th August, and we wanted to mark it for her, but despite our desperate calculations, we couldn't agree on the date. The men who delivered our food refused to tell us. I suggested we celebrated her birthday the next day, in an attempt to add a touch of light to it, and to give her small presents. I still had the jewellery in my kameez pocket and picked out a small ring, from my wedding. Ushma still had some clothes and shoes she had wrapped in a bed sheet, before she left home, and she would allow Noor to pick anything she wanted.

'They're beautiful clothes, you have,' Maa said as Ushma knotted the sheet and put it back in the corner of the room where she slept.

'I was due to get married, and these clothes were to form part of my dowry,' she said, picking the dirt from under her fingernails.

'How did you become separated from your family?' Kareena asked.

'We were trying to get onto one of the army buses, which were going to the border. My family had got on and I was following, when a crowd of men pushed forward, blocking the doors, and leaving me behind. Ammi and Abba were pleading with them, but they didn't listen; everybody was shouting, trying to get their own relatives on. The bus was filling up and I desperately tried pushing to the front, but before I did, it drove away. I ran after it, begging for the driver to stop, but he wouldn't.'

'They say the buses were the most reliable way of getting to the border, so your family must have reached the other side safely. You will join them,' Kareena said reassuringly, 'they would have left your details with the army officials.'

Aman refused to speak for almost a day after his return. He woke screaming in the night and Kareena would calm him by softly singing to him and cradling him in her arms. He hadn't spoken about what occurred during the few days he was taken away. Each of the women took it in turns to keep him occupied because there was nothing for him to play with. He befriended Rajendar and they occupied themselves. Their laughter was the only sound which warmed our hearts and brought smiles to our faces. Since her son was taken away, Shanti had stopped

175

speaking and kept her head buried in her arms, isolating herself from us. Aman was a constant reminder of him. I tried to block out what had happened, I couldn't think about it, but in the night that vivid scene repeated itself again and again. It wouldn't stop. I yelled, I shouted, I closed my eyes tightly, but the nightmare would not go away. The sun was beginning to set and there was still no sign of dinner arriving.

'I'll ask the guards outside,' Kareena said.

She opened the door, looked out, and then without speaking a word, hurriedly returned and closed the door behind her.

'What's wrong, Kareena?' I asked.

'All those men are coming up the stairs, I've just seen them.'

'Which ones?'

'Those who captured us.'

The door opened and six men entered; each of them clean and well-shaven in their best clothes, not a glimmer of remorse in their bright eyes. They were savage animals: able to take human life with such barbarity. My chest started wheezing and my temperature was rising.

'We've brought you dinner,' the small man with the brown scar said. I turned my head for I could not look them in the face. 'Distribute it to these wonderful women, Waqas,' he ordered the man to his right.

Waqas was a tall, slim man, no older than twenty, but with bushy eyebrows. He put a plate in front of Noor and whispered something in her ear. I don't know if she heard him, because she made no response. She immediately began to eat the rice with her hands.

'You too, Aleef,' the man said when Waqas returned.

Aleef was much older than Waqas and of average height. He looked around at each of us and when his dark eyes met Ushma's he smiled, revealing a set of rotten black teeth.

'I've picked mine, Razak,' he said to the man.

Aleef slowly walked to the corner of the room where Ushma was seated and placed the plate carefully in her lap. He stroked her face with his filthy hands. Maa cursed him under her breath.

'Get off me, you bastard!' Ushma shouted at him. He stood back and smiled at her again.

'I hope you won't be so harsh with me later.'

'What is this?' Maa asked Razak. 'Why have you brought these men here? Have we not suffered enough?'

'Not at all,' he replied. 'You women have not suffered half as much as the Musalmaan women across this supposed border. Trains are coming in with every single person slaughtered; breasts chopped off, that's what I call barbaric. Think about that, an entire train butchered. You women have actually been spared!'

After distributing the plates and bringing a jug of clean water, they left us to eat. I couldn't remember the last time I had seen or smelt a hot meal. Hot chapattis with steam coming off them. I held one in my hand and it stung the wounds my nails had left in the palm of my hand, but I continued to break off small pieces to give to Rajendar. She looked at it, smelt it, slowly took the light fluffy chapatti to her mouth and licked it, but then put it back down on her plate. With a little encouragement, she picked it back up and chewed on it, and then she didn't stop until the entire chapatti was gone. My baby was eating again. I sat and watched her enjoy each mouthful. Aman did not move from beside his Ammi, he ate more than he usually did; even he recognised that this was not the usual food.

Half an hour later, when we had all finished and piled up the plates beside the door for the guards to take away, the men reappeared. There were only three this time, and were headed by Razak.

'Two at a time, we're going to allow you to shower and refresh,' Razak announced. I was sceptical about what he said. I scanned the room for everyone else's reaction. 'You and you, come with us, we'll show to the bathroom,' he said, pointing to Noor and Ushma.

'Where are you taking them?' Maa asked.

'You may not want to shower, but I'm sure these girls do, look at them, they're unclean,' he remarked. Waqas and Aleef sniggered, like snorting pigs, behind him.

'I'm going to come with them,' Maa ordered.

'No! Now shut up or you won't live to see the rest of this night,' he threatened.

'Kill me, I don't care. There is nothing left for me in this world. Just leave the girls,' Maa pleaded, but Razak took no notice.

'I don't need to wash,' Ushma insisted.

'Yes you do, now come on.'

He pulled out a pistol from his shalwar pocket and forced the girls out of the room. We didn't utter a sound, Kareena and I held onto our babies. They closed the door and this time locked it.

Hours had passed by but Ushma and Noor had still not returned. Two days grace was all we were given and now the torment had begun again. Deep within me a rage of anger ignited fiercely, like a volcano on the brink of eruption; but I was forced to contain myself because Maa had told us not to risk anyone else being hurt or worse even. Aman and Rajendar were also quiet, they were not playing or laughing. The door unlocked and we all sat up, waiting to see what news they brought back. Slowly the door opened and Noor and Ushma entered. It closed behind them. They had washed, that was evident. Their skin now brighter and more youthful. Their hair wet and dishevelled, but they were clearly not refreshed. Noor was shivering, her arms tightly folded. They walked slowly to the centre of the room, where Maa was sitting, and slumped next to her. I left Rajendar on the floor and took Noor in my arms and cradled her, I wrapped a scarf around her, to cover and protect her; even if it was too late. She was so young to be ruined like this. All the pains of my giving birth, which I had somehow blocked from my senses, came flooding back as refreshed agony for me.

'It hurts,' she whimpered to me, crushing any hope I was hanging on to, wanting to have understood it all so wrongly. Those wild beasts had exploited her innocence; adding to all the traumas she had faced so early in her life and all over a period of days or maybe weeks. I wished suffering upon those animals for continuing to inflict such torment on us all. 'He asked how old I was, and I told him I would be thirteen on the 11th,' everybody quietened and listened to her account. Her voice quivered and she was still shaking, her face as white as the snow-capped mountains. Ushma still wailed uncontrollably, her head buried in Maa's lap. Shanti came closer too. The other four women listened, but they did not move forward. 'He told me it was 9th August today and that he would give me an early present. He will marry me, because I look like a doll,' she muttered, before being violently sick.

We barely slept that night, and the next morning we woke early. Maa went to use the bathroom first; she quietly opened the door, careful not to wake Aman and Rajendar who were still sleeping. Leaving the door ajar, she looked around and then returned.

'There's nobody out in the hall,' she whispered. Everybody immediately sat up.

'Are you sure?' Ushma asked.

'Positive,' Maa insisted. 'Noor, come here,' she said. 'Quietly look around that corner and make sure nobody is there.'

'I don't want to go, Maa, what if they take me again?'

'They won't my child, I'm here. You're smaller than the rest of us and you'll be quieter. Don't make any noise.' Maa waited at the door, while Noor inspected the hallway.

'There is nobody,' she reported.

Maa whispered quickly as she gave her orders.

'Ushma, Noor and Shanti, this is your opportunity to escape. You're younger and fitter than the rest of us, go.' There was a disconcerted look on everyone's face, as we all exchanged glances. This was surely too good to be true. I felt anxious but also excited; was this a trap or was it an opportunity? For a moment my head was buzzing with thoughts of freedom and escaping from this torturous chamber; but then there was a tumultuous thudding in my chest as I didn't know what my life was anymore.

'How, Maa?' Shanti asked.

'Just go. Go quietly, and the three of you work as a team, keep a look out and don't make any noise until you are out of this village. Find the police station and report what's happening.'

They stood before Maa, carefully listening to her instructions. Ushma began gathering her things.

'Leave it, Ushma, your life is worth more than your possessions,' Maa insisted.

They were ready to leave, but before they went, Maa looked out of the door to check that the guards had not reappeared.

'Go,' Maa directed, and the three of them tip-toed out into the hall and down the staircase.

Maa came back into the room and closed the door, she smiled. I couldn't believe what had happened. There was a faint hope that they would safely reach the police station and bring them here to rescue us.

'If those men come in and ask where the girls have gone, we are to remain quiet, and tell them we know nothing,' Maa whispered. 'As far as we know, they were here when we went to sleep, but had disappeared in the morning.'

I got up to use the toilet next door and when I reached the hall, I saw that there was still nobody there.

'They're still not there, Maa,' I said in a low voice. The four women, who seldom acknowledged us, instantly got up with a renewed sense of energy in them. They were middle aged women, probably about my Ammi's age.

'Come on, let's go!' One of them shouted.

'Be quiet,' Maa said. 'You'll get caught.'

They quietened. Another peeped out of the door and motioned for the rest to follow; I watched them run down the staircase and escape in the same direction the others had. Kareena, Maa and I, looked at each other dumbfounded; I questioned if anything over the last week had even been real. I must have imagined it all. The room was bare again, just the three of us left with the children.

'Why are we still here?' Kareena asked, with her eyes dancing.

I picked up Rajendar, while Kareena woke Aman.

'Come on, Aman, we're going.' He mumbled something and whined. 'Come on, Aman,' she repeated.

'I want to sleep.'

'Kareena, carry him,' Maa suggested. 'You girls go, I'm going to stay here.'

'Why, Maa?'

'I'm not going to be able to escape, how will I run? I'm not quick enough. I'll get you all caught and I can't do that to you.'

'No, Maa, you're coming with us,' I insisted.

'There is nothing to run for, I have nobody left.'

'Aman, get up!' Kareena shouted.

Aman eventually rose when he heard the anger in his Ammi's voice. After a brief but tearful farewell, we left Maa and escaped from the house.

*

The breeze gently touched my face and blew through my hair, it danced with me celebrating our release. The farm animals were exchanging morning greetings; bleating goats, cackling hens and snorting horses. The smell of manure was strong, coming from the nearby farms. My eyes were strained trying to adjust to the natural sunlight again. My senses had been liberated, just as my mind had been. We followed the straightforward route back to the mountain edge, where we had been captured. Not a single person was in sight. I expected the villagers to be up, tending their crops and animals, but this village lay as motionless as when we arrived. A long pathway ran beside the mountain edge, leading out onto the long road Maa had told us about. I still had some difficulty running, as the pains had not totally subsided, but we continued nonetheless. Kareena suddenly jerked back, having seen a woman coming out of one of the huts with clothes draped over her arms. We hid behind a tree, praying that she wouldn't see us. After hanging the washing on a line, she went back inside and we continued to run. The end of the village and the beginning of the road was in sight.

'We're almost there,' Kareena said, encouragingly.

Just as we were stepping onto the road, we blundered into a tall bearded man.

'I've never seen you around. Are you lost?' he said. Neither Kareena nor I spoke. He had a travelling bag in his hand as if he was returning from somewhere. Perhaps he doesn't know what is happening, I thought. 'You must be part of the group they've captured here.' I felt like I was being gagged with a noose around my neck.

'Please, let us go! You've no idea what those men have subjected us to. They're evil, twisted, scum! They've murdered our men and raped some of the girls!' Kareena howled. He listened.

'We are no use to you, we're married Sikh women, why would you want to keep us here?' I tried to negotiate but as I spoke it slowly dawned on me, I was not married: I was a widow. An unfamiliar word which had the power to instantly make me feel numb.

'Come, come with me, you girls are clearly distraught.'

Kareena and I locked eyes as all hope of escaping slipped away.

'Let us go, we won't ever bother you. We won't even tell the police what has happened, just let us get to our new homeland,' Kareena now pleaded.

'You have young children, it's not safe for you women to try and cross the border alone. If I let you go, someone else will find you.' We had truly been defeated. 'My name is Safdar, I'll take you to my house, my wife is there too. I won't harm you,' he claimed.

He led us back to that ghastly village.

Safdar's wife was a dainty woman with shining green eyes and fair skin. I'd heard about the Kashmiri women's fairy-tale beauty, but had never seen it for myself until now. They seated us on some stools in a tiny bare room. It was dark and windowless, and lacked any natural or artificial lighting; it could easily have been mistaken for a cellar three feet underground. Young children were running about, unaware the country was in turmoil, that men were being murdered just yards away. The eldest was ten; he looked at us and sniggered. Safdar's wife tried to speak to us, but her speech was halting and she stuttered on every other word. Although neither Kareena nor I understood what she said, she leaned forward and stared at my lips, waiting for a reply.

'She's asking, what's your name?' Safdar said.

'I'm Taji and this is Kareena.'

He then loudly repeated our names to his wife and she nodded her head in acknowledgement.

'And your name?' I asked.

'Aminah.' Safdar replied on her behalf.

I felt uneasy: they were looking at us as if we were strange creatures. Safdar gazed at me, his eyes moving swiftly up and down, a gentle nodding of the head occurred simultaneously. I turned slightly towards

Kareena and she turned towards me as he did the same to her. Rajendar and Aman did not utter a sound.

'How old are you?' Safdar asked me.

'Eighteen.'

'How about you, Kareena?'

'Twenty-two.'

'You're both married?' he asked.

'Yes,' I replied, clearing my throat.

'Where are your husbands?'

'They're dead!' Kareena snapped, after a momentary silence, unable to take his interrogations.

He didn't ask any more questions. I thought about Maa, we needed to tell her that we hadn't escaped: we were captured again, like we hadn't been punished enough.

'Why is he keeping us here, Taji?' Kareena whispered, as Safdar and Aminah left the room.

'I don't know.'

'We were so close,' she wept.

There was sudden outburst of shouting outside, the sound of men quarrelling.

'Safdar,' a familiar voice called.

'Yes.'

'Those Sikh and Hindu women have escaped, have you seen them?'

'All you brave men, raping and killing, but you can't even keep a few women under control?'

'They've left that old hag,' another man shouted. 'What can we use her for? She's no use.'

'Have you seen them or not, Safdar?' the same familiar voice asked. It sounded like the man who had first captured us all those days ago; I pictured him out there, with his flaring nostrils and dark face.

'Yes, I have, Ejaz.'

'You have? Where? Where are they?' he questioned.

'Oh no,' Kareena whispered. 'They're going to take us.'

My heart was beating rapidly as I waited for Safdar's response.

'That's none of your business, they're out of your hands now.'

'What do you mean?' Ejaz blustered. 'We captured them.'

'I don't care, capturing them is one thing, but raping and killing is another matter. You must stop this dirty game you're playing. And as for the group you captured today, let them go.'

That was why there had been nobody to guard us in the morning; they were busy capturing more innocent people, to satisfy their own sickening desires.

'But where are the women?' Ejaz quizzed. 'Did you see them?'

'I have two in there, they are with children.'

Ejaz approached and stood in the doorway.

'Why are you troubling yourself with these women? Leave them to us.'

'Get out!' Safdar ordered. 'Don't come back here.'

Ejaz left with the rest of his group, who were waiting outside.

'Maybe Safdar will let us go,' Kareena said.

'We thought he would let us go when he met us outside the village, but he brought us back in. Why should he free us now?'

'Where are we, Ammi?' Aman asked. Kareena didn't know the answer.

'I'll send a note out to Asaff immediately telling him to return home,' Safdar said to his wife as he re-entered the room. 'There is not enough space for you both to stay here, so I'll take one of you to a family relative's house.'

'We don't mind where you put us, but please, keep us together,' Kareena politely asked.

'That's not possible, the houses are small and we have large families. Kareena, I'm going to take you to a safe place.'

'Please, let us go,' Kareena begged. 'Allow us to go back to our families.'

'You have a new family now,' he said, smiling. 'Come along, they're waiting for you.'

Her eyes filled with rage, I embraced her and at the same time whispered, 'Remember what Maa told us.' She nodded and they left.

The breeze blew sand and dust through the door. Rajendar was crying, unaccustomed to such dusty surroundings. Aminah said something I didn't understand. She made a drinking motion with her hands, she was probably asking if Rajendar needed feeding. I turned my back to the door and lifted my kameez to feed her. She soon calmed down and fell asleep. I held her in my arms for there was nowhere to put her down. Aminah stood and motioned for me to follow; we went out into the small yard and into another room next door. This room was slightly larger and held two charpais. It was the bedroom. I lay Rajendar on the charpai closest to the door. There was no room to walk to the far side, they probably had to climb over. There were no cupboards or dressing tables, just piles of clothes on the floor.

'Is she asleep?' Safdar asked, entering the room. There was barely space for us all to stand.

'Yes, she's tired and she hasn't eaten for the last few days.'

'I think you need a change of clothes and a wash,' he suggested.

I must have smelt badly, although I wasn't aware of it. Perhaps I had got used to it. He told his wife to find me some clothes. Aminah said something to him angrily

'How far is Kareena?' I asked.

'Only a few houses away,' Safdar informed.

Aminah looked through the pile and picked a worn out, grey shalwar kameez. She thrust it into my hands.

'Aminah will take you to the riverbank, you can wash there,' Safdar instructed.

The riverbank. It might be the one where I left my baby. Perhaps I would be reunited with him. Perhaps I would once more have a son and Rajendar a brother. That sense of hope was building up inside me again.

'Yes, let's go now,' I said.

I didn't want to disturb Rajendar, so left her sleeping and Aminah led me towards the river. Some villagers were going about their daily business returning from the wells with buckets of water or going to tend their animals at the farm.

'Who is she?' many of them asked. I don't know what she told them.

All the houses looked the same, I couldn't tell one from the other. I looked for Kareena in each house we passed, but she was nowhere to be seen. The route to the riverbank was complicated: Aminah made left and right turns, passing through winding paths and tiny alleys. At last we reached the water, but this was a stream, not a river. It wasn't where I had left my baby. I looked up and down, but this wasn't it, this was a totally different place. There must be a river here somewhere. My baby, I promised I'd go back for him. I must find the river.

'Is there a river nearby?' I asked Aminah, but again, I could not understand her reply. 'There is a river here somewhere, please help me find it.' She shook her head, trying to explain there wasn't one. My lower lip and chin started trembling like that of a toddler. I breathed heavier, gasping for air, but there was nothing to take in, I felt a sense of suffocation. The rawness of leaving my baby was still there, the fury boiling within, I was unable to contain it any longer and I sobbed uncontrollably.

Aminah kneeled down and tried to calm me, but I was beyond calming now. She said something and gently stroked my wounded arm. I looked up at her, she was concerned: I could see it in her eyes. I could run away from her and she wouldn't be able to catch me. But I had left Rajendar at the house. Why couldn't I think straight? Two chances of escape in one day; both lost.

Aminah sat by the riverbank and began to undress. She washed herself by cupping her hands together and scooping the water from the stream. I copied her although the water was ice cold. She gave me some soap and I scrubbed my body rigorously, removing the blood and soil stains. Aminah used the soap in her hair and so did I. Dija used soap in her hair, because she couldn't afford shampoo, and I used to think, how strange… but here I was doing the same. Aminah finished and changed back into her clothes, she didn't even dry herself as there was nothing to dry with. She picked up the clothes I had been in for the last week or more. My gold was still in the kameez pocket.

'Leave it,' I said, not wanting her to discover the jewellery. It was too late, she felt the pocket and gazed at me, stunned at the amount of gold. She spoke quickly with a sense of urgency. 'Please, leave it, that's mine.' She spoke again and almost shrilled, she felt the jewellery as if she had never seen gold before. She probably hadn't. I quickly changed into the clothes she had given me. I tried to take my kameez from her, but she wouldn't let go until I forcibly pulled it from her, then held onto it securely. We walked back to the house, Aminah was almost sprinting; she clutched my arm, just in case I tried escaping.

Safdar was in the yard, washing his hands and face in a bowl. Before we even entered Aminah began speaking to him, her voice was getting louder and louder. He stood up immediately and looked at me.

'Come inside,' he ordered, Aminah followed and closed the door. 'You have some gold?' Safdar asked. I didn't know what to say: if I lied he would just take the kameez from me and look for himself.

'Yes,' I replied reluctantly.

'Let me have a look.'

'This is my wedding gold, my parents gave it to me, it's the only memory I have, please don't take it.'

'Take it out.' I slowly removed some of it from the pocket and held it in my hand. Safdar reached out and took it.

'And the rest,' he said.

He put it in his lap and inspected each item. Aminah's mouth gaped open, her eyebrows rose a notch. She took a ring and put it on her finger. I wanted to shriek and rip it off.

'This is worth a lot,' Safdar observed. His wife spoke to him and he nodded his head, 'A brand new house.'

'I will allow you to keep my gold, if you let me go.'

Safdar did not speak. He wrapped up the jewellery in my kameez and took it away. I begged for him to let me keep it, but he didn't respond, he walked out of the room and closed the door. Aminah was playing with the ring, twisting it around her finger and looking at it proudly. She had nothing to be proud of, she'd stolen it. Rajendar was crying in the next room, I went and lay beside her and watched the rhythmic movement of her chest rising and falling. Holding her in my arms I fell asleep.

A ghastly smell woke me late in the afternoon. I looked around, but Safdar and Aminah were nowhere to be seen. Rajendar was awake playing with her hands and feet. Stepping out, I saw smoke rising behind the house they had kept us in. The smell was vile, like they were burning dead animals. I covered my nose and mouth with my hand and went into the room next door, where Safdar was sitting with a slate and chalk in his hands, making some calculations. He quickly turned over the slate when I entered.

'What's that smell?' I asked.

'Some of the villagers are burning bodies,' he replied casually. I was dismayed with his matter-of-fact response.

'So, they're being cremated.' I confirmed, wanting their bodies to be respected through the final rituals.

'Of course not. There is no other way of disposing them. Burning is the easiest way.'

My body was paralysed; unblinking eyes staring right at Safdar, my brain felt scrambled, trying to make sense of such demonic behaviour.

'Have you been to see?'

'Yes, I went about an hour ago. An old woman is gathering the human remains and piling them up to make the fire.'

I wished Maa had escaped too so she wasn't tormented with such a hideous task. To have to identify the remains of her own husband and know others belonged to the loved ones of those women she'd spent so many days with comforting.

'Take a seat, Taji,' Safdar said. I slowly sat down on the edge of my seat, thinking about what was happening to those bodies, where were they being piled and how? The foul smell still lingered heavily in the air. 'Where in the country have you come from?'

'Mirpur.'

'You were from a wealthy family,' he commented. 'But you have no family now, do you? Your husband is dead.'

'I have my parents,' I objected. I was not totally abandoned and alone.

'Where are they?'

'Lahore.'

'They won't be there anymore,' he said calmly. 'Lahore will fall within the Pakistan side of the border, the majority of Sikhs have escaped from there.'

I wondered where Ammi and Abba would be, whether they had escaped Lahore, or whether they were suffering like me. How would I ever explain to Gurpul's parents that their son had been murdered.

'They may have crossed over to Amritsar, which is only an hour away to the east of the country. What did your father do for a living?'

'He's an engineer.' Aminah made a comment, almost as if she had been impressed by what I said. 'Very wealthy,' Safdar said to his wife.

'What is she saying?' I asked.

'She says you must come from a wealthy family because your father is educated, and also, a lot of wealthy Sikhs lived in Lahore.'

'Where's my gold?' I asked.

'I have kept it safely, it's extremely valuable.'

'You can keep the gold, just let me go,' I pleaded yet again.

'I would like you to meet my cousin brother, Asaff, he will be coming home tomorrow. He is in the army, he's twenty-one years old and a good looking man.'

I didn't understand why he was telling me this: I was a Sikh woman, with a child.

'Can I see Kareena?' I asked. We had to escape together, we couldn't remain with these people.

'I think the mullah is still at their house.'

'Why is there a mullah there?' I asked concerned.

'Kareena has converted to Islam, she's a Musalmaan now,' Safdar said proudly.

How could she have converted? She was born and brought up a Sikh and had lived the life of a Sikh woman. She can't just adopt another religion on the say-so of these people! I needed to do something to help her.

'She will be married soon,' Safdar added.

I tried to stay quiet but I couldn't.

'How can you do this? She's a widow! Just let her go. Why do you want to keep us here?' I yelled at him.

'Calm down,' he said, watching me with amusement. Aminah was in the yard providing Safdar with a running commentary of what was happening at the house Kareena was at. 'The mullah and some of the men are walking back to the masjid, which means the nikkah has been completed. Your Kareena is a married Musalmaan woman now.' He stepped out into the yard. 'Nikkah complete?' he shouted.

191

'Yes.'

'Mubaarak,' he congratulated them. I tried taking a glimpse but he blocked my view. 'What's her name now? Have you got rid of the Sikh name?'

'Khadeeja,' a man shouted back.

Aminah looked at me and made a comment. Safdar returned and took a seat on the stool again.

'She's married, and she's called Khadeeja now. A nice Musalmaan name, better than Kareena.'

'I preferred Kareena, it suited her,' I said assertively.

Safdar and Aminah's children had disappeared. I hadn't seen them since the morning. They had nothing better to do in the village, except play. There were no schools for children to go and learn: they were seen as a waste of money.

'Aminah is going to make dinner, you can help her,' Safdar ordered.

'I don't know how to,' I explained, 'I had a cook at home.' They laughed.

'She's a rich girl, what do you expect?' Safdar said to his wife. She said something back to him.

'Aminah says, how are you going to manage in the village?'

'But you will let me go?' I asked, hoping that my gold had persuaded them.

'Stay in the village, it's a good life. You can learn how to cook for your husband and plough the weeds in the farm and milk the cows. It's a good life.'

I felt sick just thinking about doing all those things, I would not know where to begin: house staff had always handled the upkeep of the home. And how could I cook for my husband when he was dead? My soul was numbed the day his heartbeat stopped.

Aminah sat on the ground and lit a fire in the yard with small pieces of wood. She placed an old rotting cooking pan on a metal stand above the flame. She gave me an onion to chop. I peeled it slowly, careful not to cut my hand. I had never cut onions, and especially not cut them in my hand: there were no worktops or cutting boards to use. My eyes were watering and I could barely see. Aminah glimpsed at me sniffling while she was examining the lentils, taking out the black stones. She pushed me aside with a curse and finished chopping the onion herself. She chopped it quickly and effortlessly. She gave me some flour in a small bowl and told me to make the dough for the roti. I had never made dough for roti either; I had never needed to. I poured a whole jug of water into the bowl, almost flooding it. I mixed it with my hands, so that it blended with the floor, but it was too watery. Once Aminah had poured the lentils into the pan, she lowered the flame by taking out some of the wood. She looked at me, saw the fluid-like batter and began screaming.

'What's happened, what's happened?' Safdar asked running outside. Aminah pointed at the bowl in my lap and shouted loudly.

'That was the last of the flour!' Safdar yelled. 'We have no more, Asaff has not sent any money home, how are we going to buy more flour?'

'I told you I couldn't cook.'

'Don't answer me back!'

'You have my gold, sell it and buy yourself some flour,' I said unconcerned, washing my hands in the water bowl.

From the corner of my eye I could see them both staring at me, shocked at what I had said. They had probably expected me to remain quiet, but I wasn't scared any more. I couldn't live life like that.

Rajendar and I fell asleep that night, hungry. They did not feed us; they all ate but told me there was not enough to go around. I lay awake on the cement floor without any sheets, re-living the events of the last few days. The absolute reality of what had occurred juxtaposed with a dream like state, my mind blurred. I felt hollow; I was merely a shell now. I wanted to mourn my husband, I missed my son, but no tears dropped from my eyes; now robbed of all feeling too.

The room was dark, like it was in the hut, the only light entering was through the gap in the door. The light had been getting brighter and brighter, but Safdar had still not unlocked the door. I needed to use the toilet. I tried getting up, but my back was aching, after spending the night on the floor.

'Open the door,' I shouted, banging on it, purposely making lots of noise.

'Coming,' Safdar said. He unlocked it and let me out into the fresh air.

'Assalaam Alaikum,' he greeted with the full Muslim address.

'Sat Siri Akal,' I replied, intentionally using the Sikh greeting.

His face turned red and he disapprovingly shook his head, 'you're very disrespectful, but I'm sure Asaff will come home and get you in order.'

'I thought you were different from all the other men in this village, but you've turned out to be just like them. You're only interested in money: you've stolen my gold and you probably sold Kareena to your relatives!'

'Safdar bhai,' somebody shouted from behind, just as Safdar lifted his hand to hit me.

'Cousin Asaff,' he said, turning around.

So this was Asaff. A tall, well-built man, with lightly tanned skin. I didn't wait for him, I returned to the room where I had spent the night. The children and Aminah were still sleeping peacefully on the charpais, while they kept me on the floor. The children woke and were jumping up and down saying, "Asaff chacha".

'Be quiet children,' I heard Safdar say. 'I need to speak to your uncle Asaff about something important.'

I tried listening to what he said, but he spoke quietly. I know he said something about coming from a wealthy family, and he mentioned the gold as well.

'Let us see, let us see,' the children protested.

Safdar must have been showing Asaff my gold.

'But she's Sikh and she has a child,' Asaff protested.

'That doesn't matter, she can convert, she can become a Muslim. Akeel has married one as well, she's converted.'

'When did he marry?' Asaff asked.

'Yesterday. Go and take a look at her and tell me what you think.' Asaff entered the room. He took a quick glimpse at me and returned. 'What do you say?' Safdar asked.

'You are like a brother, and I'll be eternally grateful that you looked after my Ammi and I when my Abba died, and I was too young to provide for my Ammi. So I'll accept any woman you chose for me.'

'Well done. This is wonderful, Asaff, with all this gold, we will be able to buy so many more animals. It can form her dowry; that is not stealing, we are entitled to one. The villagers will be so envious.' This was a triumphant victory for him, a business deal coming to a close. 'I will go to the masjid right away and call the mullah.'

They didn't ask me if I wanted to marry Asaff, this stranger being imposed on me. He hadn't been vetted by Ammi and Abba, like Gurpul had been. This was a business transaction, all so they could keep their consciences clean: if he married me it would not be classed as stealing. I was a free labourer for them. I would not allow this to happen, they couldn't force me to convert and surely the mullah would not allow it. I could hear the water outside, Asaff was washing.

'Asaff bhai, when did you return?' A man asked.

'A little while ago. I hear you are married, Mubaarak.'

195

'Don't congratulate me, I've lost her. I got back from praying Fajr this morning and she wasn't there. Have you seen her? I've searched everywhere. I've even reported her at the police station.'

'Only married one night and she has already eloped,' he mocked.

I felt my eyes sparkle, with a racing of the pulse and a smile growing on my face. She had got away, she was free! I prayed that she had not forgotten me.

'Akeel, how is your new bride?' Safdar asked, having returned from the masjid.

'She's run away.'

'What?' He exclaimed. 'How could you let her get away, are you stupid? You could get us all into a lot of trouble.'

There was no response from him. They were all quiet. I heard footsteps approaching, but I was unsure whom they belonged to. Safdar entered the room where I was sitting. He closed the door and took out a knife from his pocket.

'Don't say a word,' he threatened.

I didn't understand why he was holding a knife to my neck, why now? He had the gold, there was nothing more for me to offer him. I obeyed his orders and remained quiet, petrified. An authoritative voice spoke.

'We've had a report that there is a Sikh girl and a baby being held against their will.'

The police! I was about to be freed from my captors! Kareena and I would reach the other side of the border and find our families. My skin was tingling, my heart racing and pupils dilated. It was all over, the nightmare was over.

'There's no one here, Sahib,' Asaff said. 'We'll let you know if we hear anything.' I wanted to scream, but I knew the knife would pierce through my neck, leaving my poor child orphaned.

'Thank you,' the officer replied.

'Where's the girl who gave you the report?' Akeel asked.

'It's nothing to do with you. You had no right to hold her here. We need to stop these revenge murders taking place all over the country. Britain finally quitting India should not be reason for us to turn on one another.'

'Officer, I'm an army official. I don't want this anarchy either and I'll ensure the village men are not part of any violent behaviour.' Asaff said.

The sound of the officer's boots faded away in the distance. Asaff knocked on the door, signalling that the coast was clear. Safdar put the knife away and left me crushed. Kareena had done everything she could, but the inadequate police officer had not even bothered to search. My veins swelled, ready to explode, the blood rushing to my head.

'Looks like your wife has gone for good, Akeel,' Safdar teased. 'The mullah's coming in twenty minutes for the nikkah.'

'I hope your luck isn't as bad as mine,' Akeel said to Asaff.

'Aminah, get ready, the mullah will be here shortly,' Safdar shouted.

There was laughter coming from the next room, I could hear everything because they were so loud. It was incomprehensible to me how I could feel like I'd been crushed to pieces and then trampled upon and they could be celebrating.

'What about Ammi?' Asaff asked.

'I've sent a messenger and she says to go ahead. The earliest she will be able to return home is tomorrow evening.'

I wondered how many people actually lived in this house. There was Safdar, Aminah and all their children, and Asaff and his Ammi. Aminah entered with a small plate. She mumbled something and sat down beside me; it was henna, lumpy dark brown mendhi. She took my hand and with a wooden stick spread it all over.

'What are you doing? I don't want this,' I snapped, but she ignored me. She had applied a thick layer. She quickly exited and then reappeared with a red scarf. She tried placing it over my head, attempting to make me a bride, but I ducked away. 'Leave me, I don't want to marry him, I

197

won't marry him.' I insisted. She stormed out and summoned Safdar to threaten me again.

'Do what we tell you to do.'

'Why are you making me do this? I don't want to become a Musalmaan nor do I want to marry your cousin. I'm a widow and I still love my husband.' He raised his hand and aimed for my face, but I moved and he missed.

'Safdar bhai!' Asaff shouted from the doorway. 'What's going on here?'

'It's nothing Asaff, you get ready.'

'Let me speak with her, alone, please,' Asaff said. Safdar and his wife left us, but listened from outside.

'If you really don't want to marry me then say so,' Asaff said in a calm voice. 'But in the current situation I think it is best you do, otherwise you will merely be used as a servant girl here in the village. I have no reason to take a Sikh woman with a child, but I don't want any more harm to come to you.'

I listened, but my mind was disturbed. I didn't know what was happening to me and was unable to think logically. I nodded, knowing that some of what he said was true. He then left me alone and Aminah reappeared; washed, changed and refreshed; proudly posing with my gold. My bangles and the long necklace I wore on my wedding, the only reminder I had of my special day; now blatantly being worn by a woman I didn't know. I wanted to feel rage, but the numbness refused to leave me. I couldn't take my eyes off the necklace, I admired its workmanship and the precious stones. The bangles clattered as Aminah placed the red veil over my head and covered my face. It took me back to my wedding day, the day I met Gurpul; and now here I was being forced into another marriage. The mendhi was still on my hands. I told her that it needed to be washed off, but she did not respond.

A few of the village women came and seated themselves on the stools scattered around the room; they were clearly poor women, everyone in the village was. They admired and commented on Aminah's gold. She proudly displayed it by kneeling over, allowing them to take a closer look, as she ran her fingers around them. She lifted the necklace from her chest and allowed one of the women to touch the stones. I watched their expressions as eyes lit up and jaws dropped in amazement. I hadn't even changed or washed, I was still wearing Aminah's old shalwar kameez, while she had changed and looked glamorous; glamorous in the eyes of the poor. The mullah entered. He was an old man, with a long orange beard, which had been dyed with mendhi. I didn't look any further up his face, my eyes remained fixed on my lap, where Rajendar was sitting, observing all that was happening. He stood before me.

'Repeat after me,' he ordered. 'I bear witness that, there is no God,' he paused and waited for me to repeat the words, but I didn't speak, a lump in my throat was preventing me from doing so. The women whispered among themselves. 'Repeat after me,' he said again. 'I bear witness that there is no God but Allah and that Muhammad is his messenger.' I remained silent, I wouldn't accept the oath: I was born a Sikh girl, I was not a Musalmaan, nor did I want to be. The women were choked by my disobedience. 'You either take the shahadah or you die, it's simple!' The mullah declared. At first I thought I didn't care whether I lived or died... but there was Rajendar.

'I bear witness that,' I began, to the mullah's delight, 'there is no God but Allah,'

'And that Muhammad is his messenger,' the mullah prompted.

'And that Muhammad is his messenger.'

'Mubaarak, you're now a Musalmaan,' the mullah rejoiced.

There was a brief cheer from those around. I felt suffocated, my lungs were caving in, I took deep breaths, it didn't help. The mere uttering of a few words which meant nothing to me, did not make me a Muslim.

'A name now, who will pick a name?' The mullah asked.

'Rasheed Begum and Zainub, for the daughter,' Asaff said from the doorway.

'Rasheed and Zainub,' the mullah repeated.

I was not Rasheed Begum, nor was my baby Zainub, we were named Taji and Rajendar according to the Guru Granth Sahib, and I was not going to accept this name they had forced on me. Taji Kaur I was born, and Taji Kaur I would remain.

'And now that you are a Musalmaan, we can conduct the nikkah ceremony,' the mullah said.

He began reading strange verses from the Quran, which was held open in front of him. I didn't understand the recitation because it was in Arabic. After a few minutes he closed the book and asked,

'Do you accept, Asaff Khan to be your husband?'

Looking up I saw those fierce eyes burning through my red veil and I looked straight back down at my mehndi-smeared hands. He must have taken the look as a yes, because he then walked outside to where the men were standing. Wedding vows were then taken by this stranger, who was to be my new husband. He was standing tall, washed and clean, allowing his mixed hazel and sea green eyes to glisten against the reflection of his skin; while I was wearing somebody else's dirty clothing. I watched him through my veil, even his relaxed posture and gentle movements stung me like biting mosquitoes, sucking the blood out of my skin. Now a cheer came from the crowd outside; the deed was done. There was no end to all that was being taken from me, slowly, torturously, literally and metaphorically; for now it was my identity that had been savagely snatched. This was the beginning of a new life, a life I did not want. I had become a prisoner.

PART III

Chapter 1

May 1979, Islamabad, Pakistan

The passengers sighed in relief as the Boeing 747 hit the runway at Islamabad International Airport, the end of a long ten-hour journey from London. Unbuckling of seat belts and gathering of hand luggage from the overhead cabins began, despite announcements from the pilot asking passengers to remain seated. Red lipped air stewardesses paced up and down the aisles, ordering those onboard to take note of the pilot's instructions; but they failed miserably. Outside, the sun was blazing on that summer's day and dust from the sandy roads filled the air, adding to the humidity and heat. Rasheed looked out of the small window, delighted to be back home, less than a year later. Her heart was beating rapidly, her stomach churning nervously, her mind busy with the excitement of seeing her parents after thirty-two years. Over the decades the resilience Rasheed had built up had meant not much overwhelmed her any longer, but being so close to looking them in the eyes, feeling them, smelling them, was causing a mixed emotional reaction. The biggest fear was how they'd react to her and how it would feel being inside a gurdwara again among thousands of Sikhs. This year, pilgrimage for her parents, Kishin and Kulgeet Singh would not be the same.

On the runway the heat burned Asaff and Rasheed's skin and irritated their eyes, but it was a relief from the English rain. A bus waited at the bottom of the staircase to take passengers to the main airport. Immigration officers sat in highchairs at their desks, scrutinising each traveller. Asaff held open the green Pakistani passports at the photo page and gave them to the man on the right, whose spectacles sat on the edge of his nose. He read the details and then looked at Asaff over the rim of his glasses; standing up, he saluted, having taken note of Asaff's former occupation as Major in the Pakistan Army.

'This is what I love about our country,' he said to Rasheed walking along.

'What?' she asked.

'Respect. Citizens have respect for the army, for the people who endangered their own lives to defend this country, to make this country.' She agreed with her husband's remarks as she had been a part of his dedication to the army. They both proudly displayed all his awarded medals in their home in England and as Asaff always said, his biggest medal was his wife.

After the nikkah in 1947 Rasheed had joined Asaff at the Army quarters where she really got to know him. Of course, it took many years for her to come to love him, but she accepted that he treated her well and took his role as a husband seriously.

Asaff placed the passports inside his suit pocket. He still walked like an army Major, with his head held high, shoulders stiff, taking long strides. Rasheed stopped for a moment, watching him: Junaid's Abba had a similar posture, she recalled as she remembered the day he came to visit Dija for the first time. Junaid, Dija, Babu and baby Ali, sometimes appeared in her dreams, at other times random passing thoughts in the day, and on occasion, when Rasheed was feeling desperately low, they spent days with her when she secretly reminisced about her old life. Their brown leather suitcase was circling on the carousel, which was jerking every few seconds, throwing off a case or two each time. Placing it on a trolley, they followed the exit signs out into the arrivals hall.

Despite notices ordering them to wait behind the barriers, the collectors still crowded the aisles, leaving passengers to fight their way out. The airport was dirty with litter scattered about and people sitting and lying in every corner. With no seating arrangements, people were left with no choice but to use the floors. The smell in the hall was stale. It was the smell of Pakistan, clinging to people and luggage alike. Rasheed used part of the scarf, which covered some of her stray white hair, to mask her mouth and nose. Asaff's relative, Akeel, waited by the exit doors, to take them back to the village for the night.

'Asaff bhai,' he shouted, having caught a glimpse of them.

They finally saw him but had to force their way through the crowd. The chaos outside was even worse than inside, with cars and vans and scooters and bicycles, all piled up, bumper to bumper, waiting for luggage to be loaded.

'Salaam Akeel, good to see you.' Asaff said whilst shaking hands, still bemused by the lack of organisation at the airport. 'Let's get into the car,' Asaff interrupted, as he greeted Rasheed. Akeel laughed at his impatience.

He had aged considerably and his hair had turned completely white; his skin that of a poor man's, over-exposed to manual work and the sun.

'You've become an Englishman, have you?' Akeel teased. 'You're a follower of their law and order?'

'If there is one thing I love about England, it's certainly the sense of organisation they have.'

'Sahib, do you have some English change to spare?' A young beggar girl of no more than nine, in ill-fitting clothes asked, holding out her soil-covered hands.

'Give her something,' Rasheed said, feeling pity for her and always wanting to help the less fortunate. Asaff searched his trouser pocket for some loose coins.

'No, no,' Akeel asserted. 'Beggars like her are employed by greedy men, who take all the money themselves. It's not going to a good cause, and plus they say charity begins at home, people in the village would appreciate that change so much more.'

'Yes, charity does begin in the home, but that is only so if they actually appreciate what you give, and not demand more,' Asaff replied sarcastically, referring to common village behaviour. He handed the girl some change and she ran away telling the rest of her child beggar friends, who then collectively approached in a large group.

'Please, Sahib, will you give us some change too?'

'Get away you rascals, what is this?' Asaff shouted at them. It made no difference, they still pestered and engulfed him, ensuring he didn't escape. Rasheed held her handbag securely under her arm,' now feeling intimidated.

'Hush, get away from here. Go!' A police officer yelled, threatening them with his stick, which he was not reluctant in using. They quickly dispersed, before being beaten or arrested.

'Where's the car, Akeel?' Asaff asked, sweating after walking such a distance.

'Just here,' he said, pointing to a white Nissan.

Asaff and Rasheed stared at the car which was severely dented and damaged on both sides, front and rear. There was also a large crack in the windscreen. The boot was held down by a rope; Akeel untied the knots, loaded the suitcase and then kneeled down to tie it again.

'Climb in,' he said, proudly. Asaff sat in the back on the torn seats with Rasheed.

'Have you been chauffeuring animals in this car?' Asaff asked.

'Top of the range this is.'

'It doesn't look very top of the range to me, it looks like you've picked it up from a scrap yard.'

Akeel drove towards the exit, sounding his horn and popping his head out of the broken window to swear and curse at other motorists and pedestrians. A traffic controller signalled for Akeel to stop in order to pay a parking charge, but he drove on almost knocking the man over.

'I have a Major in the car,' he shouted through the window, as Asaff and Rasheed glanced at each other uneasily.

'What is the temperature?' Asaff asked agitated.

'Only one hundred degrees: it will get much hotter between June and August.'

'I don't know how these people cope, I'm glad I'll be back in England by then.'

'You've survived hotter months in poorer conditions, Asaff bhai, I think you've just forgotten.'

'Ten years of English weather and I used to say I can't wait to get back home to the heat, but I've had enough already,' Asaff complained. 'Turn on the cold air vents.'

The vents only succeeded in absorbing the sweltering heat and blowing it in their faces, making them feel nauseous. Asaff hadn't prepared for such intense heat: his English suit and shoes were inappropriate. He removed his tie, unbuttoned the shirt and took out the cufflinks to roll up his sleeves. This cooled him for half the journey, but the further they drove from the city, the hotter it got. When he warmed up again, he removed his shoes and socks, sitting barefoot, with his head tilted back. Rasheed remained quiet as she remembered a similar journey she took with her Nanni just under thirty-five years ago, when her Abba's chauffeur drove them from Jhelum to Lahore for her wedding. It was a similar type of heat she had endured then, even if it was a luxury car. Images of her Ammi running around frantically arranging the wedding were before her again. She imagined what her parents would look like, how they may have aged. Were her siblings married, did she have nieces and nephews? How would her Abba react not only to her converting to Islam, but to her accepting the religion as a way of life? During the dark days, when she felt isolated and trapped, she would pick up the Quran as a means of escape. She read the translation with the help of women in the village and over the years came to accept that the religion was one of kindness, love and peace. She then also made peace with the fact that her initial experiences were not in the name of religion, but a consequence of politically charged civil unrest.

The rolling hills were before them once again, the lush green gradually losing its colour in the build-up to summer. They began to descend the dangerous snake path, where so many vehicles had driven off the cliff. There were no barriers to prevent such fatalities; it required skilful manoeuvring, which could be mastered by few drivers. Rasheed watched for the first sight of the valley river, uttering a prayer to her angel baby and sending him love; she knew he waited for her in heaven.

They stopped outside Asaff and Rasheed's house and unloaded the boot. Asaff looked around the familiar surroundings, stepping into the yard. The house was double storey now, with a staircase at the side. Safdar appeared at the top.

'Safdar bhai,' Asaff said, delighted to see his cousin after ten years apart. He was still as tall as he was in his youth, over six feet, but he now used a walking stick. Holding the side of the wall, he came down. They both embraced warmly.

'I've been waiting for this day,' Safdar said. 'I didn't want to die without seeing you one last time.'

'Don't speak such nonsense, please,' Asaff said.

'Rasheed,' Safdar greeted, stepping forward to embrace his sister-in-law. Although Rasheed respected Safdar as her husband's cousin brother, she still detested him for not allowing her to escape when she and Kareena bumped into him outside the village that morning, so many decades ago.

'Welcome home!' Aminah shouted.

Over the years Rasheed had come to understand her speech. She still remained a slim, petite woman with immense beauty, but was now looking old.

Dinner was prepared at Asaff and Rasheed's home, in the lower storey of the building. Aminah had taken out Rasheed's dinner set and glasses, and placed them on the dining table. When Rasheed left for England she had locked the doors and cupboards, so nobody could get in, but all the bolts and keypads had been broken and her furniture damaged. Safdar and Aminah's children and grandchildren were probably responsible: they didn't have their own house, nor did they work for a living, so Asaff's wages were required to provide for them too. Rasheed was willing to allow them to use her house, as long as they kept it clean and in order, but they didn't even do that. The frames which once held photographs of Parwez's wedding had been stolen, and the curling pictures were collecting dust on the cupboard. The covers Rasheed had made for the settees had been deliberately torn. They stole from her on the day she arrived, and to this very day they were still doing so.

'How are Zainub and her children adjusting to life in England?' Safdar asked at the dining table.

'They are settling. Her husband is driving buses, her boys have started schooling, the girls are too young for school yet, so she spends the day with them.'

Aminah had prepared a basic dinner, consisting of vegetables and roti.

'I spent twenty rupees, preparing dinner for you,' she commented, waiting for Asaff to compensate her.

Rasheed almost exploded: Aminah had spent no more than five rupees on dinner at the very most. The villagers believed money in England was easy to accumulate; they preferred to forget that Asaff and Parwez spent twelve hours at a time at work.

'Here is ten and don't ever ask us for money again,' Rasheed shouted. She was not subservient to them any longer, those days ended a long time ago.

Rasheed cleared the dishes and washed them in the kitchen sink, despite feeling exhausted from the journey. She was in her own home and did not want to be treated like a guest.

'Get some rest,' Safdar said, seeing her washing the dishes. 'Aminah will do them later.'

'And charge me twenty rupees for them?' Rasheed replied fully accustomed to their tricks. Aminah returned to her quarters upstairs, leaving Safdar and Asaff to speak.

'Why are you reuniting her with her parents?' Safdar asked. 'It's ludicrous. After so many years, she's going back to her roots? She should have forgotten about all that now.'

'They're her family, her parents; Zainub's grandparents, they can't be forgotten.' Asaff argued.

'What if they take her back with them? What if they poison her mind? We have not accepted her into our family for them to now take her away.'

'Safdar bhai, you are worrying for no reason. She's been my wife for nearly thirty-two years and I have loved her and cared for her as much as I can. I love Zainub as much as I do my own children. This is one dream she has longed for: do you think I will allow it to be shattered?'

'But they are Sikhs.'

'You know since partition we've all forgotten we lived as one, when religion didn't matter. Remember my friend Mohan? Hindus, they were, but we spent all of our time together. His Ammi would bathe and feed me, like she did him. Religion didn't matter back then Safdar bhai.'

'Suppose they try and take revenge on you?'

'We are meeting at a gurdwara, they're not going to do anything in a place of worship; more importantly, they are my wife's family.'

'I'm just warning you, Asaff, you are like a younger brother and it is my duty. If you choose to listen to your wife instead of me, then do as you please.'

'She could have chosen to go back home when her father wrote to the General Commissioner of Kashmir, begging him to locate his daughter. When he came to the village looking for Rasheed, do you remember what her reply was? "Write to my father and tell him there is no record of Taji Kaur, she must have been killed during the riots." She did that because she was married to me, a Musalmaan, and was carrying my son then. If Rasheed made such a sacrifice that day, then I'm prepared to risk my life for her. I was an Army Major, I'm not scared.'

'You aren't thinking straight Asaff, I'm telling you.'

'I owe Rasheed this, and I'm going to take her to the gurdwara tomorrow morning.'

Rasheed listened to the argument from the kitchen, and bumped into Safdar as he stormed out.

'You…' he said pointing accusingly, 'You're lucky to have a husband like Asaff. He's going against what I say, for you. I don't know how you have poisoned his mind, but you will be punished for it.'

'And you will be punished for selling Kareena to Akeel, for stealing my gold, for threatening me and holding a knife to my neck, for forcing me to convert, for not allowing me to get back to my family when I tried to escape for the second time, you'll be punished for all that too. Now get out of my house!' She shouted, pointing at him exactly as he pointed to her. Rasheed had never confronted Safdar about what had happened following that day he captured her and Kareena; and then again when he caught her trying to escape one night after her marriage to Asaff. For the first time she had felt strong enough to stand up to her captors, who treated her like an outcast for decades. Rasheed was relieved she was able to express herself and tell him what she really thought.

Safdar's eyes turned red, his entire body was shaking as he ascended the stone staircase, outraged that Rasheed had insulted him.

Rasheed left Asaff alone. She didn't interfere with their arguments and problems: this had been her philosophy since she married him. He rarely got angry because he was such a kind-hearted, gentle being, but when he did, she allowed him the space he needed, before she comforted him. Unpacking the suitcase in the bedroom, she picked out the clothes they were going to wear the next morning. For Asaff she chose a plain blue shalwar kameez and for herself, a violet printed kameez and a white shalwar. She bought the suit in England and had it tailored especially, so her parents could see that Asaff kept her well. She even had matching sandals; her signature look. Her parents would never know about the hard times she had suffered, they would see her as the old Taji, with her perfectly coordinated outfits. Rasheed plugged in the travelling iron and pressed their clothes, so there was not a single crease. She hung them up in the wardrobe, ready for the next morning.

Evening fell and Safdar and Aminah had still not come back downstairs, nor had Asaff visited them. He remained adamant and would not allow anybody to influence him. The indoor rooms were warm, despite the fan they had brought from England, and so they pulled the charpais out into the yard and slept under the stars in the cool breeze of the night.

At the crack of dawn the azaan sounded from the masjid. The morning call for prayer echoed in the village, waking everybody, announcing the arrival of a new day. Rasheed lay on the charpai looking up at the dark blue sky, watching the brightly shining moon fading and the sun appearing on the still summer's morning. In the background she listened to the beautiful legato phrases from the Quran being pronounced, each syllable and vowel recited with such devotion. When the pace slowed, signalling the end of the azaan, she got up to wash in the bathroom.

'Asaff, time for prayer.'

He woke immediately, despite the jetlag. After dressing, he walked out into the narrow, dark alleyway, closing the gate behind him, so that nobody disturbed Rasheed praying in the yard. In the darkness, he still found his way to the masjid: the alleyways were the same ones he used for over forty years, before moving to England. It made Asaff proud seeing the village had progressed considerably since his childhood. Many of the village men had emigrated to England, worked long shifts in manual jobs so they could send money back home and better the standard of living. The small room in the masjid was already full, village men in their positions ready to begin the prayer.

'Allah o'Akbar,' the mullah recited.

They stood shoulder to shoulder in two rows, one behind the other. The morning prayer was a short one, just under five minutes. When it finished Asaff greeted all his relatives and then sat back down again, observing the room. It used to be bare when Asaff attended as a teenager, but now thick green coloured satin had been nailed down to cover the mud walls. The solid cement floor had been covered with a brown padded mat, which the women in the village stitched for the men to pray on. Asaff remembered that all of this was down to his wife: she had written to him while he was in England, telling him she had gathered the women to complete the task after she saw what a dull and uninspiring room it was.

At home, Rasheed had already prepared breakfast and left it on the table: tea and three rotis covered in fresh butter from the village cows. Rasheed changed in the bedroom, putting on her new clothes and shoes, using some English moisturiser on her face. Although she should have been excited, she felt a sense of unease, something was bothering her, but she didn't know what. After breakfast Asaff shaved and also changed.

'Are we ready to go?' he asked Rasheed when he heard Akeel's car outside.

'Yes,' she replied, still without enthusiasm and made her way out.

'Akeel, can we stop at the graveyard first? I've not been to pay my respects at Ammi's grave.' This was a ritual Asaff always followed.

The graveyard was behind that grand house where the Musalmaans had kept the captured Sikh and Hindu victims. Akeel drove past the familiar huts further on to the graveyard. Asaff brought some fresh rose petals from the man sitting outside. Before entering he stopped at the gate and prayed for all those who had left this world; most of them family in this cemetery. Rasheed allowed Asaff some space to mourn privately and so she took a walk around the grounds of the house. She walked slowly, her feet dragging behind her as if her brain was not connecting with her movement. Her eyes examined the dilapidated house, no longer pristinely white but rusty and tired; doors ripped out, overgrown grass, cobwebs. A part of Rasheed wanted to get out of there and run back to the car, but she involuntarily walked the route she took to the back of the house all those decades ago. She had locked away the most nightmarish of her experiences and refused ever to unlock what remained in that box. Today those memories stared her in the eyes, having found their way out somehow. Looking up at the room where she'd been held, there was the cracked window pane and through that the reflection of the hills and mountains. Taller than she remembered, they reached far into the heavens, the tips not even visible. Turning around, she was before the same hills, dwarfed between the force of nature and the grand mansion. She felt suffocated. She closed her eyes, not allowing any memory to play before her. "Go away!" she shouted, tightly squeezing her eyes shut, raising her hands to her ears to block the sound; but this time she couldn't hold them back. Having relived and accepted what had happened, she opened her eyes to see Asaff standing before her.

'Are you ready?' he gently asked, taking her hand in his, knowing what had just flashed before her. She wiped her eyes, nodded and walked towards the car.

Chapter 2

May 1979, Hasanabdal, Pakistan

Some three hours later Akeel brought the car to a halt, along the gridlocked road where over-flowing rickshaws, mini-buses, coaches and scooters had stopped in precarious positions to allow their passengers to alight. Thousands of Sikhs obtained special permission to cross the border from India into Pakistan to visit this sacred site: home to a boulder which held the perfect handprint of the founder of Sikhism himself, Guru Nanak. The line of partition had meant this particularly significant gurdwara remained in Muslim-majority Pakistan. A gently flowing river of pilgrims headed to the entrance; steps taken in unison as strangers were united in reaching one common destination. The free-flowing chiffon dubattas around the women's necks and shoulders were being rearranged to cover their heads. The men with turbans casually walked on, whilst those without slowed down to tie orange or white coloured cloths over their heads. Although Rasheed couldn't remember the last time she was amongst so many Sikhs, she felt at ease. The petty quarrels she was overhearing, reminded her of the childhood visits to the gurdwara with her siblings, where her Ammi would be herding the crowd too, trying to get everyone in. The sheer volume of people meant there was pushing and shuffling, but none with bad intent. There was chaos, but a peaceful chaos, and enough to distract from the intense sun's rays beginning to beat down through the wispy clouds.

In their last letter exchange over a month ago, Rasheed's Abba had said they'd meet at the main entrance early in the morning. In her mind she had already built up images of them, she had imaginary conversations with them. The little voice in her head re-told her story again and again because she'd missed some vital piece of information or occasionally because she'd shared too much. Rasheed didn't want them to know everything and so she wanted to be guarded; but what she did want them to know was that Asaff was a good man. He truly respected and loved her. He helped her settle into village life and protected her from the awful villagers who couldn't accept her as a widowed Sikh woman with a child. He worked hard and provided for her, and although she never went back to living the luxurious life she had with Gurpul, she had a simple but comfortable life with Asaff. Asaff owned a house in England and one in Kashmir and earned enough to support the family that were still less fortunate than they were. Being in their seventies now, Rasheed expected her parents to be frail, especially after the heart attack her Abba had suffered six months ago when Balminder broke the news. Balminder had written to her to explain what had happened upon his return from England: Kishin had spent time in hospital and then months recovering at home before he was able to accept that Taji was still alive. During that time no one was permitted to speak of Taji in fear that it might have triggered a fatal second attack. Over a month into his recovery at home, he woke suddenly from a deep sleep, in the early hours of one morning, having dreamt of his eldest child. It was in that moment he turned to his wife, Kulgeet, and said they would travel from Delhi to Gurdwara Panja Sahib in Pakistan to meet with their daughter. He explained this place of worship was the safest place to meet given that post-partition conflict between the nations was still rife. Rasheed began doubting whether she'd even recognise her Ammi and Abba; she also feared her Abba's reaction to her Muslim husband. A complex web of thought had been woven and her pulse raced, despite her taking deep breaths in an attempt to calm her nerves.

As they followed the crowds, Asaff admired the imposing white dome and gleaming spire of Gurdwara Panja Sahib, which was visible a short distance ahead. It was a beautiful double storey marble temple, with intricate gold patterns woven into the arches and domes. The reflection of the sun and the green mountainous backdrop enhanced the stunning building. Rasheed and Asaff both covered their heads, removed their shoes and washed their hands as they entered the holy site. They had never visited a gurdwara together; she glanced at him, wondering how he felt amongst the Sikhs, but he seemed to be taking it in his stride. For Asaff, supporting Rasheed on such a momentous day was at the forefront of his mind. They walked through the main entrance and stepped aside. Rasheed studied the faces of those around her, she didn't recognise any of them as being her Abba or Ammi. She listened intently to the pilgrims reciting verses from the holy book, the Guru Granth Sahib; it all sounded distantly familiar and triggered memories of major life events that took place in gurdwaras pre-partition.

'Shall we sit along this wall?' Asaff suggested, 'there is a good view of everyone coming through the main entrance.' Rasheed agreed and they took a seat on the floor, watching the crowds pass them by. In any given moment Rasheed felt a range of emotions, from fear, to nervousness, to excitement, to regret and then nothing. As she watched the pilgrims enter, she was excited, because she knew she would see her Ammi and Abba as soon as they walked in. She wondered if her Abba held a walking stick now.

The gurdwara was getting busier, the crowds larger, so much so that keeping up with studying each face had become impossible. There were elderly pilgrims, youthful pilgrims, children, disabled pilgrims even; and each face told its own story. Some held a relaxed demeanour with smiles and bright eyes; others were sad, the worry evident through the frowning foreheads or gravity-drawn shoulders; and some just content. As Rasheed studied each face, she wondered how many had been displaced during partition, liked she and her parents had; forced to leave their homes in the newly created Pakistan to start over again in India.

Rasheed's back was aching from sitting on the marble floor, so she stood to stretch.

'They did say the main entrance, didn't they?' she checked with Asaff.

'The letter was written in Punjabi so I couldn't read it, but that is what you said.' Asaff replied. Rasheed tried to pace in the restricted space she had to move, now that others had joined them on the floor. Over two hours had passed and there was no sign of them.

'They will be here soon.' Asaff reassured, watching the concern on his wife's face. He stood up too. 'Let's take a walk. Although this is the main entrance, there are a number of other entrances too, let's just be sure they aren't waiting at another.'

Asaff looked out of place amongst the many bearded and turbaned Sikhs; he too felt a sense of anxiety about meeting his parents-in-law. He wondered if he'd been a good enough husband to Rasheed, could he have done more? Did he support her enough? As they walked from one entrance to the next, Rasheed remained wide eyed, not daring to blink, in case she missed them. Every so often she wiped her eyes with her dubatta; Asaff watched her helplessly. The torment on her face took him back to that day in 1947 when he married her. It wasn't that he'd immediately fallen deeply in love with her; he saw a vulnerable woman with an innocent child, who was victim to civil unrest and who would have been tortured, raped or murdered if she'd stumbled into the wrong hands. Being a man of the army at the time, he'd directly witnessed all the atrocities that were occurring on both sides. Asaff hadn't classed himself as a martyr for saving her life, by marrying her: such heroic and selfless behaviours were demonstrated on both sides. Neighbours and strangers helped one another by taking in those of other religions, those whose lives were at threat because overnight they'd been ostracised on the grounds of religion; hundreds of years of peaceful living, ripped apart. Sikh and Hindu men married and protected Muslim women and

219

their families to help save them; not everyone had bad intent, many acted in good faith too. For Asaff, being in the gurdwara, this place of worship that was once so sacred for Rasheed, meant he could feel just what she must have gone through when she converted; how gruelling it must have been for her. Asaff had merely spent a few hours amongst the Sikhs, where no one had imposed anything upon him and yet it felt isolating, but Rasheed had spent most of her life in a village full of Muslims, all alone. Asaff had felt some hesitation when Parwez embarked on his quest to find his Ammi's family, but he was now thankful to his son for doing so.

Rasheed wondered if her Abba had fallen ill again and therefore hadn't been able to travel.

'Asaff they must have changed their mind. We've been here for several hours now.' Rasheed said in a low, quivering voice.

'I believe they're here, Rasheed,' he reassured in his calming manner, placing his hands on her shoulders. 'We will find them.' Asaff promised, looking her in the eye.

Asaff approached the volunteers in the gurdwara and asked if they could make an announcement for Rasheed's parents, but they weren't able to because it disturbed the peaceful surrounding. Rasheed was furious for allowing herself to become emotionally vulnerable, where she felt like everything around her was about to be crushed again. She reminded herself of that day she wholeheartedly gave up trying to escape from Asaff's village: the day she found out she was pregnant with Parwez. Not only had she taken on another religion, but she was carrying a Muslim man's child, and coming from an orthodox Sikh family, she knew her Abba would never accept her back. She felt that she had failed and betrayed him; she wasn't able to fathom that her Abba would have understood that his daughter was a victim of partition. Rasheed was convinced her Abba would have an easier time accepting she was dead than knowing she was living another life. Clenching her fists and grinding her teeth, she cursed under her breath. She felt strongly that this was all a mistake: for three decades she'd lived without them and she could have continued to do so because she had lived through the worst of it. She'd won the hearts of the villagers, she'd forgiven those who needed forgiving, she had been blessed with many more children and grandchildren, and most importantly she had a husband who loved and respected her immensely.

'Asaff, let's go, they're not here.' Rasheed asserted.

'They will be here. The crowds will begin to disperse and we'll find them. I'm sure we're just missing each other amongst all these people.'

'I really don't think so. I know they're not here. I'll write to them and we'll arrange another meeting.' She spoke so matter-of-factly; but Asaff felt his wife's pain like a needle pricking his chest slowly and deeply.

'I'm going to go and get us something to eat. You wait here. We'll decide what to do when I get back.' Rasheed's stomach was locked tight, there was no chance of anything going in. Asaff left her and scouted the crowds, desperately wanting to reunite Rasheed with her parents. In an act of desperation, he asked every man that looked like he could be Rasheed's Abba's age, 'Are you Kishin Singh, Taji's Abba?' but he had no joy. He must have asked thirty men, aimlessly walking around, having forgotten about the food. Over an hour later he returned, praying that Rasheed would be standing with her parents, but she was not. Her face was drawn, her eyes red, her chin dropped.

'Let's go Asaff, seven hours we've been waiting. If they were here, we'd have found them or they'd have found us.' Asaff had nothing to say. Maybe they needed to accept defeat, maybe her Abba had changed his mind. He wrapped his arm around her, he felt he had failed her, and they walked towards the exit, both of them silent. Rasheed's heart had been torn to pieces like it was all those decades ago. Her stomach swirled with nausea, her head blurred with confusion as she tried to understand why her Abba had betrayed her like this. As she vowed to pick herself back up and not re-live the pain from partition, she looked ahead and saw an elderly man standing tall with his back to her, a light blue turban tied high on his head, in a white kurta pyjama. He was steady on his legs, but those broad shoulders were hunching with age. He was blocking the view of an elderly woman who stood facing him.

'Abba!' She said in almost a whisper. She struggled to focus her eyes.

'What did you say?' Rasheed didn't even hear Asaff, she stopped and stared; her mouth slightly open, her jaw continued to drop. Her eyes were wide, her pupils dilated. Rasheed was completely numb, she couldn't move; her muscles had frozen. She felt Asaff's hand on her back, which sent a shiver down her spine. She blinked hard and slowly, and then opened her eyes and focused again.

'That's my Abba,' she pointed to the man in the distance. They looked at one another, the blood drained from their faces.

'Are you sure? You recognise him from his back?' she nodded with absolute certainty. 'Go, Rasheed. I'm going to wait right here.'

She approached the man, but stopped just a couple of feet behind him. The sweat droplets around her temples ran down her face, her hands trembled. She stepped forward, tapped his shoulder, she could feel his bones, 'Abba?' He turned around. He studied her face: no longer youthful, but now lines of sorrow around her eyes, not as bright and shiny as they were; her complexion darker than he remembered. A mature face, she looked more like her Ammi.

'Taji?' he finally stuttered. His hands were shaking, his lower lip trembled, she held onto his frail hands, not strong and firm as they used to be, but that connection ran straight through her. Even if her eyes were firmly shut, she would have known it was her Abba.

'Yes Abba, it's me.' He took her into his arms, repeated her name again and again, like he did when she was a child. She allowed him to take her weight as she fell into them, rested her face on his chest and allowed her tears to fall.

Rasheed's Ammi came closer, 'My Taji!' The three of them embraced, not saying more than each other's names; her Abba held her hand tightly; her Ammi stroked her face, wiped away her daughter's tears. 'The Guru's have reunited us, Taji.' They wept and sniffled and blew their noses.

Asaff watched from a few feet away. The flecks of green were shining through the swollen, blood-shot eyes. He sent a prayer to his son for being fearless when standing up to the villagers who had thought him idiotic for digging up bad history.

'Taji, I've got a train ticket for you,' her Abba said, reaching for his pocket, 'come back to India with us, come home, Taji.' She took the blue-veined hand holding the ticket to her lips and kissed it.

'Abba, there is so much we have to catch up on.' She looked around for Asaff and he took that as the signal for him to join them. 'Abba, Ammi, this is Asaff.'

'Sat Sri Akal.' He greeted in the true Sikh manner which brought a smile to Rasheed's face. Her Abba and Ammi took him in their arms.

'Let's go sit down,' Rasheed's Abba said. 'We've been pacing the gurdwara all day; we thought you might have changed your mind.' Asaff and Rasheed smiled at each other as they exchanged glances. Her Abba's arm around her shoulder, her Ammi's hands sandwiched between hers.

THE END

Afterword

To find out more about my grandmother, Rasheed, my grandfather, Asaff, and my father, Parwez, and how this incredible true story continued to unfold, read on.

After meeting with her parents at Gurdwara Panja Sahib, Rasheed kept in touch with her family through letter and telephone. Some years later they arranged a second meeting at Gurdwara Nankana Sahib also in Pakistan, where she was able to meet some of her siblings.

The tense political situation between the countries meant that it wasn't easy for individuals of Pakistani descent to obtain Indian tourist visas; however, in April 1991 Parwez and Rasheed made their first visit to Delhi, India. Asaff wasn't comfortable with the visit because he felt there may be a threat of revenge from the more conservative Sikh family members. Parwez was father to five young children and Asaff did not want to risk him not returning. There were months of family discussions on whether the trip should go ahead, but Parwez was not going to be held back. He had embarked upon the quest to reunite his mother with her family and was determined to ensure she was able to meet them all again. The reception they received in India was one of overwhelming love: they were family after all, and blood was stronger than religion.

Rasheed had become a practising Muslim and continued to offer her daily prayers whilst in India with her Sikh family. Upon seeing Rasheed praying one day, her younger brother quietly wiped away his tears. Parwez was sensitive to how difficult this must have been for his uncle and comforted him; to which his uncle responded, 'there's only one God, we just call him different names now.' The impact of his words were profound and the beginning of what would be a strong bond between the uncle and nephew.

Gurpul's parents were still in touch with Rasheed's parents and came to hear of their daughter-in-law's story. Sensitive to her new life, they asked if they could meet with her when she arrived in Delhi, to which she agreed, with Asaff's blessing. Shashi and Roopa had unanswered questions about their son and the last days of his life; and they also wanted to hear about their granddaughter, Rajendar. Rasheed shared what had occurred, allowing them to finally mourn their son. Parwez and Rasheed shared photos and videos of their grandchild.

Rasheed's father died shortly after her first visit to India; her mother had died in 1985. Rasheed made her second and last visit to India in 2001.

After marrying Asaff, Rasheed went on to have five more children. She was blessed with twenty-seven grandchildren and was great-grandmother to more than ten at the time of her death.

Asaff and Rasheed continued to live a simple, but happy life after emigrating to England. They never moved out of the house they first purchased, and I have fond memories of visiting them there during the school holidays. It was during these holidays I frequently heard my grandmother tell me and my siblings stories of her life; and it was in my early teens I made a promise that I would write the story she shared so boldly. To capture the details she sometimes skimmed over, I interviewed Rasheed over a period of two years between 2002 and 2004. In July 2004, I completed the first draft of the manuscript and we celebrated together because her wish had been fulfilled.

Asaff died in August, 1997 and Rasheed died in March, 2010 at the age of 81. In the months leading to her death she often spoke to my mother about the son she left behind. She shared for the first time that images of his face flashed before her; and she didn't know how she'd answer to God when asked about why she had left her son. This haunted Rasheed until her dying day. Raising a family and being a part of a family, became the focal point of her life. Lying ill in hospital, she remained good-humoured and promised, when the angels came to take her away, she'd refuse to leave until her entire family surrounded her. Her dying wish was granted: she peacefully took her last breath, as her children and grandchildren prayed over her, we held her hands and stroked her hair, telling her we were with her. At Rasheed's request, she was laid to rest next to Asaff, in the very village where she was captured over sixty years earlier: it had become her home and she had truly earned the respect of the villagers. She was mother, daughter, sister, grandmother to the entire village and beyond.

The absolute impact of Rasheed's sorrow for her son was not felt by my siblings and I until we lost our beautiful nephew, baby Sami, on July 9th 2014. The tragedy that hit was unbearable and totally unexpected; and that was when we truly appreciated what leaving a child behind must have done to our grandmother. We missed her terribly because she was our pillar and if anybody could console our little sister, it was our grandmother.

Rasheed was an incredibly strong, resilient woman, with a great sense of humour and a kind heart, despite all that life had thrown her way. She had great intelligence, was extremely articulate and had a zest for life. She tried to learn English in her 50s, she was an amazing cook, an incredible seamstress and loved to knit and crochet – every family member was gifted an item of clothing made by Rasheed. She learnt Arabic and could recite long sections from the Quran and went on pilgrimage to Mecca with Asaff. She had no photos from pre-partition, but frequently told me I was the spitting image of her in her youth!

Rasheed has left a legacy which will never be forgotten by the generations to come. My siblings and I feel immensely blessed to call her our dadi ji. She taught us to be strong, resilient and independent and encouraged us to pursue our dreams.

She died a blessed and happy woman.

The publishing of this book marks the ten-year anniversary of Rasheed's death. This is a celebration of who she was and the life she lived.

Picture Gallery

Rasheed, Kashmir, 1976

Rasheed and Asaff when he returns to Kashmir for the first time after emigrating to England. Kashmir, 1968

Parwez and his wife the month he meets with Balminder Singh. England, 1978

Asaff, England, 1965

The Author

Fozia Raja is an author, creative writer, and corporate Human Resources professional. She was born and brought up in Manchester, UK, where she has fond memories of pursuing her passion for reading - carrying a heavy backpack to the local library each Saturday to pick out her next seven books for the week ahead.

She has vivid childhood memories of the stories shared by her grandmother about her surviving the partition of India. Fozia would listen to these historical narratives in rapt attention – motivating her later in life to complete a master's degree in Creative Writing. Her grandmother's wish that Fozia "write the story of my life" came to its fruition with this publishing.

Fozia is an avid reader, foodie and gym-goer; and when she's not travelling, London is home.

For more information visit www.foziaraja.com or find her on Instagram @foziaraja_books or Facebook @daughtersofpartition.

Printed in Great Britain
by Amazon